MUSTARD SEED

MUSTARD SEED

a novel

BRIAN HOLERS

GIRL FRIDAY BOOKS

This is a work of fiction. Names, characters, organizations, places, events, and incidents are either products of the author's imagination or are used fictitiously.

Published by Girl Friday Books™, Seattle
www.girlfridaybooks.com

Produced by Girl Friday Productions

Design: Paul Barrett
Production editorial: Abi Pollokoff
Project management: Sara Spees Addicott

Image credits: cover © iStock/ H.Takemoto

ISBN (paperback): 978-1-954854-88-8
ISBN (e-book): 978-1-954854-89-5

Library of Congress Control Number: 2022946228

For Jody and Ben
and Mama and Daddy

ACKNOWLEDGMENTS

I wrote much of this book while traveling in Kenya, Tanzania, and Israel. It would not have been possible without the space my family afforded me. Many thanks to Leslie Miller of Girl Friday Books who sent me back to the table many times; she and her team helped turn this chunk of coal into a diamond. *Toda raba* to Ari Brown, my Jewish friend who understands Christianity better than many Christians. He not only named my business, he also named this book. Finally, I'd like to acknowledge the friendship and contribution of Joe "Head" Thiels. You'll recognize some of these stories. I hope I did them justice.

CHAPTER 1

Vernon hates pennies. He knows it's ridiculous, the surge of dread he feels in his stomach when he holds a penny in his hand. But it's like just about everything these days, deceptions and crimes and perversions of the sort you never heard of way back when. What can he do about it? After sixty-one years, Vernon allows himself his feelings.

When the rain shower stops, he stands from the seat of his truck and takes the coins from his pocket. He reaches back inside, drops a quarter, a dime, and a nickel into the open ashtray. Vernon looks across the parking lot at the Branden Parish Hospital. The afternoon sun is well into its long descent, and though it is not yet April, steam from the midday shower rises in clouds off the pavement.

He holds one of the copper coins out in front of him, holds two others in his hand. Vernon loved these when he was a boy, when EL used to give him a few cents to buy candy or gum with Pearl or Leonard. Leonard, his only brother left, in there in his bed. Hard to believe they used to be so special, back when a quarter still filled the palm of his hand. Now they're everywhere. Free in convenience stores. Vernon reads the date on the penny—1975. His stomach burns, not just from the whiskey. The year Billy was born. It was an overshined penny just like this one that had worked its way out of his pants pocket one day, wedged itself under the agitator of his washing machine, and stripped the gears so thoroughly that the innards just froze. Vernon was working on it that night when the sheriff came by. A four-hundred-dollar washing machine dead, because Vernon tried to hold on to something worthless. Something absolutely worthless.

Finally, he closes the door of his truck, walks toward the hospital. He throws the three pennies in the briars as he passes. Vernon smiles at the red-haired receptionist in the lobby, shuffles up the stairs to his brother's room. Leonard is asleep. The hospital blanket is bunched at his feet and he's covered by nothing but a gown.

Vernon stands over his sleeping brother, tsks at the yellow pall creeping into Leonard's face. For a moment Vernon thinks he's looking into a distorted reflection of the Davidson family chin, the wide upper lip. He feels a crush of sympathy for his brother, so strong he starts to reach out his hand. Just then Leonard stirs, opens his eyes, smiles.

"How you doing today, Leonard?"

As Leonard's eyelids flutter, the pictures inside them fade quickly, snap off midmotion like a frozen camera shutter. Yet he knows in an instant what his dream was about, and a warm, contented feeling he has only recently begun to know seeps into his joints as he wakes.

Leonard settles into the bed. "I was dreaming."

"Yeah? What about?"

"Pearl."

"Hmm."

"Yeah. I've been dreaming about him a lot the last few days. Vernon?"

"Sir?"

"What do you think about what Daddy used to say?"

"Hmm. What was that?"

"About why he done it."

Vernon reaches into his empty pocket, grabs a ball of lint, pulls it out, looks at it. "Done what?"

Leonard struggles to sit up, settles back, then kicks what remains of his blanket onto the floor. "You know what I'm talking about."

"Well. I haven't thought about that in a long time."

"Vernon. That's not true and you know it."

"Probably just what he said, then. That was his job. His responsibility."

Leonard reaches for the plastic pitcher by his bed, pours himself a cup of water, drinks it. "That's what he said. But I don't see how that taught Pearl anything. Or us."

Vernon walks to the window, his back to the room. "It don't matter now. He just done what he done, I guess."

For a minute they both are silent. Leonard pours another cup of water and drinks it, blows out a long breath. "You know what I think, Vernon?"

"Hmm."

"I think Daddy done the best he could. What he thought was the best thing for us."

Vernon looks out at his truck in the parking lot. "You think so?"

"Yeah I do."

"Well. I'm not going to argue with you."

"Why not? Because I'm dying?"

Vernon doesn't answer.

"Don't look so sad, Vernon. You're not the one dying here."

"You think that if you want to, Leonard." Vernon snatches up a magazine from his brother's bedside table. "But I guess we'll never know why Daddy done the things he did."

"I hear you. I thought that same way. That there's things we'll never know."

"And now?"

"Now I feel like I know something."

"Well, good for you, Leonard. Good for you. What the hell makes you think that?"

"I don't know. I just do. Isn't that something? Layin' here on this bed before I figure things out." Leonard pauses again. "The good Lord spoke to me, I guess you could say."

Vernon starts toward the door. "I've got to get on home."

"Come on, brother. Stay awhile. This may be the last time we get to talk."

Vernon feels himself blush. "Don't say that, Leonard. Please don't."

"All right. All right. I apologize. I shouldn't have said it." He raises a hand in accordance.

"I've got to go. Got to get on home. I'll stop back tomorrow."

Leonard reaches for his brother's hand. "Vernon?"

Vernon stops.

"I need you to do something for me."

Vernon stands still, looks out the door into the hallway. Waiting.

"Find my boys for me."

Vernon exhales loudly, as if lowering himself to the ground. "I figured eventually you'd ask me."

"You think you can find them?"

"Jody . . . I knew where he was out in California last year. I can probably track him down. He hasn't been back since . . ."

"No. Been twelve years now. Matter of fact it'll be his birthday in a week or so."

"He'd be thirty then." Vernon grimaces when he says it.

"You got it."

"I'll see what I can do." He steps again toward the door.

"Vernon?"

"Yessir?"

"Find Scooter too."

Vernon pops his lips, considers a response, decides to leave Leonard his peace. "You've never asked too much of me I guess. I can make some phone calls."

"I appreciate it. You always were the best finder."

In the waning daylight Vernon drives his truck through Branden. He passes the paper mill, where he's spent most of his life for the last thirty-six years, bumps over the railroad track, and thinks, as he often does, of his father. He tries to imagine the day the train brought the man to Louisiana, the deeds he ran from, the future that must have held such hope, now but a distant blink in the past. Vernon feels a pinch of sadness blindside him, then reaches for the bottle on the floorboard, takes a long pull at the stoplight, begins to feel the numbness again before the light turns green.

He rolls past the abandoned shops at the edge of town, guides the old truck along the mile-long stretch of broken sidewalk that stops at the highway, shifts through the light blinking red, and crosses the bypass road. Even the Walmart lot is mostly empty.

Outside town, Vernon slows down in the curve that fronts the old home place. A porch light is on, and for a moment he considers stopping. But, as he does every day, he decides against it, pilots the truck back onto the road and continues toward Natchitoches.

Vernon slows again to read the sign out in front of Mt. Olive Church. The preacher there had hauled in one of these chest-high signs on wheels and was always changing that sign, trying to say something witty to the people passing by. This time Vernon rolls down his window, stops in the middle of the road. Humidity and the roar of crickets pour in. Vernon reads:

If you meet me and forget me
You have lost nothing.
If you meet Jesus and forget him
You have lost everything.

He slides back into gear and continues. Then he feels the truck slowing, feels his hands jerk the wheel all the way to the left, sees the sign approaching again and the white concrete of the church's parking lot. He reads the words once more, leans his head back, laughs out loud, shouts.

You believe that if you want to, Leonard. Doesn't matter to me. Doesn't mean anything. Not one thing. He punches the gas pedal to the floor. The words of the sign grow larger.

Vernon screeches the truck to a halt. *You have lost everything.* No sense ruining his truck too. No sense letting everything go. He backs off a few feet, jumps out, runs over, lifts the handle of the sign. Then he lifts it until it flips over and he hears the crash. By the time a light switches on in the vestibule of the church, Vernon is back on the road, headed home.

CHAPTER 2

Jody takes the stairs down into the parking garage three at a time. He goes straight to Art's car. Isolated bits of his conversation with Vernon reappear for an instant, then disappear again, as if the words he exchanged with his uncle won't find purchase in his mind, cast about for a place to settle. *Happy birthday. Your cousin. Chicago. Daddy. We've missed you. Dying.*

He opens the door, steps inside. The seat, as always, is perfect. He touches the shift lever, the radio dials, the louvers of the vents, counts the number of years he's wanted a car exactly like this. He looks around, forgetting for a minute where he is. *Take it from me. You don't want to leave anything unsaid.*

Jody starts the car, gets out. He opens the hood and stares inside. The vibration of the carburetor tells him the timing is within a hundredth of a second. Valves purr smooth as a spring afternoon. After a minute he feels the heat in his hands. The whole engine begins to blush.

Jody closes the hood, sits down again in the driver's seat. He leans back and watches the movie that begins to play in his mind. At first it's just his father holding the baby, fumbling with the diaper, safety pins. Then the baby is grown and Daddy stands cooking at the stove, wearing his bright red apron. Uncle Pearl sits at the table in jeans and a flannel shirt, eating bacon and eggs, flapping his gums like he always did. The picture changes and they're all at the church; even Pearl is there in his short-billed cap. Jody's father waits at the back holding the collection plate, his hair all over the place. Uncle Vernon stands up from the pew. He is dressed in a three-piece suit and he sings the hymns the loudest. When the singing stops the minister begins to speak. Everyone is sitting down, listening, murmuring along with the message. Except his brother, Scooter. Scooter watches the stained-glass window. The late-morning sun comes through and casts an orange glow on his face as if he's on fire.

Then everyone else is gone; only Jody, his father, and Scooter remain. They're back in their work clothes. It's fall, early fall, and they're out in the truck hauling firewood. The tangy smell of fresh-cut hickory billows in the gloaming. They drive back toward their house. Leonard stops the truck at the crossroads, cuts the engine, stands up. He stares out through the slanted September light. The only sounds to be heard are the muted barks of hunting dogs, chasing squirrels in the cutover a mile away. Leonard starts the truck again and they drive into town, stop and wait at the railroad track for the train to pass, carrying hardwood logs to the lumber mill in Lidem, Texas. The same track that carried Jody's grandfather to Louisiana all those years ago.

CHAPTER 3

The night before Vernon's phone call, the men drive toward their apartment. Art turns on a jazz station, leaves the car running as he parks in front of their building and steps inside to change his clothes. Jody waits in the car. Snowflakes fall on the windshield with a muffled roar. He relaxes into the seat. Jody imagines his friend inside, buttoning his shirt, brushing the lint off his pants, slapping cologne on his face. The two have lived together so long he can practically see the man through the walls, going through every step of his motions. By the time Art returns, the windshield is covered, softening the street light.

"Want me to drive?" Jody checks his friend's eyes, can't help but notice the gob of mints rattling around in his mouth.

"I'm fine, pal. Don't worry about it."

Jody watches Art's motions, guides himself once again through some mental calculus. He decides it was probably only one drink.

"Some snow, huh?" Flakes come at the windshield like giant butterflies, scratch the glass, a whisper. Jody cracks the window, smells the cold.

"These late snows. I have to say it's pretty," Art says. Dusky spring light holds on in the west. Ahead the sky is black, the lights of cars crisscross with one another and all the other glow to give the air a purposeful blue tinge.

"This place is beautiful."

"I'm with you. I like the city lights."

"Same here, brother. Nothing like city life." Jody stretches, squirms in his seat. "Man, am I tired."

"Another week gone." Jody doesn't answer, only smiles. Art has been his boss for the nearly twelve years the two have known each other, and the men have learned to communicate mostly without words.

"Dad says you're doing a great job."

"That's nice. Like I was saying before. I do all the work anyway. You should give me the bigger office."

"But I like to practice in there."

"Of course. Your trumpet."

"You got it." Art turns instinctively and eyes the brass instrument in the seat behind him, belted in place like a passenger. He turns up the radio. The shrill, silvery notes punctuate the evening. He raises one hand to the melody, works his lips on the imaginary mouthpiece. Art slowly increases the music's volume until Jody begins to feel himself drawn into another place. They drive in silence past miles of shopping centers, apartment buildings, houses, churches, streetlights. The snow begins to change to sleet, ice pebbles pecking against the windshield. Jody turns the blower down; a momentary pinch of cold sneaks into the car. The wipers swipe the window intermittently. Then Art slows, switches on his blinker, and waits for the traffic to clear. He pulls into the parking lot of what appears to be a Chinese restaurant, bamboo dividers lined up in the windows, neon sign blinking.

"So it's Chinese, is it?"

He parks. "They have both Chinese food and all kinds of barbecue. Not kosher, I know."

"I'm not the one supposed to be keeping kosher. And hey, you're taking two spaces."

Art smirks, restarts the car, and moves it over. "What would I do without you?" This time he parks on top of the line. "Speaking of keeping kosher, there's a perfect example of why you don't want to be Jewish, Jody. We have 613 commandments to keep. Your people have what, ten? I probably keep thirty, maybe forty of them. Which is a lot more than ten. But do I get any credit for this?"

Inside, Jody just stands there, breathing. Behind the counter is a huge Samoan guy in some sort of traditional dress, tossing the steaming meats around on a platter. Next to him a tall girl arranges a dim sum cart. A woman yells at the two of them from the back, through the hole in the wall of the kitchen.

The men scan the room for their party. Art spots his father and Karen talking jovially at a corner table. The two are engaged with one another and do not look up at the entrants.

Art backhands Jody playfully on the chest. "I can't believe you're dating my sister."

"*You* can't believe it?" Jody giggles then, pleased with himself. "She is lovely tonight, isn't she?"

"Shut up. That's my sister."

Finally, Cyrus and Karen look up. Cyrus grins mightily, while Karen appears suddenly drawn.

Art waves, heads back toward them. "She better be nice to me. She looks bored already."

But Jody knows this look, has known it, he thinks, forever, since the moment they met, as if some lovers' code only he can recognize. Her makeup is a perfect combination of dark and light, her beauty a contrast to Jody's plain looks. The skin of her face is smooth, slightly flushed. Her inky black hair reflects the room's dim light. The air around her is infused with the smell of lavender. She turns her eyes up to him, the lower lip slightly extended. He bends down to kiss her. Karen scoots forward and he takes a quick look down her dress. She has known other men, sure, some certainly more handsome than this small-town guy. But none who looked at her the way he does, as if he knew her from the start. Karen thinks her chest will just explode at the tentative way he reaches down to her, the unexpected firmness of his lips.

"How's your heart tonight, Karen?"

Karen blushes, appears demure, laughs at herself. The question has come to be a shorthand between them. When they met she had told him, as she had told many others, as if she somehow needed explanation, of her humble beginnings as a blue baby, born with a hole in her heart.

She moves to an adjacent chair to make room for him, continues looking through him with her dark, mysterious eyes. She kisses him again and this time he nearly blushes.

"Happy birthday, Jody."

"Thanks. I guess I have to grow up, now that I'm thirty."

She reaches out to rub his forearm. "You're about the most mature young person I know. Dad and I were just talking about you. He's so impressed with your work."

"Oh. I just work for my money. That's all."

She shakes her pretty head. "Jody Davidson. You do beat all. I've never known anybody else like you."

"Be grateful for that."

Karen pulls him close, once again. She loves his little sayings, his down-to-earth, slow talk. She loves so many things about him.

After the meal, Art stands, hands Jody a gift from a pile of brightly wrapped presents on the table. From Cyrus, the package contains a picture of Jody with Art, Cyrus, and three of

Art's uncles. *To Jody, the newest member of the Gellert family.* Cyrus wipes his eyes with a handkerchief. Karen's gift is also a photograph, a framed picture of the Chicago skyline at night. *Country boy come to the city.* As Jody turns to thank her, Art picks his own gift up off the table, unwraps it, and tosses onto Jody's shoulder a button-up Cubs jersey.

"I was hoping you'd give me the car, but I appreciate the jersey."

"Maybe next year. If you put up with me that long."

Jody swells at the thought. "Maybe next year." He raises his glass. "To birthdays."

The two stand outside her apartment. Jody reaches both arms around her, and Karen settles them inside hers, at her waist. She moves one onto her hip and holds it there. He imagines her later, when the lights are out and the night is quiet, dreams forward to that world where no worries survive, only the immediate, rhythmic motion of their bodies. As if sensing his thoughts, Karen turns herself toward him, bathes her face in the soft white light of the streetlamp. Even in this grainy picture her beauty is piercing.

"Aren't you cold, honey?" Karen doesn't even wear a coat.

"Never. I'm hot blooded."

He breathes onto her neck. "I just wish we could hear frogs and crickets in the city like what I grew up with."

"I'll do an imitation if you'd like."

"Go ahead."

Karen giggles, turns and presses her back into him. Jody holds on to her, Karen's warm-blooded hands on top of his own.

Inside, she goes to the entry closet. Karen removes her dress, hangs it, smooths out wrinkles with her hands. She wears nothing underneath. Jody knows she does this to tease him, but still he intercepts her as she walks toward a sheer green kimono, hung on a nail by the entrance, which she likes to wear when she paints. In the two bedrooms in back she keeps all her supplies, along with a sofa and chair. On the floor of the hallway lies a rolled-up futon. The only part of the living space she uses is an open room with a bare plywood floor.

She slips away and puts on the kimono, walks to the middle of the floor, and opens three cans of paint. Karen dips her brush into a can, looks at the paint on it, then dips it into another can, pulls it out and flings color onto the wall. Quickly she dips the brush twice again into a can of dark blue paint, flings a splotch of it onto the wall in two spots, both above and below the first target. Then she steps back, wipes her hands across the stomach of the kimono and smiles.

"Why are you painting the walls?"

"I wondered how long it would take you to ask me that. You're quicker than I expected."

"It's hard not to notice."

"It's just for practice. I'm stuck. I'm trying to get some new ideas. I thought maybe a bigger canvas would open my mind up."

"Well, I wish I could give you some advice." Jody makes a show of pretending to think, taps one side of his head with a finger. "Maybe try to paint something that looks like something."

Karen laughs once again at his quick deduction. She has always worked in abstract, but lately has considered a change. Especially since her last show was such a thorough bust.

She sets the brush down on one of the cans, looks at the open white walls. "Maybe you're right. That's what my agent says. She says I'm getting too old for all this angst. I might actually have to paint something pretty." She hangs her head, but playfully. "Oh my god, don't tell me I have to grow up!" Once again, Jody has no idea what to make of this beautiful, mysterious girl.

"Oh! I've got an idea for you! Okay, here it is. Get a big

canvas. Like, five by five feet. Just paint it solid white. Then paint some type of a trim all the way around it, make it look like some fancy molding. You can just call it *Wall.* See if some sucker will drop twenty-five hundred on it."

Karen moves toward him, reaches an arm around and lays on a kiss with a passion that disarms him. "You are an artistic genius, Jody. Just a genius! Maybe you should paint."

He bends down to pick up the brush sitting on top of the can. "Wait a minute. That is a great idea. I would love to. Hold on just a minute." He parts from her long enough to pull a hardback chair into the middle of the floor. "Great idea. Just take off that dress and sit down here. I'll get started right away."

"I want to show you something." She pours a healthy dose of white into a plastic quart container, then adds a similar amount of dark green, stirs the colors together with a flat wooden stick. She opens another can, this one a pulsing red. She stands next to a bare white wall, the only clean surface now in the whole apartment.

"This is you, Jody." She rubs out the shapes of trees, grass, a cold green ocean. "You're the color in everything alive, and everything alive is in you." She works slowly, shaping each image before moving on to the next.

"And this is me." She picks up another brush, dips it into the red. "I'm the wild one." She draws a life-size figure in the blank center of the wall, a hollow form in red, red hair hanging over the shoulders and energy radiating out, surrounded by everything green and all the life it contains. She draws the shape of a heart inside the body, and then, in what appears to be an afterthought, a small circular hole in its center. She drops the brush and moves toward him, squats down onto the bed.

"You're all around me. You're in everything." She moves herself to straddle him, begins a slow, hopeful motion as their two yearning bodies, filled to bursting, become one.

. . .

Later, they lie together. Jody fills himself with her, squeezes her tight. His skin warms at Karen's touch. He fingers the faint remains of the scar on her chest, puts an ear to the blemished surface, loses himself in its rhythmic beating.

"It's amazing you're alive."

She lies, content, in the room's dim light, hands behind her head. She wants to reach out to him, but feels so perfectly comfortable she doesn't move.

"Maybe that's what made me so expressive. I wonder sometimes. It's like I always knew life was precious. I remember thinking that even when I was just a little girl."

"I had similar feelings. After my mom died." The two look at each other then, a look that means much more than either could say. Karen continues.

"I grew up with so much fear. And then had lots of therapy." She sighs. "I don't feel so crazy anymore, that's for sure. Only problem now is, my work sucks."

"Here's my well-thought-out idea. Try something different."

Karen gasps, covers her mouth. "That's brilliant! You're such a wise old man, Jody. Now that you're thirty."

"You'll be there soon enough, honey. Are you ready to go to sleep?"

Karen stands. "I think I'm going to work some more."

"Okay, baby. I'm going to sleep. Wake me later if you want. I've got more work to do too."

In the night, Jody stirs. His heart is pounding fast. Karen calls out to him in a velvet voice, half a whisper, half a cry.

"Jody? Wake up, sweetie. You were shouting."

He shakes himself awake. All the lights are off. Forced-air heat blows its throaty wind from the gold-plated register on the floor. The shadow of a massive oak moves on the wall, and falling bits of ice tap on the frosted window. Karen bends over him, squats naked on her toes, inky black hair in front of her. Her pale skin glows in the fractured light.

Jody reaches out to her.

"You look like a ghost."

She touches his face. "I'm not a ghost."

He sits up, tries to shake off sleep.

"I'm not a ghost," Karen says again. A blast of wind rattles the panes of glass. "I'm right here with you. But look. I have something to show you."

She turns on the light, but it's way too bright. She cuts it and stumbles to the shelf for a flashlight as Jody looks on. Then Karen directs the beam onto the sketch of herself from earlier in the night. Jody rubs sleep from his eyes, squints at the wall, then takes her soft white hand to his lips at what he sees. Added to the picture, surrounded by radiant red, is a swatch of green, the color of life, the color of earth, the color of Jody, there, in the center, where there once had been a hole, in the middle of her heart.

CHAPTER 4

Cyrus sits in his car, looking out at Lincoln Park. He drinks from a large paper cup of coffee, the plain black kind, not this fancy stuff with milk and chocolate and flavorings the kids all spend their paychecks on these days. Though he can have whatever he wants, Cyrus still goes for the simple things. He considers the irony. Yet he knows he can only have whatever he wants because he has learned to want so little.

He takes another sip, prepares himself for the cold. Twenty-five times they've done this now, every year on the twelfth of December, and he doesn't remember a colder one. This is the first year his lovely Lydia won't be with them; he lost her too, last summer. But at least Art is finally back, after all those years away. He waits for the others in the car. When he finally sees his beautiful daughter—*god* how much she looks like her mother did—walking across the grass with her head down, he braces himself and opens the door.

He meets her at the picnic table, the one they always use.

"Hey, love." Karen only smiles. Cyrus begins to spread the box-frame kite on the table, sets the tangled spool of string off to the side. He ties on the fluttering tails, eight-foot pieces of ribbon that hang from each corner. Those were Robert's favorite. Colorful kites of all varieties were the one indulgence that child allowed himself in his short life. Though he only lived eleven years, he never went for much in the way of extravagance.

Originally, it was the rabbi's idea. Cyrus had never given much thought to God in his younger days—he just figured a man learned to work and to make his own way. They didn't even belong to that synagogue. The youthful rabbi had come to see him when Robert's first *yahrzeit* approached, the anniversary of his death, bearing words Cyrus at first resented. *You have to find a way to keep him alive in your heart.*

No doubt about it. This is the coldest one yet. He pulls his coat higher, tugs his hat lower down on his ears. Karen stands with hands in her coat pockets, lost in thought. Cyrus never did like the cold. As hard as Chicago winters were, Cyrus spent the first forty-two years of his life slogging through them, angry nearly every minute. What was it the rabbi said? *God works in mysterious ways.* Somehow, someway, through the death of his beautiful young son, Cyrus learned to stop hating winter.

Today, he actually feels good.

"So Art's coming, Daddy?"

"He'll be here in a minute. He's bringing his friend Jody with him."

"Aah. So I'm finally going to meet this mystery man."

Cyrus finishes tying on the tails, holds the kite up for inspection. "You'll like him. He's been friends with your brother a long time. He doesn't seem to have any family. Hey, there they are."

Cyrus raises an arm in salute to the two men as they make their way across the grass. He looks on at them as they approach, continues talking to Karen.

"There's something about him, honey. He makes me think of how Robert would have turned out."

"He looks nice." Karen takes him in, the narrow, flat nose, almond-shaped eyes, paints his picture in her mind. She is drawn to his grace, his smooth, upright gait. Art draws her into a hug.

"Karen, I'd like you to meet Jody. Jody, my sister, Karen." She extends her hand softly, and is certain she feels a jolt when he takes it in his own. He doesn't turn away, looks right into her eyes, as if he knows what she is thinking.

"Well, boys and girls, it's cold. Let's get this bird in the air." They all murmur in agreement. "Karen, can you get that string straightened out?" She takes the roll of string, pulls off a good portion of tangled mess as the men talk to one another, then begins to wind it all back on.

Jody sees her struggling and asks if she wants help. She stares at the mess of string in both hands.

"I'm having a little trouble here. I'm not sure why."

"I could show you, if you like."

"Sure. Help."

"See, when you wrap the string around the spool, you keep twisting it. You need to hold the string in place, then turn the spool over and over." He offers both hands, and she gives him everything. Jody repositions the line and begins to roll it up cleanly.

"How do you know so much about kites?"

He continues working. "I don't. I only know about string." Karen smiles, mystified for the first time of many by this strange young man.

Cyrus takes their finished product, ties it to the kite with a simple bowline. "Everybody ready to fly a kite?" The three agree. "It's cold. The party's waiting. Let's get it up in the air."

"Thank you for coming, Art." Cyrus stands on tiptoes to kiss his son on the cheek. "You too, darling." Next, he and Karen embrace. Without hesitation he reaches for Jody, who is glad to be included.

"And you as well, Mr. Davidson. Thank you for joining

our little—celebration. This was one of Robert's favorite things."

"Thank you for having me."

"You are surely welcome, Jody."

Cyrus holds it out at arm's length, begins to let the string out in inches. Within minutes the kite is high. He feeds it slowly, until the entire spool is extended. Except for the wavering tails, it would be nothing but a speck. The four take turns holding the line. For half an hour it stays like this, never moving, never diving. Just like Robert, holding perfectly steady in the sky.

Finally, once again, as he does every year, Cyrus feels a little more of the leftover grief settle out of him, this feeling that has lasted more than twice as long as the boy did. The wind and cold tell him he's had enough, and he begins to reel in the line. Just then a gust spits out and he feels something in his hand, the slightest little tug, as if he were fishing and his hook had been taken by a minnow. Slowly, gracefully, the string falls back to the ground. The kite rises higher, higher, it rises ever higher, until it just flies away.

A large party has formed by the time the four return to Cyrus's house. Cyrus greets his guests, tells a few about the kite. Everyone settles in with food and drink and the din begins to build. Jody and Karen talk to one another in a corner, appear from the outside to be longtime friends. Art converses with a cousin across the room, who nods along as Art talks. His gestures are animated and he stamps his foot rhythmically as he speaks, as if the story he tells demands meter.

Finally Cyrus disappears into the kitchen and returns with a book of matches. He tells the crowd that things are about to begin. Everyone takes seats, and Cyrus moves toward a bank of switches and turns off the lights. He returns to the front of the group. Then he strikes a match and lights the candle he holds in his hand.

"We're ready, O great and wise teacher," a man says. He grins in a familiar way.

Cyrus scans the room, looks at twenty-five or thirty of his brothers, sisters, cousins, nieces, nephews, and children, smiles his approval.

"Greetings once again, and thank you, everyone, for joining our Hanukkah celebration." The light of the candle flickers on his face. "As all of you know, we gather on these nights to celebrate a miraculous event. An event in which *Hashem* honored the Jewish people with the gift of light.

"Hanukkah celebrates the liberation of the Jewish people from the oppression of the Syrian Greeks, led by the evil king Antiochus. Antiochus, you'll recall, had taken over the temple and outlawed many of the practices that made our people who we are, from circumcision of boy children to our dietary laws to our habits of worship. All of this as part of his effort to secularize and assimilate the Jewish people. In the year 165 BCE, our great leader Judah Maccabee and his badly outnumbered army led a successful revolt against Antiochus and his men. Judah Maccabee and his army were able, by way of this effort, to reclaim the temple, which had been destroyed by the Syrians.

"When they went into the temple they were horrified at the destruction. They went into the holiest place, the place where the temple priests had always kept a light burning for Hashem. They found that the menorah had been stolen and only found enough lamp oil to burn for a few hours."

Cyrus stands and approaches the kitchen, still holding the candle, a tiny shadow jumping all over his face. He closes the door to the kitchen and returns to his seat at the front of the group.

"But the men did not fret. They did not wring their hands and wail at God. They simply got to work. They made a replacement menorah and lit the remaining oil, giving no thought to how little they had or wondering whether they should save it until more could be secured. After this, because of their faith, they experienced the miracle we now celebrate. The light didn't burn for a few hours or even for a day. Or two days. With the intervention of our God, the light burned for *eight days*. During this time Judah Maccabee and his courageous men were able to cleanse and rededicate the temple.

"Hanukkah celebrates only one of the many ways God lives with us, of the many small miracles God sends to help us. When we light these candles, their burning is a sign to us. Their light is a reminder that the God we cherish holds us as his people under his protection. These lights help us remember.

"And now if you'll join me." Cyrus lights another candle with the first one, and the room begins to sing.

Baruch atah Adonai
Elohenu melech ha'olam
Asher kid'shanu b'mitzvoh tav
Vetzivanu, l'hadlich ner
Shel Hanukkah

"Blessed are you, Lord our God, King of the universe, who has sanctified us with your commandments, and commanded us to kindle the Hanukkah lights." The flame grows and everything is silent. Then, slowly, the space begins to brighten. Still Cyrus faces the floor with his eyes closed. He is whispering. Finally, he lifts his face and looks around the room at the mass of flesh and blood therein. Then Cyrus smiles, blinks, and lifts a hand to wipe his face, to brush away the pools of tears cupped like sacred droplets at the corners of his mouth.

CHAPTER 5

Sunday is Vernon's wash day. And though he has enough money to buy a dozen of the nicest washing machines known to man, Vernon Davidson washes his clothes by hand. For his washing, as for everything else Vernon does, he has a system. As far as Vernon is concerned, his clothes come out looking cleaner and newer than any machine could get them. He wears all of his clothes during the week according to the schedule he has printed in black marker on the insides of the garments. Five sets of work clothes, three sets to rotate before or after work on those five days, and two sets for the weekend. When he wakes each Sunday and slips off his underwear, his drawers and closet are completely empty. If the morning is cool, Vernon goes out and washes his clothes wearing only a cotton robe. But if any warmth hangs in the air, as it often does by the first of March, Vernon goes out in the yard and washes his laundry naked.

Vernon wakes on the first Sunday in April with a nagging headache. He rubs his temples and lies thinking about Leonard. Finally he shakes it off, opens his eyes, and stands up. Though spring is well along, a touch of chill is in the air, so he puts his robe on after kicking his underwear into the giant laundry pile, then goes into the kitchen to start breakfast.

For the last dozen years, since he quit going to church, Vernon starts Sunday mornings with a large breakfast of eggs, bacon, French toast, orange juice, and coffee. He could have started working Sundays years ago if he had wanted, just to fill the time, but he never has. Sunday is the only day of the week he eats anything besides fried bologna-and-cheese sandwiches, which he makes twice a day for himself in the same greasy cast iron skillet he uses on Sundays to make his breakfast.

Once the coffee is going, and the bacon and eggs, Vernon walks back into the bathroom. Though he usually doesn't stop by the mirror in the hallway, this time he does. He turns and looks at himself face on. He opens his bathrobe, stands and flexes the long corded muscles that still run through his torso after sixty years, pats the flat part of his stomach. In the bathroom he grabs a comb, comes back to the mirror and quickly whips it through his long gray hair. He works the comb through, notes again that he hasn't lost a single strand. Then he combs through his thick gray beard and fluffs it just a bit. He smiles at himself wide, taps his perfect teeth. "Better to turn gray than turn loose," he says to the reflection as he pulls on a chunk of his hair. "I'm still looking good."

He goes back to the kitchen, takes his squeezable bottle of yellow mustard from the refrigerator and squirts a quarter inch of the oily yellow substance into a glass. Then he unscrews the lid of a bottle of Jack Daniel's, smells it out of habit, winces, and pours in three fingers' worth. His stomach gags, as it often does, with the first sip. Vernon lowers the glass, catches his breath, and raises it again. This time it all goes down, and the bitterness radiates out through the hinges of his jaws, his stomach, the top of his head. He slams the glass down on the counter, proud of his effort. After a minute the sour taste goes away, and the whiskey begins to do its work on the rest of him.

Everything starts to settle. By then the food is ready, and he slides it all onto a plate, pours a large cup of coffee, and sits down to eat.

By the time the food is gone, the good part of his drink is leaving him, as it seems to do earlier and earlier these days. He goes back to the kitchen for another round of the whiskey and mustard. Then he clears the dishes from the table and, with the sink already full, puts them on the counter. "Leave those for the cleaning woman," he mutters to himself. He eyes the mess in the rest of the house, papers all over, dust on the floor. Vernon likes to pretend.

Back in the bedroom, he picks up all the clothes and places them in the proper piles. Then he carries them all to the rear door, steps outside, and looks across the creek running through his backyard. Vernon smiles. Everything in his yard is the deep, rich green of spring, and not a weed is anywhere to be found. He's thought about planting flowers once or twice, something to break up the single note hue that soon enough will turn to brown. But, though everything outside is as it should be, nearly all color is missing from Vernon's yard.

Nevertheless, things are looking good on his side of the creek. On top of that, a few days earlier someone showed up while he was at work and cut the grass at the Baptist church camp on the other side of the creek. Funny how things work out. Vernon sold that property to the church fifteen years ago, back when he was still part of it.

The arrival of spring means a lot of things. It means the mill where he has worked for thirty-six years will bring some young guys in, guys Vernon will harass into doing his work for him. It means the bullfrogs that sing their throaty songs as he lies in bed at night will be back in tune any time now. And it also means Easter, and the Baptists he loves to terrorize will be showing up for lunches on the grounds at their camp across the creek starting in two more weeks. And when they come, the men to stand around and talk about fishing or hunting over fried chicken and beans, the women to compliment one another on their new dresses, the boys to run around the playground and wear grass stains on their new Easter pants, Vernon will be there washing his clothes in the yard, in all his bearded, gray-haired glory, as naked as the good Lord made him. And that's exactly what he'll say to whichever one of those do-gooder men comes to the edge of the creek to complain about it in response to the shrieking of their children or the pecking of their wives.

"This is the way the good Lord made me!" he shouts into the air, shrugging his robe to the ground and spreading out his arms. Practicing for the first confrontation of the season. He can already picture the guy standing over there, usually Jerry Reeves or Tom Staples or Donnie Lyles. One of them is who they usually send. He just loves to see the looks on their faces as they stand there in their Sunday best, striped or polka-dotted choke chains hanging from their necks, trying to look him straight in the face and not to let their eyes wander downward.

They always say the same things. "Come on, Vernon, it's kids over here. Come on, Vernon, put some clothes on, brother, my wife . . ." Sometimes they even try to guilt him. "Look at you, brother Vernon, look what you've turned into, you orta be ashamed of yourself."

But Vernon Davidson cannot be guilted. Not after what he's been through. And certainly not after the four or five glasses of whiskey and mustard he'll have in him by Sunday noon.

Over the five or six years he's been playing this little game, the church group has tried a few things to keep Vernon's nakedness from being exposed to their side of the creek. They once planted a hedgerow but didn't water it and everything died. Another time they even put up a six-foot wooden fence, but they had to build it close to the edge of the creek to keep from shrinking their playground. The way their property and Vernon's are elevated, it made no difference whatsoever.

After Easter, Vernon's friend Tommy Robichaux, too, will be pleased. Tommy is the owner of the Ragin' Cajun, a watering hole not far from Vernon's house and a place where Vernon has passed many an evening over the last dozen years since he emphatically gave up the Baptist church. Tommy always keeps a bottle of mustard in the cooler just for Vernon's visits. Tommy loves the stories Vernon tells about his exploits with the Baptists, and each time Vernon comes in with a new one, Tommy asks him to tell it over and over and howls at each telling. Tommy and his family are Catholics, and Tommy has never understood how anyone can call himself a Christian but not go to *his* church. Baptists in particular he thinks of as imbeciles who deserve to be made fun of in any way possible. Besides that, not many of them come in for drinks in his bar. A few, but not too many.

"Vernon, my friend," Tommy had said. Vernon was leaning on Tommy's bar at the time. "You gon' get after them Baptists this year, huh?"

"Yeah, planning to," Vernon said. He motioned for another drink.

"Good, glad to hear it," Tommy replied, as he opened the case. "Be good for you. Get some new life in you."

"What you mean, Tommy?" Vernon had known Tommy for a dozen years and was a good twenty years older. He wasn't accustomed to anything but kind words from the man.

"Get a little pep in your step, Vernon buddy," Tommy said. "Be good for you."

It eats at him, thinking about it, but Vernon knows Tommy was right. For some time now, he can't say for exactly how long, he has not been feeling his best. Could be for a year, maybe longer.

Maybe just since he got the news about his brother. Vernon has been an outgoing, backslapping man all of his life, and the personality that made him a fine deacon in the Baptist church he now hates has never left him. Not until recently. The energetic person he has been all of his life is suddenly confused and so, so tired. He's certain nobody can see it yet, no way has he let his guard down. But he surely knows it.

Not just tired, but edgy. Everywhere Vernon goes he keeps up a steady monologue, a repeating series of topics to gripe about, a practiced handful of ways to keep the talk going whenever he's around other people. Anything to close down the yawning hole he knows will suck him in unless he fights his way outside it. The night Tommy said that to him had not been a good one. Vernon had had a disagreement with one of the other regulars, a man not quite his age named Ben something, Vernon never could remember. Just another drunk jackass in the bar. Whatever led Ben there couldn't have been anything like what Vernon had learned to live with.

But Ben was the only other patron there that night, and Vernon was trying to explain to him the simple rules of weight conversion. If there is nothing else to talk about, Vernon falls back to whatever subject is in his head at the moment. Usually numbers. Vernon is always thinking about numbers.

"It's real simple, Ben," Vernon said, accenting his points on the bar with the edge of his hand. "Kilograms to pounds, it's like this. Just double the number of pounds and add ten percent. Five kilograms, double it to ten, add ten percent or one, that makes eleven pounds."

Ben just looked at him.

"Pounds to kilograms, little more tricky. First you have to subtract an eleventh, then halve it and there's your answer. Take the other example, it's easy. Eleven pounds, just subtract an eleventh or one pound, leaves ten, then halve it for five kilograms. Takes some practice but before long it's easy."

"That don't make no sense," a drunk Ben said.

"Of course it does. Those are the exact formulas, Ben."

"Naw," Ben said. With effort he lifted his head off the bar. "Don't make no sense."

"And why not?" Vernon asked. "A kilogram is 2.2 pounds—2.21, to be precise."

"It don't make no sense."

"I'm not understanding you, buddy." Ben stood up quickly, slammed his glass on the counter. "It don't make no sense! It *don't*—SLAM—*make*—SLAM—*no*—SLAM—*dayum*—SLAM—*sense*!" Then he shuffled toward Vernon and whispered the words again, his breath hot and putrid in Vernon's face.

Tommy Robichaux grabbed Ben and shoved him out the door, but not before he noticed a wild look in Vernon's eyes. Later, when Vernon thought about it, he was glad he had not punched or shoved the man. But he knew that, if not for Tommy, he would have. And the thought of what had almost happened ate at him like a cancer. That a worthless drunk like Ben whatever-his-name-was could get his goat like that. What right did that fool have to be in there drunk on a Tuesday night anyway? Ben what's-his-name's son was alive and well and living up in Arkansas somewhere, and Ben hadn't seen him in twenty years. Twenty years! Vernon just got madder when he thought about it. He should have pounded the sorry jerk just on principle. And then when Tommy Robichaux told Vernon he was dragging, why, that just made it worse.

But his Easter show, as he's been calling it, his Easter show in two weeks, that's going to bring Vernon back. Get him out of his doldrums. Get his juices flowing again. Get some new stories to tell in his repertoire. He can barely wait.

Vernon sorts all the clothes into soaking tubs and goes back in, fixes another drink, and sits down in his chair. He considers his plan for Easter again, goes through it all as he has done many times already. He is expecting to get a real thrill out of the day.

Hopefully nothing like that one time last year. Sure, the guys came over and asked him to stop it, and he shouted back at them like he always did. What happened next, though. Vernon was playing naked basketball on the concrete court he had poured for Billy years ago when his son was still a boy. The backboard and rim had deteriorated quite a bit over the years, and one of the straps holding it to the pole had rusted through. As a result the rim was only eight feet off the ground, and even at sixty years old and naked, Vernon could jump eight feet high to make a monster dunk for the Baptists' entertainment, whether they wanted it or not. He had just finished dunking the ball, and the ball had hit the base of the pole, rolled down the hill into the creek, and lodged in some brush. As he stood in the water reaching for it, a new face appeared.

"I'm David Adams," the man said, stepping into the water and extending his hand. "I'm the minister at First Baptist now."

Vernon was caught off guard by the young man's approach and instinctively reached out his hand. Vernon could see that the minister had removed his shoes and stood with his pants rolled up in the water. In an instant his composure returned.

"You're on my property."

"Oh," the young man said. "I'm sorry. I was given to understand that this creek was the dividing line of the two properties. You ever catch any fish here?"

Once again Vernon was caught off guard. "Yeah, a few, when it swells in the fall rains. Sometimes even in the spring."

"Wow. You're a fortunate man. There's nothing like God's own bounty, right in your own backyard."

Vernon quickly regained himself. "What do you want?"

The young man looked right at him then, right into his eyes. For an instant Vernon felt embarrassed about being naked. "I didn't want anything, sir, just to meet you. I understand at one time you were a deacon in our church, but that you haven't been part of our congregation in a few years. I thought maybe I could come over and speak to you sometime. Is that a possibility?"

Vernon was stumped. He couldn't speak. He kept his eyes on David Adams as if the man were a grizzly bear as he reached down and picked up his basketball.

"God is here for your pain, Vernon," the minister shouted as Vernon walked backward up the hill. "God's family is here for you."

Those were the last words he heard as he backed away and up the hill into his house, where his whiskey waited.

Vernon gets up from his chair and makes another drink. He's had more and more of those lately, these long periods where his mind goes off somewhere and blanks out. In some ways he's always done it, gone off into his memories. Vernon has a sharply detailed memory for the things people say, how they look, how they talk, a particular accent somebody uses. And of course for numbers. When he isn't remembering things from his past, Vernon's mind is filled with numbers that swirl around in his brain like a mathematical tornado. Vernon Davidson does not forget. He is aware, in a general way, that he drinks too much, certainly more than he wishes he did, but he often reminds people that he didn't start drinking until he was almost fifty years old. Especially when someone suggests that he might be losing some of his memory, that he's over sixty now and might want to cut back on the drinking. Just something to think about, they always add. When Vernon glares at them.

But that thing with the preacher, that was just a fluke. The young minister had surprised him, that's all. Nobody from that church had tried to talk to him in years. Well, some had tried, sure, but not for many years. Those that do, now, only try to talk to him from the other side of the creek. And only to try and shame him. For several weeks after that day with the preacher, Vernon kept his .22 loaded and propped up behind the door where Misty used to keep her broom. Each day when he came home from work, he mixed up a whiskey and mustard, grabbed the rifle, sat down in his chair, and stared at the door, waiting for a knock. Some nights he just flat-out prayed, as best he remembered how, that the presumptuous young fool would come. So he could stick the point of his rifle into the young man's chest.

Then one night, the minister did. Vernon was well into his whiskey that night when the minister knocked on the door. He still isn't sure, when he thinks about it, if he invited the guy in or not. He vaguely remembers a sound at the door and, when he looked up, there the young man stood.

Vernon stuck with his plan. He beckoned David Adams closer, pretended he wanted to shake his hand. And when his visitor came closer, Vernon stuck the barrel of his rifle into David Adams's chest, and pointed at the door with his other hand.

People can say what they want; Vernon Davidson is still as sharp as he ever was. He has replayed that scene with the minister a hundred times since then, until he can feel his legs standing there calf deep in the running water, can look up and see the man's face. He remembers how he slipped, how he had a pleasant moment with Adams before telling him to leave. But he goes through the scene again and sees something this time that somehow escaped him before. David Adams's eyes. It was his eyes, staring at Vernon. So open, so harmless. So kind.

Vernon finishes his drink and stands up from the chair a little shaky. He looks out the window at the camp across the creek. Somebody is walking around over there, a short man in overalls and a straw hat, and when Vernon opens the door he can hear the sound of the man's weed trimmer. *Easter,* he thinks, and smiles. He goes back outside, bends down into the tub of water, and begins rubbing his shirts together, working detergent deep into the spots and stains.

CHAPTER 6

Back at his apartment, Jody staggers outside later that morning, bewildered by Vernon's phone call and his first contact with Louisiana in a dozen years. The sidewalks, now, are nearly clear of snow as he travels through a Saturday morning slowly groaning to life. A man walks a dog, which alternately barks ferociously and stops to pant and wag its tail as if begging to be patted. A jogger says hello as he passes, a bald man whose head bursts with sweat. The leaves of an oak tree seem to open in front of him, the deep green hue breaking out in all directions.

He returns to his apartment. Jody surveys the room, feels only an emptiness, a blankness, a swirling sense of nothing in particular. When he can't decide what to do next, he simply sits down.

He lifts a book of pictures from the coffee table, idly turns through its pages. He stops at a photograph of the two of them taken in their office, returns easily to that moment. Jody touches the side of his own frozen face.

Jody joined the army days after he left home. His life as a soldier lasted two weeks.

No one knew exactly why he couldn't shoot a gun. Jody didn't care to discuss it. Why the feel of metal made him sweat, the sound of firing spun his head in circles so strong he had to lie down on the ground. His drill sergeant, a short man from Oklahoma named Watters, recommended he be discharged as untrainable. But Watters had already taken a liking to the skinny kid from Louisiana and, knowing Jody had nowhere else to go, gave Jody high marks when he referred him to a personal contact he had with a defense contracting agency. There Jody met Art, who had also backed into the job on the basis of an undergraduate psychology degree.

"Davidson, look. You're a kid. You'll recover from this. It's a good job, an opportunity. You're what, not even nineteen years old? You'll learn some skills. Not everybody was meant to be a soldier."

The project consisted of interviewing new army recruits as part of a long-term data collection project. Art Gellert, the lead researcher, had been there three months already, and all his paperwork was a mess. Jody was annoyed with him at first, a grown man who couldn't put his pens back where they belonged on his desk. But he kept his mouth shut, did his job. Jody knew Watters didn't have to help him. And, after all that had happened at home, he didn't have anywhere else to go.

They interviewed the new recruits by bringing them into a room and asking them a series of questions. After the paperwork was done, one of the two presented a longer interrogation, to get more detail about what their lives at home were like. Why they wanted to be in the army, and what sort of asset they would be.

Most of the talks were routine. Only maybe one in ten answered more questions than they were asked. Even fewer actually opened up and detailed stories of their lives at home, of abuse, neglect, hope lost at young ages. Or in some cases, storybook lives. In the course of the years on the project, Jody watched himself slowly change, put his own past behind him. He learned to understand people, to put his hands on them, touch them, to tell them, at times, when to let things go. Art was better at getting the conversations started but he never got any real information from anybody at all. With Jody, though, the young recruits often wanted to talk.

He returns to the picture. They were out in California then, a Friday at the end of a busy week. In the picture, Art's trumpet sits, upright, on the table. Jody can't remember a single day since they met that his friend hasn't had that trumpet nearby.

That night was the first time he ever actually heard Art play. A large group of them were there at the bar, to drink beer and talk too loudly to one another, Art and Jody and a number of their friends from the base. After a couple of drinks Art was holding his glass in one hand, his instrument in the other. They sat together, talked about what led them to the army. Art, like Jody, had wanted to be a soldier but had settled for working around them instead.

"I left just to get away from home," Art tells him. "My dad wanted me to go, to get out, see some things. Thought it'd be good for me. He's real proud, feels like I'm serving the country." He lifts his glass.

Then one of the other guys asks him to play. At first Art is sheepish, stays in his chair, shakes his head. Then a dozen guys are chanting. "Trum-pet, trum-pet, trum-pet, trum-pet." Finally he lifts his glass, empties the dregs down his throat, stands up on his chair.

When he hits the first note the place goes quiet. Glasses clink together for just an instant more. Murmuring stops. Everyone in the place looks up at him. Even the bartenders.

He plays. And plays. And plays. Art blows the sound of a gentle breeze, of songbirds, of a springtime afternoon, of shrill, silvery streetlights on a dark and rainy city street, the horns of cars passing by, the boisterous chatter of hatted smokers in doorways. Jody feels the sunshine on his skin, raindrops on his face, imagines the boxy notes of Scooter's harmonica, smells the verdant grass in which his brother lies back, playing his ode to life on the cowboy trail, the faraway focus of the player's thoughts reflected in each note, a perceptible syncopation. At that moment Jody knows, and knows he knows, that he and Art will be friends. Finally, Art steps back down from the chair. Someone hands him a drink. He sucks it down and laughs before he finally sits again.

"Wow," Jody says. "I just want to touch you."

"Oh. It's just my horn."

A few guys sit listening to him play back at the apartment. After an hour, Jody excuses himself and goes to bed. When he wakes in the morning, Art still plays in the living room. He says he's been up all night, blowing softly. He says good morning. Then pulls the horn back to his lips.

"So, Jody. I was thinking more about your brother. Didn't you say your mother died in childbirth?" Art drives him to the bus station early that evening.

"I did."

"That must be some guilt to live with."

"What do you mean?"

"Just knowing that the fact you're alive means your mother is dead."

"I never really thought about it that way, Art." Karen settles her head into Jody's chest. Art continues to check the reflection of the two of them in his rearview mirror. He turns into the parking lot of the bus station and pulls into a spot.

"Jody, I'm real sorry about this. Just get down there and see what you can do. And we'll be here when you get back."

"Thank you."

Jody and Karen step out. Art reaches through the window, pulls his friend into a hug.

"Good luck. I know it's hard, dealing with family, with things like this. Don't forget you're one of us now. Don't forget where you come from." He grins at his joke.

"That's funny, Art. I'll call you in a couple of days."

"Are you sure you don't want to take the car? The Mustang?"

"Nah. I still know how to ride a bus. Soon enough that car will be mine. I'm not driving it until it's paid for. Till every dime is paid."

"All right. Up to you."

Karen walks with Jody to the bus. Two guys are stuffing luggage into the belly of the machine. Jody hands over a bag that contains most of his possessions to one of the guys. The porter scratches his forehead with the back of a gloved hand, then writes out a ticket, tears it off, and hands it to him. Jody turns back to Karen. She lays on a kiss with disarming passion.

"Jody, my good man." Her eyes, once again, cut through him.

"Yes, darling?"

"I'm going to miss you."

"I'm going to miss you too, Karen."

She grabs his hands and yanks them down repeatedly, like a small child. "I can barely stand the idea of being away from you."

He kisses her forehead. "I'll take that as a compliment. Sometimes it's just magic between us. Something bigger than both of us put together."

"It's you, Jody. You do it to me. You love me just as I am."

"That's exactly how I love you, Karen. Just as you are. I'll call you in a couple days. Okay?"

"I can't wait." She pulls him close again, nose to nose, flutters her eyelashes to mingle with his. "I can't wait."

CHAPTER 7

An apocryphal Louisiana legend tells the story of a Caddo Indian named Natchitoches, who stood on the banks of the Sabine River, now part of the border between Louisiana and Texas. He stood by the river with his father and his brother, Nacogdoches, sometime in the early 1700s. In an effort to expand the territory of the nation, the chief instructed his two sons that day to take a group of people each and form new settlements. The father gave each of his sons specific instructions. Nacogdoches, he said, go west for three days, find a place to settle and form a village. Natchitoches, you go east, and follow the same plan. Thus, as the story goes, a young Caddo Indian founded the first settlement in what came to be the Louisiana Purchase. And, with the influence of the French, prevalent in the area at that time, his name took on the pronunciation "nack-a-tish," which it uses still.

From the first time he heard the story in school, Vernon felt a connection to it. Like the two sons in the story, Vernon imagined himself one day moving away from his family, from his father and brothers, turning his back to the river, cutting his way through the underbrush.

Vernon stayed in Branden a few years after he finished school, driving a delivery route for a small farm-equipment manufacturer in north Louisiana. Like his brothers before him, Vernon didn't have the stomach to even try working for his father. Before long, the owner of the company took note of Vernon's behavior, of the clean-cut, driven young man from Branden, and offered him a position in their main office, in Natchitoches, fifty miles away.

The week he was offered the job, before he even started, Vernon's truck died, a truck EL handed down to him in his last year of high school. Vernon was young then, heady, serious about things in the way a young man is, before the crushing realities of life set in and make him content just to get his job done, to get up and do what needs to be done each day. And so, with no vehicle of his own, the day he left his family home, left his mother and father and his brothers to live in Natchitoches, Vernon followed the example of the city's founding father; he walked. Vernon set out that day at first light with a pack on his back, a head full of possibility. Late that spring evening he arrived to start his new life, exhausted from fifty miles on his feet, and checked into a hotel, where he stayed for a week until he found his first house.

In his initial days there, Vernon bought a new truck, began to settle. But within a few months the company, which was paying him handsomely, fell apart suddenly when the accountant left town in a hurry with the owner's wife and $75,000 of the company's money. EL, to help out his son, made some calls and landed Vernon an enviable position at the paper mill back in Branden.

But Vernon loved Natchitoches and began to find a peace there as a bachelor he had never known in his parents' house. After a couple of years sleeping late or fishing on his days off, Vernon met Misty DuBois one afternoon in a local café. Her father was minister of the First Baptist Church, and before long Vernon belonged to a church again, where he settled in and eventually was asked to be a deacon.

Though Vernon has returned to his hometown five days a week for thirty-six years since, he has never for a minute wanted to live there again. Each day he leaves his house, points his truck north. Though Natchitoches has grown, and a bypass has been built, though there are a number of shortcuts that would save him a few minutes driving, Vernon prefers the old ways. Each day he drives past the college, rolls down the old brick-lined, bumpy Front Street. Often, if he has a few minutes to spare, he likes to pull to the side of the road and look out, down the hill to the holiday light displays on Cane River. Sometimes he even parks and gets out of the truck to stand on top of the levee, crunching his boots over piles of dry brown leaves from previous years in the lives of the live oaks lining the road, embedded in every possible crack in the ancient brick street.

A few days after his phone call to Jody, Vernon drives in to work. Coming into Branden, Vernon passes the old home place. Even after fifty-something years he can't look at that place without getting the picture in his head. He can't forget what it was like to stand there and watch Pearl fight those other boys, in the horse corral out behind their barn. To watch the fights EL had set up for his own son. Like Pearl was EL's private trained animal. Vernon can't forget the words their father always said when he and Leonard helped Pearl stumble back up to the house afterward either.

"That'll teach you boys to take care of yourselves." That's what he said. In Vernon's memory, EL wears denim jeans and a Western-style plaid shirt, his breath a knife blade of whiskey. Vernon mouths the words. "And you two," he liked to add, pointing to Leonard and Pearl, "keep yourselves looking good like your younger brother and you'll have a lot less problems in life." Just thinking about it brings back the mix of warmth and revulsion Vernon felt when EL moved toward him, put an arm around Vernon, pulled him close.

Vernon thinks about all that nearly every day as he drives past the home place on his way to work. The house where he and his brothers grew up is set back from the parish highway at the edge of Branden. Vernon looks out at the place every day, at the horse corral that still stands on the back side of the barn. A new family has been living there for the fifteen or sixteen years since EL and Hazel died. Vernon stopped in with Billy and met them once not long after they bought the place, a couple that had relocated from Tennessee. They didn't have any kids of their own but they did have horses. They always had a horse or two wandering around that old corral.

When he pulls up on the street in front of the mill, Vernon puts on his blinker and waits for the traffic to clear. By now the bitterness from his predrive drink is completely gone and most of the good part is gone too.

Vernon's mind drifts back to EL. In Vernon's memory his father is not the wasted, thin-skinned old man he became at the end of his life. The father Vernon imagines is the ruddy, thick man in the black-and-white photograph he still keeps on the mantel of his fireplace at home. In the picture EL smiles, stands behind his three young boys beside their old flatbed Chevy truck, the water of some lake or pond reflecting the light of a day fifty-some years ago in the background.

That's the EL he pictures when he talks to Leonard about him. Leonard is the only one left who can talk with him about their father. Not that he and Leonard have talked that much. In all the years that Vernon has driven within a mile of his brother's house every day when he goes to work, he had only occasionally stopped in. He's seen his brother more times in the last month than in the last five years combined, probably.

Twelve years. That's what Jody told him on the phone. That he had been gone twelve years. Dang how it gets away from you. And that means Billy and Pearl and EL and Hazel have been gone even longer. As he finally makes the left turn into the paper mill's parking lot, Vernon spots a rolling cloud drifting across the sky. Maybe they're all in there. He doesn't know where they all are. Only that they aren't with him anymore.

Still, he has to work. Thirty-six years he's been working there, and in a couple more months he's set to retire. Vernon pulls into the lot and cranks his truck down the lane toward his parking spot. Then he sees Robert Millie's old green Chevy blocking the way, and Robert underneath it. Robert slides out, looks up at Vernon with both arms crossed in front of his face and smiles. A lot of the guys greet Vernon this way, a sign of respect, they tell him, for the shine that still bounces off his nearly forty-year-old truck, the same one he bought when he first moved to Natchitoches. Vernon never has seen the sense in letting anything run down.

Vernon has witnessed this scene with Robert Millie before; in fact he's even been under that truck himself. Robert's old truck is a column shift, and the external linkage is worn out so bad that the truck gets stuck in a gear sometimes and has to be yanked back into neutral from underneath. As he waits, Vernon reaches down to the floorboard and pulls a bologna-and-cheese sandwich wrapped in a baggie out from the cooler and places it along with a large bag of pork rinds and a thermos of black coffee into a smaller cooler. Then he repositions his jar of mustard in the ice, pulls out the bottle of Jack Daniel's, opens the lid, takes a little swig of it with his head down near the floor, and buries it back in the ice. By the time he looks up, Robert Millie is coming out from under the truck and waves at him. Then he gets in and moves out of the way, and Vernon starts back for his parking place.

He turns the corner of the lane and sees his spot is

taken again. He stops and stares at the blue pickup with the Confederate flag in the back window. That Summers kid has been parking there lately. This time, though, Vernon is stumped. Vernon had talked with the kid about it and thought they had the misunderstanding cleared up. Vernon thought they were through talking.

But, apparently, Vernon has more talking to do. Johnny Summers has only worked there for a few months, and Vernon has been pretty easy on him. The kid has had his own problems in life, that's for sure. On top of that, he's just a kid. A large one, but still just an overgrown boy. On the other hand, Johnny Summers has left Vernon's parking spot alone for the last week or so, and Vernon sits and wonders why the truck is there today.

In point of fact, it isn't really *his* parking space. But he has used it for as long as he can remember. And it isn't even that great of a spot. It's nowhere near the building, out at the edge of the lot. Vernon likes being out there by himself. Most of the guys who work at the mill are way too lazy to walk an inch farther than necessary. The lot is only close to full a couple of times a year, when they double the guys on shift so they can shut down one of the paper machines. Even then nobody else ever takes it. Everybody knows that's Vernon's spot. On some days, like today for instance, there isn't another vehicle within fifty yards of it. Yet there sits Johnny Summers's truck, all alone.

The first couple times it happened, Vernon asked him about the drive-through wash, if he just wanted to be close to it or what. While the spot is not close to the entrance to the mill, it's about as close as you can park to the drive-through wash. At the edge of the lot stands a water structure the guys can drive their vehicles through when they finish their shifts and rinse off some of the crap that falls on them while they're in working. And it's true, there are some days, not many but some days, when it's dry and there's not much wind to blow the ash and soot away, when a lot of guys want to use the wash and might have to wait ten or fifteen minutes in line. All you do is drive up, push a button and drive through, there's no soap or anything, it's just a half-minute rinse. So he had asked Johnny if he wanted to be close to the wash. Except for that Confederate flag, the kid does have a pretty nice truck, Vernon has to admit, and he was planning to tell Johnny that if they ever got there at the same time he'd be glad to let him go through first. *Just please don't park in my parking space.*

"So what do you say, Johnny?" Vernon asked a couple weeks back.

"About what?"

"About what do you think?"

"What? *Your* spot again?"

"Come on, Johnny. I mean, what are you doing, kid? You know it's mine. You just want to be close to the wash?"

"To the what?"

"You're trying my patience, kid." Vernon poked him in the chest. "I been parking there since your daddy was your age."

"Hey." Summers turned on his heels. "Screw off, old man. I park where I want to."

Vernon started at the comment, and backed away immediately. His first thought was of Pearl. If Pearl had been there he wouldn't have listened to that even once. Never mind the kid was twenty-five years old and big as a gorilla. Never mind the kid had played football in college and even a couple years in the NFL before blowing his knee out and ending up back at home working at the paper mill. Never mind his arms were as big around as Vernon's head, and he liked to talk about how he could still bench press five hundred pounds. No sir. Never mind if Pearl were alive he'd be nearly a seventy-year-old man. No sir, no way. He would have hit that big monster in the time it took Vernon to think about it.

Vernon pulls forward and settles in next to the kid's truck, grabs his lunch, and bends down for one more little swig before he goes in. That doesn't do the trick, so he takes another one just to be sure. Then he gobbles a handful of mints and puts two sticks of gum in his mouth to cover up the smell. For some time now the alcohol hasn't been tasting the same, hasn't given him the satisfaction it has so many times before; in response, he's found himself drinking even more of it. After he closes the lid and puts the bottle back in the ice and closes the truck door, he feels that way once again. Not satisfied, as he has so many times before. Not numb, which is even worse. Just a little foggy and not quite steady, and more irritable than he wishes he did.

"Good morning, Caroline."

"Hey, sweetie. How's Leonard?"

Vernon blows out. He just looks at her, shakes his head.

"I'm sorry, sweetie." The receptionist puts her hand on top of his on the counter between them. Just by standing she releases a cloud of perfume into the air.

"You come see me if you need to talk about it." She turns and marks a big X on the calendar for the previous day, then another big X across the entire month of March.

He goes into the locker room, sits down on the bench, and puts on the rest of his clothes. Though Vernon still has the personality of a church deacon, he keeps it turned off most of the time at work. Over the last many years he has found the person he enjoys talking to at work the most is himself.

When he sees the Summers kid at the other end of the room he steels himself, turns his charm back on. He decides what he'll do is remind the kid that he'll be retiring soon. That old Vernon'll be out of there in just two more months and then Johnny Summers can have the parking spot and maybe keep it himself for his own thirty-six years. Thinking this gives him a moment's lift, and then the kid sees him.

"What's up, old man?"

"Hello, young man." Vernon sallies over, reaches up and squeezes the kid's massive shoulder. He can't even begin to get his fingers around it. Touching the kid's shoulder is like trying to put his hand around a wall.

"Listen, I see you took my spot again. I was thinking of something. I'm going to be retiring here at the end of next month. How about you just give an old man a break until then, and then it'll be yours for as long as you want it?"

Summers jerks his arm away. For an instant Vernon sees a trace of something different in the young man's eyes. Maybe fear?

"I park where I want to, old man. Like I told you."

"Come on, Johnny. We've all got to get along here. I've been working here thirty-six years. You're just playing games."

Summers turns and walks toward the door. "Like I said before. Screw you, old man."

Eventually Vernon gets his boots laced and goes out of the locker room to work. He takes a deep breath, smells the stench of burning iron and sulfur. He puts on his hardhat and in the instant it takes him to flip the earmuffs down, Vernon feels the drowning noise of all the working machines vibrate through him. He walks toward his worksite. With the first step his whole body moistens from the heat. The noise is only one of the many signs of danger. Whether the grinding lull of the giant chippers that pulverize whole trees in a second, or the hiss of one gas or another pressurized to a thousand pounds per square inch. All of it was out to get a man. Even Leonard had not got out of the mill unscathed, and spent his last fifteen years limping from a broken leg he got when he fell off a scaffold one cold winter day. Over the years Vernon has seen dozens of men get injured, and fifteen men who have died at the mill, whether chopped into pieces by one of the chippers or cut in half by a vapor explosion. And he knows enough about math to know more men will die. Which means of all those guys walking with him or around him or toward him in the hall, most of whom plan to spend their careers working there, one or maybe more of them is a dead man walking. It only takes a second to die.

All morning as he does his work, the exchange with Johnny Summers gnaws at him. When the lunch whistle blows, Vernon decides he'll try something different. Really different. He goes outside to his truck. Once inside, he reaches for the toolbox. He rummages around for a short leather punch he thought he had in there, and finds it. He sits sideways for a moment on his passenger-side seat, looking at the tires on the kid's truck, pushing himself to go through with it. He glances around to make sure no one is there.

Then he reaches into what's left of the ice for his bottle and takes a long pull. Once again he just feels foggy, and the small amount of indignation he has been feeling disappears. The kid really does have a nice truck, one he bragged he had bought with the signing bonus he got when he was drafted to the NFL. And sure, Johnny Summers probably never expected to end up back at home so fast. Vernon drops the punch tool on the floor of his truck and sits staring at the tires.

Vernon never had liked to drink. But unlike anything else he's ever done, the drinking helped pass all the time. He could be a full-time drunk if he wanted to be. All the time alone is the only reason he hasn't retired already. Everything he owns is paid for, and in pretty good shape. He has money put away and could have quit any time in the last few years and still drawn a pretty good pension. So far he hasn't, and the only reason he's planning to leave the first of June is that the mill bosses really like to get guys out after thirty-seven years. Seems arbitrary to him, but they have their reasons. His thirty-seven years will be the first of June. When he first started thinking about it a few months ago, Vernon decided he would fight it, that he didn't want to retire after all. But then he found out about Leonard, the days kept passing, and when he does stop and think about it, he figures maybe he'll fight after all.

After a minute Vernon walks around Johnny Summers's truck out to the street. He pauses and looks at his tree, reaches out and runs his hands over the bark. The sugar maple wasn't really planted for Billy. But it was planted the week after the accident, and when Vernon showed back up to work after a week of grieving, there it had been, right next to his parking space. Since then Vernon has unofficially adopted it. He takes a few minutes after work each day to touch it, talk to it, to keep the grass pulled back from the base. To water it in the summer from barrels he carries in the back of his truck. To give it lots of room to grow. It must be a foot in diameter now, and strong. Vernon's head is swimming. Today he wants desperately to hug the tree but stops himself, instead puts his hands around the trunk at about the height Billy's shoulders would have been.

Vernon runs his hands over the bark. All the trees he has seen chopped up, thousands and thousands and thousands of them. But not this one. This tree was just there when he showed back up for work that day, planted between the street and the sidewalk. Vernon took an immediate liking to it, just a sapling then. Over the years he's watched it grow. More than once he has come out to his truck at lunch or at the end of his shift to find the city workers about to prune the tree, these dimwits barely qualified to pick up garbage, who had about as much common sense as the sputtering chainsaws they held in their hands. He always chased them off and pruned the tree himself when it was needed.

In his dreams Vernon sometimes stands by the tree and watches as it turns into his son, who then opens up and talks to him just as he always did. In Vernon's dreams the two of them get into his truck and go to the lake to fish. Billy always lands a stringer of bass and holds them up proudly, that wavy forelock of brown hair in his face. At times, Vernon feels like those dreams, waiting to see his son in that other world, is all the life he has left. And at other times, when the days take forever to pass, he feels like he's already dead. Dead a long time ago.

When the whistle blows, Vernon starts back in to work. On a whim he opens the truck door and reaches for a screwdriver down on the floorboard. He stands and looks at Johnny Summers's truck, considers what it would feel like to run the screwdriver down the length of the body, to dig it deep under the paint. As he gets into position, Vernon looks up and sees Robert Millie, probably out there fooling with that shift lever again, eyeing him. He throws the screwdriver in the bed of his truck. He heads back toward the entrance to the mill. As he's walking he notices a scuff mark on his boot where the leather is wearing thin. "Got to get these things oiled," he says to himself, and continues toward the gate. He's been meaning to oil the boots for ages. The kind of thing he has always kept up with, even after Billy died, until just lately. The second whistle blows and he goes back in, flips down his earmuffs, and gets back to work. Three more hours and he'll see his brother, stopping by the hospital on his way home.

CHAPTER 8

At the step of the bus Jody feels queasy, hollowed out. The driver looks down the steps at him. Sunlight pours through the window behind him and Jody can't make out his face, only the outline of a head with a fringe of hair around it. Jody walks up the steps onto the bus. The driver sits in his seat, taps on the microphone. He has big red sideburns and he turns to look as Jody makes his way up the steps, emits a radius of a smile, then goes back to the microphone. He appears friendly, though he has beady gray eyes like some crustacean. The man's lower jaw juts out from his face as if he's about to belch. He says his name is Pork Chop.

Jody sidesteps down the aisle with his duffel bag, finds a seat halfway back in an empty row. By the time the bus pulls out, he has too many things to think about, and knows he will never go to sleep.

After many years of separation from his parents and the rest of his family in Texas, grandfather EL Davidson reconnected with them when Jody was a boy. Jody's father, Pearl, and Vernon were all in their thirties and forties when the Louisiana branch of the Davidsons began attending family reunions, held annually at the house of EL's brother, Bobby Frank, back in Texas.

As a boy Jody was excited every year to see the new family he had found, and though they never talked about it, he knew his father and uncles felt the same way. Jody was eight years old but Leonard, Pearl, and Vernon were all grown men when they met many of their aunts, uncles, and cousins for the first time.

From the time his boys were small, EL talked about some trouble he had in Texas. Whatever that trouble was, they never knew until they were all adults. EL had believed for years that he'd be subject to arrest at the border if he ever returned to Texas. In fact, EL only agreed to go back, at sixty years old, when Pearl finally assured him that an anonymous call to the Texas Rangers had confirmed that no outstanding arrest warrant for EL Davidson existed in Texas. Even then, he only agreed to go when he found out his brother BF had, years before, moved several hundred miles away from their hometown of Lidem, Texas, to the Louisiana side of the state.

On the Friday before Easter, EL had one of his guys clean out a panel van he kept to haul his logging crew around. When EL got home at the end of the day, the truck was cleaned up real nice. Then he set in four folding lawn chairs and a bunch of blankets for the floor. His sons, all three, could have easily driven out to Texas in their own vehicles. But it made EL happy to drive his whole clan over there, and if EL was happy, everybody was happy.

Driving over there, they all had a certain anticipation—how would everybody look, what would Aunt Earline have for them to eat, would Ernie make the same rude comments he made the year before. As EL drove, they all played cards in the van or Scrabble on a pallet on the floor. Leonard and Vernon and Pearl and Dot, Pearl's wife, didn't really mind sitting in those lawn chairs either. This big old mean man they all had described as their father was, to Jody's eyes, a harmless, more and more sickly old version of a man he never knew. But as they drove and got closer, the anticipation built and all the complaining amped up. "Why do we have to drive out here every year, when are they all going to come to Louisiana?" EL was a first-class complainer and had taught his sons young how to bitch. In a way none of them was comfortable unless the air was full of gripes.

Once they finally got there, Uncle BF had the place all dressed up—he had made a little bit of money in oil and, though he wasn't rich like J.R. Ewing, he fancied his place a miniature South Fork Ranch from *Dallas*. The house was set nearly a mile off the road, and somewhere he had found these cardboard cutouts of the characters from the show, J.R. in his big hat, Sue Ellen with all that feathered hair. They were stationed at intervals to greet the family as they drove up the driveway. Standing by the front door, to break up the monotony, maybe, was a similar cutout of Junior Samples in his brush blue overalls and horn-rimmed glasses with that grin on his face like a pig in mud, holding his BR-549 sign. Uncle BF loved *Dallas* but Earline was the biggest fan of *Hee Haw* Jody had ever known. Which is why they all went there on a Saturday, to end with the weekly viewing of her favorite show at six o'clock.

They all spilled out of the van and into the house as fast as they could to beat the sun, or the rain, whatever was coming out of the sky that day. Even for the fifty yards they had to walk to the door EL and his boys shouted a chorus of complaints. As if the weather in Louisiana had been any different when they left.

The Davidson family all met up in a room down in the basement that was big enough to hold church. In fact, Aunt Earline said BF was always threatening to do just that, break off from the local First Baptist Church and start his own congregation with his son Eddie as preacher. Though EL and his clan tried to arrive early, they were always the last into the room. The Texas Davidsons turned one by one to see EL's end of the family straggle in, and the place broke into applause.

As they squeezed into the room, BF came over and quickly shook his brother's hand and then stepped up onto the stage, which was right by the entry door. He actually had a little stage in his room.

"Ladies and gentlemen, ladies and gemmun," BF said. "The Louisiana Davidsons are here." As his brother spoke, EL looked down at the floor with his foot shaking, waiting not so patiently for his turn. Finally, EL stepped onto the stage.

Maybe "lunged" was a better word. Even getting up that one step was an effort for him. He had been a big man most of his life—Leonard joked that when they were kids their friends used to ask him if EL stood for Extra Large—but by that time his health was failing. Yet he somehow made it up and took the microphone.

"How y'all doing over heah in Texas," he said, then adjusted the cowboy hat he only wore on these occasions. "For them that don't remember me"—Jody laughs out loud when he remembers this part, wonders if his grandfather really meant this, standing in a room with sixty or seventy members of his own family—"I'm EL Davidson. I live over in Branden, Louisiana, and I have three boys—Pearl, Leonard, and Vernon. And I'm so proud of them." Then each year he told the same story, how he was the first Davidson to leave Texas and how he had had his family and they had been such a good family, how they had always had such a nice time and were such a happy family living in Louisiana. Jody just sat and listened. Pearl and Leonard had both talked many times about how EL had just beat the tar out of both of them practically from the day they were born, but not Vernon, Vernon he always left alone. But Pearl and Leonard just stood there and hung on every word of their father, talking about how great family life had been. Like they were standing there waiting on him to say it again and say it in some magic way this time and just have it be true. Maybe change a couple words from all the years before, maybe even accent the words differently, just have it all be true. Vernon looked away, waiting for EL's speech to be finished. He was a deacon in his church and would never say or do anything to embarrass his father. But he didn't look at EL either. Pearl and Leonard, though, they ate it up.

After the annual introductions, up spoke Ernie Davidson. Ernie was Uncle Eddie's son, BF's grandson, Jody's second cousin. He was ten or fifteen years older than Jody and Scooter, but to them he was just another adult. Leonard used to say what happened to Ernie happened to a lot of preachers' kids. He never did learn to act right. Or if he ever learned how, he decided not to. He had his hair a little long and grew a bushy beard, always wore a tee shirt with either a dirty saying on it or a picture of some naked woman. So when EL finished his speech, Cousin Ernie, who seemed to get dumber by the year, said the same stupid thing he always said.

"You proud of *both* of your sons Uncle EL? Hell, Vernon don't look nothing like you. Still got all his hair too. Hell they all do." Leonard and Pearl sat looking at the floor, clenching their teeth. Vernon looked off in another direction. It was true that Vernon didn't look much like EL, certainly not like his brothers did. And all three of them had full heads of hair, while EL was egg bald.

"It's the mother's Daddy!" Pearl ran shouting as he went straight for Ernie. "Hazel's daddy, you idiot, he had a full head of black hair till the day he died! You didn't even know him, you punk!" Ernie towered over Pearl.

"I's just kidding, Uncle Pearl, take a joke, huh!"

"Kid somebody else besides Daddy, you little peckerwood!

You ain't too big for me to stomp right here!" Pearl poked Ernie in the chest as he said this, leaned back to see Ernie's face.

Most of the family sat looking down at the floor as if in prayer.

Then Pearl went back over to his father.

"You okay, Daddy?"

"What's going on?" EL responded. Then the three of them helped him down from the stage, got him seated at a table and plied him with food. Leonard and Vernon each put a hand on Pearl's shoulder and whispered something in his ear. Pearl had been hotheaded all his life, and he had had one stroke already. His doctors were always telling him to take it easy, to settle down. His brothers were just there to remind him.

Then there was Billy.

Billy Davidson lived part time with Vernon but always went to the reunions. Vernon and his son were comfortable together. While everybody else worked the room and jawed at each other, squeezing biceps and patting guts, finding ways to outdo and outtalk each other, the two of them sat in a corner, side by side, legs crossed, leaned back, talking together and laughing like old friends.

They couldn't get three minutes together without somebody trying to break it up. Maybe one of the boy cousins would come up and punch Billy on the arm. Maybe Pearl would try to pull Billy up from his chair to join a softball game in process. Even the little kids got in on it, running around the two of them, screaming, shouting names at one another and then the same names at Billy. The way the two of them, father and son, were so easy together somehow unnerved the Davidson family. Like they should have been fighting or something.

Later, at home, Leonard offered his opinion. "I've told him he's spoiling that boy." Leonard said from the time Billy was born Vernon treated him that way, always holding him, never letting him cry. There's not one picture anywhere of Leonard holding either Jody or Scooter, only bending down to pet them like long-tailed cats. Leonard said that EL had talked to Vernon about the way he treated Billy, and Pearl had talked to him about it, and that he himself had talked to Vernon about it. Yet on they went, the two of them, just like friends.

Eventually everyone got in on the softball game. It usually ended when one of the uncles hit a home run into the neighbor man's chicken yard and the chickens all squawked and feathers flew and BF's crazy old neighbor ran out to the edge of the yard with a shotgun pointing up at the sky, shouting that Jesus was about to come back. By that time, the ice cream that had been churning all afternoon was ready to eat, and Uncle Eddie called them all in together, and they went back into the basement where they were blasted by the air-conditioned chill and would have a sweet snack along with their meal.

But before dinner, there was one more thing. For a minute Uncle Eddie took over as minister, asked for everyone's attention. "Everybody quieten down and bow your heads, please." Everyone was tired from the day and ready to settle in. The prayer went something like this.

> *Heavenly Father we'd like to thank you for bringing us all together again here this year and for all the wonderful food and nourishment we've received, may we use it to strengthen our bodies so that we may be of greater service to thee. Also we'd like to thank you Father for the chance once again to have our family here together, and we ask that you help all of us as the Davidson family be an earthly reflection of your heavenly family that we all hope to join when we are called. Today*

especially we'd like to remember Aunt Allene who got her promotion to glory this last year, may she be a trusted servant to you there in heaven as she always was here on earth. And thank you once again Father for all of the good things you've done for us and for the opportunities you give each and every one of us to partake in your bounty. Through your son Jesus Christ our Lord we pray—

In unison a roomful of Davidsons said, "Ay-men." After that one of the girl cousins in jeans, boots, and hat cued up the cassette player and did a song for general entertainment, a Patsy Cline or Dolly Parton or maybe a Tammy Wynette number. Or sometimes even a hymn, "Amazing Grace," "Gather at the River," "The Old Rugged Cross." After the singing, hugs and handshakes went around the room and the men patted each other on the back, and Cousin Ernie, ever the center of attention, yelled out, "Hee Haw!"

Which meant it was time for the centerpiece of the celebration, the reason they all were gathered on Saturday, the weekly episode of what, as far as many of the Davidsons including Jody were concerned, was the greatest television show ever made. *Hee Haw.* While Roy and Buck sang the opening song, everyone would bicker and talk back and forth, what was better about the show, the music or the humor, what have you, the natural result of forty people crowded around one rabbit-eared television set. But once *Hee Haw* started, the talking was over. After that, it was all about the love. And so was everything before, really.

CHAPTER 9

The bus travels in the fading daylight of the warming spring evening. Cloud cover from a steady pounding rain has forced the streetlights on early. As they approach each pole, the light splays out, refracted on the bus window, fades, then splays out again from the next light. The rain falls mostly steady, but periodically whacks the side of the bus in splats, stops when they travel into a tunnel, and then picks up again on the other side in a drumming patter, like thousands of tiny fingers tapping at once.

Leonard and Pearl talked about EL quite a bit when Jody was growing up. None of the three brothers had any interest in taking over their father's business. Even though Vernon worked with Leonard at the paper mill in Branden, and drove within a mile of his brother's house every day, he rarely came by. But Pearl never had any kids of his own, and he visited Leonard and the boys regularly. Many days Jody and Scooter got home on the school bus to see Pearl's old red-and-white pickup parked in their driveway, usually with the hood propped open for one reason or another.

When Leonard and Pearl talked about EL, they called him Daddy. They always spoke about him in a reverent tone, usually by cutting the volume in half when they mentioned his name. Neither one ever said a cross word about him to the other. And they certainly never talked to each other about what living with him had been like. But Jody had gleaned a few things about his grandfather along the way, and once in a while either Pearl or Leonard or both of them had a cold beer or two and got to talking and they'd open up. Vernon, if he happened to be there, never said a word, though he obviously had his own thoughts about his father.

The story EL told of his life went something like this. He quit school in the eighth grade to go to work in the local sawmill. Times were tight, he liked to say, and he felt like he needed to support his family, to help his parents keep together the little horse-and-cattle operation handed down from EL's grandfather. When EL told the story, he stressed this important distinction. Nobody made him go to work, and his parents didn't expect it.

After a couple years milling logs, he went home one day and told his parents he wanted to take a trip. EL said he'd been watching those logs come in on the rail spur every day and he'd got an idea in his head he couldn't get rid of. EL told his parents that he couldn't stop wondering where all that wood came from, and he intended to hop the train and go see for himself. He told the story like some sort of mystic, as if all his life he had wondered about things. EL, bulging out of his overalls, recounted this story to his sons with a sad, almost bewildered look on his ruddy face. "I told Daddy," he said, "we wouldn't have nothing without them logs." His mother asked him to sit down to eat some chicken and dumplings, but he told them he wanted to get going. Didn't want to miss the train. He walked away from his house with fifty cents in his pocket, and left the little money he had saved on his bedroom dresser. Then he rode all night and all the next day on the train, to the end of the line in Branden.

When Leonard or Pearl felt talkative, one of them might tell a slightly different story. They never said anything like this to one another, only to Jody or Scooter, maybe Vernon if he was there. And only if they were looking away and not right at anybody. They were careful not to tarnish their father's name in any way, and without a doubt they were still scared of him as grown men. EL had talked, they said, about a mysterious man named Jack. A name he mentioned from time to time when they were boys, and Leonard and Pearl were never quite sure what he was trying to say. To scare them maybe, to tell them about himself. To explain. They were never quite sure.

EL's family, when he was a boy, had a neighbor man named Jack. Jack lived alone in a house that had been his mother's but she had died a few years before. EL's parents understood this Jack had been married once, but somehow it hadn't worked out or she had died or something, the story was never quite clear. EL thought of Jack like a second father, one who always took him places unlike his own father, who lost interest in EL once he grew too big to beat senseless. This Jack was a nice man his parents' age, and EL spent a lot of time at his place from when he was very young, learning card tricks or helping him with odd jobs around the house.

According to Pearl and Leonard, Jack was a man who never had married. "He never did marry, and one day Daddy didn't like the card tricks he showed him anymore," Pearl sometimes said. What happened after that was never too clear. As Pearl or Leonard told the story it was always with raised eyebrows and a questioning look, with quieted voices. Now they weren't too sure, but what might have happened if they had understood what EL was trying to say, was that when he was seventeen, EL left work early one day, went over to Jack's house and beat him almost to death, then hopped the train and left home in a hurry. That he didn't even stop to eat lunch at home. And both his parents died before he ever got back there.

The only thing they knew for sure was the thing EL had told them all a thousand times. That he went home on his lunch break from the sawmill and told his parents he was going to get on the train that brought the logs in, just to take a look around. Just so he could see where those logs came from, to see where everything started. Only later did he send a letter to his parents to tell them he wouldn't be back, explaining that he knew what was there for him in Texas if he had stayed.

When Pearl and Leonard and Vernon were boys, EL used the name a lot. "Jack used to act like that," he would say. Maybe it was just the way they walked or whistled or gently picked a flower. They both learned to fear the name Jack, and to fear doing anything like a girl might have done it. They both learned the hard way to control their behavior and expect the worst. Whoever this Jack was, his was not a name mentioned lightly.

Vernon, the two of them said, never saw this side of EL. When Vernon came along, their father ignored him, though Leonard and Pearl both said their father actually admired Vernon. Leonard and Pearl both said EL often pointed out the way Vernon kept himself together, kept his clothes clean. Though he was a heavy man all his life he kept himself neat, his hair combed, his shirt tucked in, and constantly sucked on mints to cover the bite of whiskey on his breath. They said that, as they all grew, EL compared the two of them more and more to their younger brother. Besides that, one or both of them would joke from time to time, Vernon was the kind of kid that never did try to please anybody else, that it wouldn't have mattered what EL had done to him. The two of them sometimes joked that their father kept so busy beating them that he didn't have time for Vernon. But all Jody knows is this: Vernon was never scared of him in the same way those two were.

Pearl, Leonard, and Vernon were grown men before EL ever went back to Texas, for the family reunions. His parents were long gone by then, and all the family remaining there were glad to see him back, this man who was otherwise merely a legend. By that time EL had begun, finally, to mellow into old age, to the place where much of the past can be forgotten. But not all of it.

Jody was fourteen years old when his grandfather died. For a long period he was sick, losing weight every month. Leonard and Pearl and even Vernon, when he came around, talked about how small he was becoming. EL, their daddy, Extra Large. At the end of his life he weighed only a hundred thirty pounds, and though the doctors never understood why, he spent his last two weeks singing and saying nice things one after another to nobody in particular, in a total state of delirium. When he finally went on to the next life, the three of them insisted on a closed-casket funeral. They said they barely recognized him. They said he just wasn't the father they knew.

CHAPTER 10

"All right, ladies and gentlemen," Pork Chop says with a clamorous grunt. He has pulled the bus off the highway and is heading into the parking lot of an all-night diner. Jody wakes with a start at the sound, surprised he fell asleep after all. "We have now entered the great state of Louisiana." Pork Chop cranks the wheel all the way to the right and eases it out in bits as the bus corrects, sidles into a parking space.

"Sportsmen's paradise. A hunter's dream. A fisherman's fantasy. A woman-lover's heaven, all these beauties we got down here. Let's see, what else. Home to cotton fields, sugarcane plantations, and catfish farms. From the Riverwalk in Shreveport"—with this he extends his right hand toward one corner of the state—"to Fat Tuesday in New Orleans." With his left hand, the other. "We've got it all, folks, all that and the cost of living ain't too bad. Even a fat old bus driver like me can make it here. As y'all can guess"—he pauses here, for emphasis—"I'm from here." The brakes whoosh as he lets out the air and the bus begins to idle. "Anyway, welcome. They's no place like it." He zips out the emergency brake and sets it. "We gon' pull out again in about thirty minutes, so ev'body be back on the bus at a quarter to five."

Jody steps out of the bus, ambles to the edge of the parking lot, out by the neon sign which, on closer inspection, reads AUNT MOE'S. Now only two letters still work, and the café appears to be named NO. The smells—pine trees, pollution, loamy earth—mix in a cloud of stale grease and the muggy exhaustion of four o'clock in the morning. Now, he remembers. It was a Saturday, his final year of high school. Jody came here on another bus that night, to this town. He may well have eaten at this same diner after the game. There are lots of things he can't remember about those games. But this one, he remembers.

For one, he almost missed it. Dad was at work that day, and as he often did, Scooter wandered away when Jody was out working in the garden. Jody had managed to find his brother half a mile away in the woods and get him safely home just as Dad was returning from work, then turned Scooter over to their father's care as if handing him the keys to the house. Then he raced to meet the ball team at school, wishing he had a faster car, and got there just as the bus was pulling out of the parking lot.

Minden High had an all-star pitcher on the hill that night, a tall right-hander named Stewart with a shoulder-high leg kick that made base stealing easy, for those few runners that ever got on base. Other than Stewart, the team didn't have much talent, and the game moved quickly as Minden's offense fell flat and Stewart mowed down the boys from Branden.

Keith Sanders, Jody's friend from school, was there with the team that night. Keith was captain of the basketball team, a whale of a kid, and everybody called him Goon. He single-handedly made up the visiting fan club. Jody didn't have close friends—as weird as his brother had always been, the oddity of living in a house without women—and no one besides family ever visited. But Goon and Jody were two leaders, team captains in their respective sports. On top of that, Goon was a fun guy to have around and knew every line from every Jerry Clower story ever told.

The big man kept him light as Jody waited his turn in the on-deck circle. Jody prepared for the at bat through a fog of worry—over Scooter, over their father, over his own future as he was about to graduate. Goon stood behind the fence, told him jokes ("Hawwwwww! Knock him out, John!"), insulted the pitcher ("You can hit that with one hand"), got him focused.

Stewart was certainly the best Class B high school pitcher in Louisiana, way beyond mature, and went on to spend seven seasons in the major leagues. That April night, everything he threw was working—his curve, his slider, and with a steady wind blowing out to center, he even had a dancing little knuckleball. Jody stepped into the box, tried to guess what the kid was going to throw him.

That's what it took to hit a baseball, as much as anything else. A good guess about what was coming. The bases were clear when he stepped to the plate, and he looked for a fastball, which Stewart usually threw him to start things off. Instead Stewart came with the curve, got Jody out on his front foot, swinging like a fool swatting flies. He looked for two more fastballs and got them, but neither was good enough to hit. He stepped back in looking for a curve, and Stewart blew by him with another fastball . . .

At 2–2, things get serious. Stewart overthrows the slider—Jody is looking for it—and it bounces to the plate. Jody knows this kid—a walk isn't going to hurt him, but Stewart has too much pride, and this is the first three-ball count the pitcher has worked all night. Jody knows the fastball is the one to look for; he sets his feet and cocks his bat.

Stewart steps off the hill, picks up the rosin bag, cleans his cleats, looks back in for signs, waves them off, then runs halfway to the plate to meet the catcher for a conference. Only then does Jody consider something different may be coming. A pitch the count doesn't call for. He knows, and knows Stewart knows, he'll be looking for the fastball. He also knows that Stewart knows he can hit it. So he just takes a guess.

Stewart unwinds his lanky frame, kicks his foot for the stars, and comes through with a changeup. Jody's guess was right. Just a slight additional hitch in his swing, and he takes the future major-leaguer deep over the left-field fence. Goon is there to pick Jody up at the plate. And since the game is not yet over, Goon breaks decorum and carries him out to his position at shortstop, to defend the bottom half of the inning, which he does with the greatest glory.

Later at home, he pulls his truck into the driveway, gets out. The softest melody plays from the tree swing at the edge of their yard. Jody walks over, sits. Scooter never stops, never looks up. His eyes are closed. He blows a tune, circular, a little twelve-bar ditty over and over, five, six, seven, eight times; he blows so quietly Jody has to strain to hear it. Then Scooter takes a run up the harmonica and now he blows harder, controlling his breath so the volume doesn't change; it competes with and intermingles with the music of crickets and the distant barks of nameless dogs; he will never play louder because the song is only meant for himself anyway. Finally he stops, looks up.

"Good game?"

Jody breathes out. For another night, he knows his brother is home. He knows Scooter will follow him in for the night, will go to church with the two of them in the morning and, maybe for a day, won't try to disappear to his own little world again.

The two boys stand, together. The moon is full and Jody can see the yard around as if he stands there in the middle of the day. From a few miles away hums the low-grade roar of the paper mill where Daddy spends his days, belching a frothy steam into the rarified blue sky. Scooter blows another note softly, discordant, takes it to crescendo, then moves up half a step and the whole thing resolves with a tone so peaceful that all Jody wants to do is go inside and sleep.

CHAPTER 11

He walks from the bus to the hospital through the slight remaining cool of the new day, his stomach still full from the diner. Jody breathes the smell of honeysuckle as he goes, looks out on a day still full of hope. The small town is quiet except for the periodic tattling of birds, muted by humid air. He passes through this ancient world on a broken, trash-strewn sidewalk that, like everything else, is filthy, run down. Jody turns in all directions, looks for something solid to balance the crushing disorientation. He passes under an oak tree; the limbs close in on him.

Outside the hospital, two women in nurse's uniforms walk past, chatting about a television show.

"That Roger is *sooo* cute."

"Cute? Is that how you pronounce g-a-y?"

"Roger? Gay? No!"

"Well. Even if he's not he spends way too much time admiring himself."

The door opens and they go in. On the side of the building a huge compressor kicks on and groans to life. In the perfectly still air the early morning sunshine becomes uncomfortably hot. The ground begins to cook, and with it the smell of decay boils out of cracks in the soil.

Leonard Davidson was a deacon in his church and involved himself in all aspects of life there. In Jody's earliest memories, his father is standing in the church laughing and slapping backs, or eating from a plate piled high at a dinner on the grounds. Scooter is there also, in body at least. All he ever wanted to do was stare out the window of the church, to sneak in Delaware Punches to drink. Jody's brother hated to go anywhere without a can of Delaware Punch; from a young age he named his intention to live in that state as soon as he could leave. Scooter assumed the red drink flowed like water in that faraway place.

The boys passed their time at home in two ways. Fishing was one. They spent more hours than either could begin to count on the pond that bordered their property, catching bass and perch, sometimes turtles, as dusk enveloped their bodies and the songs of bullfrogs were sung to gnats settling in clouds on the water's edges.

Jody's other passion was baseball. Scooter, as with everything he did, had only moderate interest in the game. But Jody was crazy about the sport. While Scooter's talent came to him naturally, involved no real effort, Jody's own was the product of many hours spent practicing. And practicing. And practicing.

On weekends or after work, with enough begging, Leonard could be persuaded out into the back forty, as they called it, to pitch the ball for his boys to hit. His pitching motion started when he dropped his burning cigarette on the ground and ended when he picked it back up after one of the boys hit the ball, as the other gave chase. On top of this practice, Jody spent hours and hours hitting the ball off a tee or throwing the ball at a target on a screen, until he could do either in the dark with both eyes closed.

Whatever they did, Scooter had more talent. Whatever Jody and his brother got into, Scooter was better, as clearly as he was more handsome, taller. Jody was always the one fixing the lures, cleaning the equipment, taking out miniature knots that had formed in the lines. When the two went down to the pond, Scooter cast out lazily into the water and pulled in fish. He often sat watching Jody take care of everything, patiently, as if nothing mattered. Scooter somehow found a way to approach right when all the work was done, pull in fish, and then wander off to the next thing.

For Jody, fishing was fun, but baseball was his world. He stayed outside year round, rain or shine, from the heat of summer to days in the frigid snap of winter, practicing by himself in the humid morning, the heat of afternoon, the cool quiet of dusk. When the water on the pond lay perfectly still, the only sounds to be heard were the ping of the bat, the *thwang* of the screen, the words of old Mr. Stringer across the pond, murmuring to his equally old mule in low tones, his ancient baritone voice skipping across the surface of the water. And while Jody spent all winter hitting off the tee, working oil into his glove, throwing balls by the thousands into the target on the screen, Scooter came out every spring, swung the bat a couple times for practice, and took up right where he left off. And when they finished playing for the day, while Jody picked up all the balls or cleaned the bats to put them away, his brother disappeared again. Nothing made Scooter happy. He could catch a fish as big as he was or hit a home run so far it was never seen again and, even at those times, his face said that whatever was next had better be better. Whatever he was doing, Scooter was already moving on, in some way, to the next thing. As if his connection to the family was just one of chance, as if they just happened to be the people around him, and their home just happened to be the place he lived.

. . .

At the entrance to the hospital Jody hesitates at the door, breathes again the smell of growing humidity. A breeze picks up, and heat rides on the back of the wind. Above, the sky is clear but doesn't look like it will last.

At the reception desk a radio plays softly, crackles with static. A large red-haired woman, a young Lulu Roman, organizes documents. She picks up a stack of papers two inches thick and tries to jam it into an envelope. Shoving, muttering. Finally the seam of the envelope tears and the papers scatter onto her desk, to the floor, into the trash can. The woman pushes her chair back, slaps her hands on her knees. She grimaces as she surveys the jumbled mess, clucks to herself.

She looks up at Jody. She grabs her chest and jumps back in the chair, scattering everything that didn't scatter the first time, and has to reach for the desk to keep from toppling over backward.

"Mercy!" she shouts, then quickly covers her mouth. "I'm sorry, young man! Listen to me, cussing like a sailor. Oh my god, you just about gave me a heart attack. You are one quiet mouse. I didn't even see you there." She smells like strawberry perfume. She reaches forward and switches off the crackling radio.

Then she leans back, twists her head, looks at Jody from one eye.

"You must be Leonard's boy. I don't remember you but he's been sayin' you was coming to see him." She shows more gum than tooth when she smiles.

"Your daddy's a wonderful man. Me and all the nurses, we've heard so much about you and your brother. We're sure hoping he pulls out of this. I've been praying for him ever' day."

"Well, thank you," Jody finally says. "I hope he said something nice about us." He is nervous, shaking.

"Aw, you quit." She lightly slaps the back of his hand. "So what about you? Where do you live? You married?"

"I've been in Chicago for the last few months. In my work I moved around a lot. And no, I'm not married."

"Chicago, Illinois? Man, I don't see how anybody can stand it way up in the north like that. All them sourpusses." She puts on a frown. "How could you ever leave such a fine place as Loo-siana?"

Jody tries to discern from her eyes what she knows about his family. He guesses from the directness of her gaze she doesn't know much.

"My uncle called me yesterday and told me what was happening."

"Vernon? Aw, he's sweet. Bless his heart. We'll just have to find you a good Louisiana woman to keep you down here this time." She slaps his hand again. "Hey, there's a lot of 'em about your age divorced with two or three kids, ready to get married again. You like a big ol' gal like me or a little skinny thing?" She squints, looks into her memory. "I got two different ones in mind for you." Then she laughs and the skin under her chin shakes.

"Anyway, it's nice to meet you. I been stoppin' by to visit with your daddy when I get off ever' day. Actually I been going to y'all's church for the last few years, that's how I know him. But your daddy, he is just so sweet."

"Leonard? We can't be talking about the same man."

"Aw, you stop. He really is. Anyway, my name's Lurleen. Visitin' hours don't start till eight but you go on ahead. Not like anybody's gonna call the police or anything. He's down in 314."

Jody thanks her, turns toward the rooms. He takes two steps, then goes back to the desk.

"Lurleen?"

"Yeah, sugar?"

"Is he really sick?"

She puts down her papers. "Yeah, baby. He's real sick."

"Thank you for looking out for him. It means a lot. I guess he's been kind of alone."

Lurleen shakes her head slowly. "Naw, sweetie. Leonard's got a lot of people that love him. That and the good Lord's been with him. He hasn't been alone."

CHAPTER 12

The hollow echo of his footsteps bounces off the walls of the stairwell. At the top he turns left, as Lurleen the red-haired receptionist instructed. In the corridor are other sounds. The numbers grow smaller—320, 319. Canned voices spill from rooms, the faint blue glow of televisions, periodically a moan, the creak of a bed. The whole place reeks with the antiseptic smell of pine cleaner, which roils off the highly polished floor like a fog. On opposite walls hang framed prints, one of a mountain lake, one a city skyline with yellow windows in the skyscrapers. The prints hang lopsided, Jody guesses from banging wheelchairs that have left their scrape marks at knee height on both sides.

One of the young soldiers Jody interviewed early on told him of a dying father. The private described his father as one whom all his friends were jealous of. How even a month before he died he had watched his son score thirty-six points in a basketball game. Who never had a cross word for anyone. The day after the basketball game, the boy's father woke up with a headache, didn't go to work that day. The son came home from school early, skipped basketball practice, to check on his father, who told him he was and always had been a terrible son and to get out of the room. The tumor was inoperable. The insults continued until the son couldn't go to the hospital anymore. The day he knew his father was going to die, he went into the room again. The father opened his eyes long enough to ask his son one question. "Who are you?"

Jody knocks lightly. He waits for half a minute and then walks in. He stands still, drawing breath. A much older version of his father lies on the bed under a thin worn sheet, snoring softly. Jody feels a welling of sympathy at the sunken face of the man. Next to the bed sits a rollaway cart with dinner on it, chicken bones in one compartment, a plastic fork stuck into a mound of gelled-over mashed potatoes with gravy, one bite missing from the center, the gravy pooled. Only crumbs remain from what was probably a piece of chocolate cake. Leonard always did like sweets. The closet door is open and inside Jody sees some of his father's clothes, a worn flannel shirt hanging lopsided on a hanger, a pair of cheap white sneakers without laces on the floor, one of them turned on its side. A blue blanket and square-patterned bedcover lie crumpled on the floor. Several greeting cards are stuck to the wall above a bureau, affixed with masking tape stretched across the corners. One of them is a picture of Carl somebody, one of Leonard's hunting buddies. In the picture Carl wears a hat with a pair of plastic antlers on it. His lips are painted with blood-red lipstick. Under the picture he has written:

> *This is Dee Dee Doe Leonard, things has got so*
> *bad I had to grow me some horns, cain't wait*
> *for you to get back out here with your big ol'*
> *gun and shoot some of these bucks off my tail.*

The room smells dirty, like a large, wet, matted animal. On the shelf behind the bed are pictures, high school pictures of him and Scooter, an old black-and-white of his mother in a pale-colored dress.

Jody steps to the side of the bed to get a closer look at the pictures. The pounding of his heart pushes his breaths out short. He hears a thumping sound and turns toward it. John David, Pearl's old spotted Labrador mix that his father inherited years before, lies with his tail rhythmically beating the floor. The dog lifts his head proudly, though his underside shoulder remains glued to the linoleum. He begins to whimper, then sneezes. The whimpering grows steadily louder as the old dog struggles to get to his feet, then gives up and collapses back into a prone position. Jody shakes his head. Same old Leonard. Convinced somebody to let him bring his dog into the hospital.

"Who's that, John David?" Leonard asks in a voice barely above a whisper. Leonard's eyes are still closed. "Bring me my gun, dog."

"It's me, Daddy."

Leonard crunches his face, opens one eye slightly, closes it.

"I must be dreaming. I better not open my eyes." His threadbare white tee shirt is sweated through, gray chest hairs limp on his sallow skin.

Jody stands over his father, who moves slightly from side to side, a catch in his ragged breathing. The years move across Leonard's face. Finally Jody reaches out and touches his hand.

Jody visited EL in this same hospital when he was fourteen years old. Near the end EL had looked so happy with Leonard and Pearl at his side, Vernon sometimes too. Though EL could barely sit up, Pearl refused to face him head on, instead stood sideways at his father's bed. EL kept saying, "I love you boys, you're the best boys I could've ever had." Leonard and Pearl looked back and forth at one another. And never said anything.

"It's me, Daddy," Jody says again. The movements of his

father's face make Jody's skin tingle. Then Leonard opens his eyes and looks up at his son.

"Where you been all these years? Did Vernon call you? I'm gonna be out of here in a few days. Maybe a week." Leonard gasps with every few words. He was always thin, but now looks bloated, as if he's been underwater.

"I've been in Chicago for a little while. I moved around quite a bit before that." Out the window rain clouds darken, move toward the hospital.

Leonard picks up the remote control for the television, looks it over. "Well, I wish you could've been here a long time ago," he says to the remote. "I've missed you." Leonard sets down the remote, looks over his bed. "Look at all these blankets, they're trying to cook me to death in here. I never did like to sleep with covers."

"I remember that. Always kicking your blankets off."

"Probably cook me and put me on the menu, judging by the taste of the food here."

Jody picks up a plastic water jug from the tray, opens the lid and lifts it to drink. The ice has formed a glob and smacks him in the face, drips water down his neck. He sets the pitcher down.

"So what do you hear from my brother?" Jody walks to the window. The hospital is built into a hill such that the third floor in back is just above ground level. Outside a man pushes two kids on swings at the same time, one with each hand. An orderly walks by the open door, pushing a mop bucket, whistling. He stops in the hall, pulls the mop out, wrings it, dabs at the floor, continues whistling. He knocks on Leonard's door, two sharp raps.

"Mornin', James." The man raps twice again, continues whistling, then repositions his mop and moves on.

"Vernon says he left here. After he got out."

Leonard begins to speak, stops, considers. "He did it this time, Jody. Your brother did it."

"Yeah?"

"Him going to that place, he didn't have any choice in that. None of that ever should have happened. But once he came back he wasn't the same.

"I'm tired," Leonard continues. "So tired. He just never was the same. Vernon says he's down in New Orleans. Somewhere."

Jody stares at his father.

"So, Jody. You're a Yankee now?"

"You could say that."

"What have you been doing with yourself?"

"Different things. Just working, making a living."

"You know I could've got you on at the mill." Leonard tries to laugh.

"You think so?"

"You like it up there? You gonna stay?"

"I like it. I've got a good job."

"You got a family?"

"No. Not like you mean."

"You married?"

"No, not yet. I've got a girlfriend. She's an artist."

"We don't have any artists in our family. Not that I know of. 'Less you count them paint-by-numbers Pearl used to do."

Leonard turns to face the wind blowing in. "Looks like rain. We sure need it. Jody?"

"I'm here."

"The truth is I've been praying you'd come. I really have. Prayin' to the good Lord every day. All these years I been wondering about you. How you turned out. If you have a good life." He reaches out for Jody's arm, squeezes it tight.

"I don't have time to change anything that happened, Jody. I can't change one thing. There's a lot I would change. A lot."

Jody shuffles, slightly pulls away, enough that he can feel his father's fingernails in his skin.

"Doctor says I don't have time left to do much. Says I may not ever leave this bed." He wheezes until he catches his breath. "And I know you don't owe me anything."

Everything floods into Jody's chest, as if he's been dipped in a pool of lukewarm water.

"I don't owe you what? What are you saying?"

"Bring your brother back to see me," Leonard says. As he speaks, the old dog finally rises and rubs against Jody's leg. The dog stands panting, putrid breath coming out in bursts. "And if it's my time, find a good home for John David. Take him up there to Chicago if you think he'd like it. He's part of the family. He's never been out of Louisiana."

"Let me get this straight. I come all this way to see you and that's what you want from me? To go find my brother again? That's why Vernon called me?"

Leonard purses his lips. "I just want us all to be together one more time."

"One more time?"

Leonard doesn't answer.

"Look. Dad. Just, just give me another year, a little more time to get settled. And then I'll come back down, find him, and get him back up here to see you."

Leonard shakes his head. "I don't have it."

"You don't have it?"

Leonard shakes his head.

"Well, dammit," Jody shouts. John David stands looking up at him and panting. The window is open now and birds scream from somewhere out there, scream even louder than all the children on the swing set. A breeze blows into the room, heavy, moist.

"Well, dammit," Jody shouts again, and turns toward the door. Just then a nurse walks in holding some pills and a glass of water. He grabs his duffel and brushes past her. He runs down the hall, past all the suffering patients in their rooms and all their friends and families walking in and out of their lives.

CHAPTER 13

A hearty rain shower is falling by the time he returns to the lobby. He stands at the sliding glass doors and looks out at the parking lot. The house is too far away to walk. He turns and goes back inside, asks Lurleen to call a taxi for him.

On the phone she is agitated. He can't help hearing as she berates the person on the other end of the line, her voice rising and falling.

"—I don't care what kind of game is on, this young man needs a ride out to the other side of Winston Road"—she presses the phone to her ample chest and looks over at him—"You did say Winston Road didn't you? Just past that taxidermy shop." She cups her other hand over the mouthpiece and tries to whisper, "Just 'cause you're my husband don't mean you drive the only taxi in town."

He waits by the doors, watches the rain pour. By the time the yellow cab rolls up it has slowed to a sprinkle. In the taxi, a blast of cold air hits him in the face. The driver, bald on top, with a ring of gray hair that is pillow-flat on one side, grins to show a missing cuspid.

"'Y god you're Leonard's boy, ain't you?" he exclaims. "I

ain't never met you but Doreen says he talks about you since he's been in here." He points with his head toward the hospital.

"Who's Doreen?"

The driver is heart shot. He hangs his head. "Did I say Doreen? Dang! Cain't believe I said that. Doreen was my first wife. Don't tell Lurleen, okay? She'd tear my butt up. Let's just keep that between the boys."

"No problem. Easy mistake. Maybe you should think of a nickname for her."

"I mean, I've made that mistake before, you know? Called her Doreen. Right in front of her face. Matter of fact it was a bad time to be calling her by my ex-wife's name. Especially since they're cousins. She'd tear me up if she knew."

"Seriously, man. Think about the nickname."

"I will." His face breaks back into a full grin. "Hey, it took 'em a few days to find you, didn't it? I run off myself once, rode the trains for 'bout a year till I just got too homesick. Ol' Branden town gets in your blood, you best be careful or you may never leave again."

Jody tries to place him, leans back for a better look at his face. "Are you from here? I don't know you."

"Aw, 'course you don't. I'm older'n you." He turns back around in his seat, looks up at the ceiling. "You musta graduated back in eighty-something."

"Ninety-three. I left right after I graduated."

"Me, I went to Branden back in '79, the year we won the basketball state championship, me and Snookie Carter and Clem Mathews and them."

"That's right, Branden did win it once. Not when I was here. The basketball team was terrible when I went to school. We only had one good player. But I remember those old trophies in the trophy case, though. Those old black-and-white pictures. You played?"

"Yeah. I played." He hesitates, repositions himself, digs his hands into his pockets. "Well no, not exactly. I practiced with 'em but in the games I was the bench boy. But let me tell you something." He turns toward Jody, wags his finger. "It hadn't been for me they wouldn't have won state."

"You must've been quite a bench boy. You have magic powers or something?"

The driver hangs his head, breaks into a grin again. Then he takes a deep breath and looks at Jody in the mirror, slowly scales back his grin until his eyes are squinted, as if looking into another time.

"See, we beat Dodsonville in the championship game that year. In '79. It was a miracle we even got that far, we was just 21–21 that year and only got to the championship game 'cause a old boy from Zwolle broke his leg and couldn't play in the semifinals. He scored fifty points a game that year and we was the first team to beat 'em, there in the semifinals. See they was 41–0 but that seven-foot skinny boy was the only one could play. Jackson I think was his name. Jefferson. No, Washington." The driver throws his hand up. "One of the presidents. It wasn't Bush. I do remember that. Fact I don't think he ever played basketball again. But anyway we did beat 'em, and went to the championship game against Dodsonville."

"Dodsonville. That's one place I haven't thought about in a long time."

"Well, it ain't worth remembering. Nothing like ol' Branden."

"Yeah, you're right, this place is beautiful. A regular New York City. A temple to the achievements of man."

"What? Are you gonna listen to my story or what?"

"All right, buddy. I'm sorry. Go ahead."

The driver resumes his distant stare. "It was a good game, both sides played pretty good. They had a big ol' boy a little over two meters tall. Not as tall as that one from Zwolle but at least the one from Dodsonville could still play, 'cause like

I say that boy from Zwolle had got a broke leg. Two meters tall, that's almost six foot eight, but I like to say two meters 'cause I been studying up on the metric system, I think it's a much better system. But with George Walker Bush and them in there we'll never switch to it 'cause they'd stand to lose a lot of money, we'd have to switch all the signs and stuff and that would cost millions, do you know I was readin' about up in Seattle, Washington, they blowed up their dome stadium but couldn't afford to take down the signs off the interstate that told you how to get to it? So the signs still tell you how to get there but the dern building ain't there no more." He turns to find Jody looking away.

"All right, I'll get to the point. Jeez, don't *nobody* want to hear a story no more. The game went back and forth all night. Clem had thirty-seven points and Snookie had twenty-three. Then Coach called a time out with ten seconds left and we had the ball. We was down by one. Then Coach done something funny. He called a kind of a trick play. See Coach Allison had a few tricks up his sleeve, he was a short little sucker with beady eyes. A crafty devil, Coach Allison. Clem was supposed to bend down like he was trying to tie his shoe, like he didn't even notice the time out was over and he wasn't even payin' attention. Then he was supposed to pop back up real quick like and take the pass and drive it in. Only thing was, Snookie passed the ball and Clem popped up right in front of our bench but he was too late and it was way over his head. The ball was about to go out of bounds!"

"Uh-oh."

"It was coming right toward me and Clem was too. I was sittin' on the edge of the bench and he was coming right at me. I mean that boy's eyes was *that big*." The driver makes an oval with his hand. "Ol' Clem had done bore down on it. But . . ." The driver shakes his head gently. "There wasn't no way he was gonna get to it. I was sittin' there on the bench with a ball in my hands like I always did during the games, see I always liked to set there and toss a ball up in the air just a little bit. I just, you know, liked the way it felt in my hands. But when I looked up that other ball was comin' right toward me."

"Now this story's getting good."

"I's just sitting there tossing that ball in the air like I'd been doing the whole game and here come Clem." The driver tosses an imaginary basketball in the air with both hands, catches it, and tosses it up again. "When I seen him coming I tried to stand up and get out of the way, I had just tossed my ball in the air but I didn't care, Clem was a lot bigger'n me and I didn't want to get no broke arm or no broke leg or nothing. Like that boy from Zwolle. See he had got his leg broke playin' basketball. But what happened was, I dived out of the way and Clem dived over to the ball and grabbed the one I had tossed up and thowed it back in to Snookie, and Snookie dribbled it in and sunk a shot from the top of the key when the buzzer went off! The game ball just fell down on my chair!"

"What! You're telling me you cheated to win the game?"

He scratches his head. "Thing is, thing is, I've never been sure. Because nobody seen it. The referees didn't see it, the other team didn't see it, I guess it fooled everybody. I wasn't even *tryin'* to fool anybody." He shakes his head. "I ain't even sure *Clem* saw it. I asked him about it after the game and he wouldn't even thank me. Acted like he didn't know what I was talking about. Like I was just the dumb sucker sittin' at the end of the bench that thowed him a towel when it was a time out. And you know what? I hate that sonabitch to this day. I wouldn't give him a ride in my cab if he had two broke legs." The driver pokes the back of his seat with a finger. "And now he's gone on to fame and fortune and sells State Farm insurance to every fool in Branden and has horses and cows and a Cadillac and everything, and far as I'm concerned some of that is thanks to *me*." The driver sticks his thumb into his chest. "That hotshot son of a gun!"

"That's a crazy story. Are you making this up?"

"No! But if you don't believe me ask my mama! Nobody around here likes to talk about it. They just think I'm nuts."

"That's crazy, man. Crazy. I've never heard anything like that. But you asked me earlier . . . I'm gonna have to leave again. I've got a job up in Chicago."

"Aw, job schmob. Your daddy could get you on at the paper mill like that." The driver snaps his fingers.

"He tried to do that a long time ago. That's why I left."

The driver's face takes on a heinous look. Jody watches as it slowly, almost imperceptibly turns into a full-faced grin. "You funny, man. You funny. I'm Gary Wayne." He thrusts his hand over the back of the seat.

"Jody Davidson. I need to go out to . . ."

"Aw hell, son, I know where your daddy lives, just hang on."

Gary Wayne fiddles with the radio as they drive and finally settles on a country station, which he turns down low, begins to sing along. Jody recognizes a couple of things—a grocery store, the train depot, of course the paper mill with the giant water tower out in front. Piles of garbage beside the road.

"Well, Gary Wayne. I see Branden's still the same old crap hole it always was. Hasn't exactly turned into Grand Central in the last few years."

"What are you talking about, man? This is a happenin' place. We've got it all here."

"Like what? Fishing? Hunting? Waterskiing?"

"Yeah, that, and we've got a lot of other things going on too."

"Like?"

"Well, we've got adultery. Violence. Intrigue."

"No way. Not in this sleepy little place."

"Yes we do, man. A Methodist lady out past the lake called the cops and said she smelt something funny going to church one Sunday morning, they come out and found a meth lab at the house down the road from her. JB Dwyer and his deputies burned it down about two years ago. Then, uh, old boy from Goldonna found out his wife was slippin' down into the colored section at night, and he went down there with a double-barreled 20-gauge and shot two of them colored boys in their asses."

"Dang. Like I say, a regular New York City."

"Aw shoot. What's so special about that place?"

"I'm just playing with you, Gary Wayne."

A few minutes later the car takes a turn at slow speed. At the sight of the house Jody feels a gnawing in his stomach. When he gets out of the car he tastes the sallow air radiating from the same old catalpa tree.

"Nice to meet you," Gary Wayne says. He takes Jody's money and begins to back out into the street. He stops, reaches under the seat, and hands over a smudged business card. Jody reads it.

"You alter wedding dresses?"

Gary Wayne laughs. "No, man, Lurleen does. I told her we should get separate business cards. Let me know if you need another ride somewhere. Anytime. 'Cept I'm usually watchin' *Jeopardy!* from six thirty to seven. Then Tuesday and Thursday they been showin' back-to-back episodes of *The Six Million Dollar Man* and *The Fall Guy* from seven to nine on TBS."

"All right, Gary Wayne. Thanks for the ride."

"You welcome. Say whatever happened to ol' Lee Majors?"

The heat of the house is stifling, mixed with dust and the smell of stale fried grease. Sunshine fills the sky again, and Jody stands for a moment in the doorway, letting his eyes adjust. Everything appears much the same, right down to the old furniture and the dark wood paneling with the deep gouge over the sink where Scooter had tried to carve his initials when he was six, green tile floor in the kitchen. Leonard had left a pile of newspapers on the table, and with the door open a wind comes in and scatters them. Jody finds the thermostat, cranks it to the cold setting, and closes the door.

The quiet of the house is spooky. One thing is obvious. No woman has lived here in a long time. Jody takes a step down the hallway of the small house toward his old room and stops. He stands and looks at the closed door but does not open it. Then he returns to the living room, sits down in one of the old recliner chairs.

The three of them spent a lot of time in that living room, Leonard in the other chair, Scooter laid out on the sofa. Jody leans back and feels almost in an instant what it was like when they were all together there, watching games or TV shows, fighting Uncle Vernon or Pearl or one of the neighbors for his spot when they dropped by to watch *The Dukes of Hazzard* on Friday nights. Usually Jody ended up sharing the chair with one of the other kids or in the lap of Vernon or Pearl or, if he was lucky, Pearl's wife, Dot, or Aunt Misty, before she and Vernon divorced.

Jody relaxes into the chair and the quiet rolls over him. He falls asleep. He wakes after half an hour and for a minute, before he is fully awake, is filled with the most pleasant feelings, with a sweetness in his joints that flows through his blood.

On the wall, a picture of him catches his eye, taken on graduation night, 1993. He falls back to sleep and dreams of that younger version of himself, the one hanging on the wall in a gold-painted frame. In a black cap and gown. Tassel hung to one side. Smiling.

CHAPTER 14

The graduation ceremony is short and simple. There are only twenty-eight kids in Jody's class, twenty-nine if you count Jimmy Everett, who dropped out of school early in the year but managed to get a GED, so the principal is letting him walk the stage with his lifelong friends. The class twins, Nicki and Vicki, had been involved throughout high school in numerous clubs, including Young Baptist Club, Friends of Jesus Club, Future Business Leaders of America, and Future Homemakers of America. And they both played basketball. For each of these clubs they received extra credit, and though their grades were no higher than Jody's they were chosen valedictorian and salutatorian by the flip of a coin.

Nicki and Vicki give their talks about the future and hope and how anything is possible with the love of your family and faith in God and how every one of them will look back on those times as the greatest days of their lives. The ceremony ends with a prayer from Joe Jones, a motorcycle gang member turned Assembly of God minister with a worn-out hairpiece, who is uncle to the twin girls. In the prayer, Brother Joe asks

God to shine his light on the young people of Branden as they enter into the next stages of their lives.

An hour later most of the kids are at a party at Goon's house. Goon, always a card, has chosen a tuxedo for the occasion, complete with top hat and white gloves. The overgrown kid has set up a bunch of lawn chairs around a firepit in the yard, then turned some big rounds of a cut-up oak tree on end to make more chairs around it. He tells everybody as they arrive how he cut that tree down himself, recreates the sound as the tree falls again, tells how he carried the two-hundred-pound logs up from the ravine in their backyard. Just for the party. In the clueless manner of youth, he misses the comic effect of retelling this story in a tuxedo and top hat.

Goon's little sister is out in the yard with all the graduates, who have removed their caps and gowns and, unlike the host, stand around in shorts and tennis shoes. Goon keeps sending her back into the house only to have her return again, saying she wants to sing with them. The fire is burning and someone adds wood, great crackles of sparks shooting up into the sky, and Goon climbs onto one of the stumps to lead the revelers in a rendition of the school fight song. A few of the kids sing with him and Jimmy Everett is crooning as loud as he can, drunk from a bottle he keeps pulling out of his pocket.

Everyone shakes hands and hugs and some exchange philosophies or plans for the future. Graduates trade yearbooks, sign names under pictures, spell out thoughts and witticisms, good luck, keep in touch. The little sister comes back out to join the party and stands on one of the logs reading a poem from a collection of T.S. Eliot. Jody stands on yet another stump talking to Goon, who has earned a basketball scholarship to a junior college in East Texas. Goon tells Jody he could almost certainly make the baseball team if he wants to try living in Texas. Maybe they could even be roommates.

Songs are sung, drinks are drunk, the party progresses as

would any other graduation night. A car pulls in at the edge of the yard just after the thump of another log dropped onto the fire. The night sky lights up in a shower of sparks. When darkness refills that space, Jody's brother gets out the passenger side of the car. After Scooter stands, Tammy Morris, the owner of the car, slides out the passenger-side door too and falls into Scooter's arms.

Jody has heard the rumors about this woman and his brother, though he's never seen them together before. But he's heard that Scooter has been spending time with Tammy Morris, a thirty-something-year-old woman with a daughter in Scooter's tenth-grade class. And a husband.

Jody jumps down from the stump. His vision tunnels. He excuses himself to Goon. He walks straight toward his brother and the woman. The windows of her yellow Corvette are down and music plays from a rock station. They lean against the car. Tammy has her hands on him.

Scooter sees Jody coming and looks off, dreamily. He lifts his harmonica—he goes nowhere without that harmonica—to his mouth, blows softly to the music, slightly tardy. Tammy is drunk, kisses his neck, pulls his arm, asks him to go over with her to join the party. "There's never any parties in this town," she says. She's wearing a low-cut tank top. Her hair is the color of her car. "Come on, baby. Let's go party."

"What are you doing?" Jody says. He smells her perfume, a scent he has noticed on his brother before, balks at the horror of what he now knows.

Scooter pulls the instrument from his face and grins, a sly smile. "Darrell says he's gon' kick my ass." Scooter giggles. He, too, is drunk.

Jody grabs him by the shoulders, shakes him. His eyes are empty, milky as old glass. "This is a mistake, Scooter. Come on. Let's just get out of here."

"Come on, Scooter," Tammy Morris says. "Let's go party."

She moves behind Jody's brother, puts her hand on his abdomen, splays her fingers low on his stomach.

"Ooh. I love this song. I was your age when she made this song." She reaches into the car, turns up the radio, holds on to Scooter with her other hand.

Jody pushes her away, pulls his brother toward him. Scooter grins. He puts the harmonica to his lips again, slowly begins to blow. Jody is disarmed by his brother's playing. The music searches. The distance of the tone is exaggerated, portentous, the syncopation an eighth-note greater than usual. He lowers the instrument again, wipes his lip.

"Come on, brother." Scooter speaks slowly, nearly a slur. "She loves me. She really loves me."

Tammy reaches around Scooter again, holds on to his stomach. She asks him again to join her. Jody grabs her wrist, flings the woman's arm away. She shrieks, then turns her face toward the lights of a truck that tears into the yard and stops just short of her car. Her eyes grow wide.

"Don't you touch my wife, you bastard!" Darrell Morris screams as he throws open the door of his truck and runs toward the three of them. Without a warning he punches Jody in the jaw with a hard, cold object, knocks him backward. Jody's eyes try to close. All he hears is ringing.

Jody forces his eyes open. His jaw is throbbing. He tries to stand up but as soon as he moves the whole world spins. Scooter jumps on Darrell, grabs his arms, pins them back. Then Tammy grabs Scooter's shirt and pulls him by the neck.

"Get off my husband!" Tammy giggles, seeming happy with the development. Scooter falls off balance and his arms flail. He grabs for her and then falls backward on top of her. Breath rushes out of her like a blown-out tire. Tammy lies on the ground, writhes, gasps, boot heels digging into the earth. Scooter for the moment is still.

Darrell Morris is shouting. Jody sees his mouth moving.

He can't make out the words, only the tinny high notes. He tries to stand again, again falls back in a swirl. Darrell Morris reaches into his truck. The open door is between them. Though he can't stand up, and can't think straight, Jody knows what Darrell's looking for.

Darrell Morris walks toward Jody with the rifle. Coolly. Jody tries again to get up, hears only the ringing. Darrell squats and pulls the bolt back. He thrusts a slug into the chamber, jams it in, and then another. Jody pushes back on his elbows again, slumps down once more. Darrell Morris slams the rifle's bolt home, lowers it at Jody's face. He is talking but still Jody can't hear what he says. Scooter the Wanderer. That's what Leonard liked to call his younger son. Always looking for something more interesting than what was right there in front of him.

For a moment, if only for a moment, Scooter earns himself a new name. He takes a few steps forward, dives for Darrell Morris, and knocks him backward just as the gun explodes in a flash of fire into the night sky. The rifle falls into the dust. Scooter picks it up, pulls the bolt back to expel the casing, closes it, then slams it back again to eject the unused slug. Then, before Jody can stand, his brother brings the butt of the rifle down once with conviction, across the spread of Darrell Morris's forehead.

Scooter stands over him. Darrell Morris's face is a bloody mess. He isn't moving. Scooter throws the rifle to the ground.

Tammy Morris limps over. She looks down at her husband. Her mouth slowly opens wide. The music is blaring from her car and Jody can begin to make out the words of "Stairway to Heaven."

Finally, Jody gets up. The world is still spinning and he shuffles, crablike, over to his brother. Tammy turns twice in a circle like a dog in high grass, begins to whine. Her husband isn't breathing.

"Scooter. Give me your shirt." Scooter doesn't move. Jody reaches out his hand. Scooter yanks his shirt over his head. Tammy Morris spins herself in another circle.

"Go call an ambulance," Jody tells her. "Turn off that radio." Jody wipes the blood away from the man's face, his mouth. He bends his ear to listen. Darrell Morris still isn't breathing. Jody begins to pump on his chest.

"Get down here and help me."

"He was going to shoot you and then me." Scooter stands straight up, shirtless.

"Shut up. Get down here, Scooter. Where is that ambulance! Someone call an ambulance!" People scramble by the firepit.

"Watch me. When I stop, you do this. Just like we learned in gym class." Jody stops compressions, bends and breathes into the mouth. When he stops the breathing, Scooter begins to pump. Begins to pump the life back into Darrell Morris's body.

Finally the ambulance takes him away. The sheriff's car takes Scooter. Goon insists on driving Jody home, even offers to come inside and wait while Jody tells his father. Jody thanks him for the ride, goes inside the house by himself.

Leonard is still waiting up. He doesn't get out of his chair when his son first walks in, doesn't lower the volume on the television. Some old Western is playing and Jody hears the canned voices and the echoing ricochet of gunfire off the rocks. Jody looks at the television. Two gunmen are sitting behind a boulder, catching their breath and reloading.

When Leonard gets up he turns the light on. The gunmen are talking as Leonard asks Jody what happened to his brother. One of the gunmen says he's been shot. He says he is losing a lot of blood. He says he can't keep the blood in his stomach with his hands. He says he needs a doctor, fast. He says he just needs some water.

Leonard's face goes blank as he walks toward Jody with both his fists. "Why did you let this happen?" The gunman says he is going to die if he doesn't get out of there fast. *I'm dying,* he says. *I'm shot in the gut and I'm dying.*

The autopsy says Darrell Morris died of a massive heart attack from methamphetamines, that the blow from the end of his own rifle only brought about what was unavoidable. But Scooter pleads guilty to manslaughter. He doesn't want a trial. At the sentencing hearing a fat deputy leads him in wearing handcuffs. When Scooter stands before the bench he doesn't want to tell his version of what happened. He wears a hangdog expression, speaks in a whisper whenever the judge asks him a question. The judge asks if he has anything to say.

"I just wanted her to love me."

The last time Jody sees his brother, the fat deputy is leading him away. He has the same blank stare he always had in the back pews of the church, lifting his can of Delaware Punch, trying to see out through the stained-glass windows.

Outside the courthouse Sheriff Dwyer approaches Jody. He fumbles in his pockets for a cigarette.

"Your brother never should have been there."

"I can't argue with that."

Sheriff Dwyer lights his cigarette, blows out a thin stream of smoke. "He never should have been with that woman. I know your daddy gave y'all a good Christian home."

Jody's breath comes out short. "Well, obviously, that wasn't enough."

He stays home with his father a few more days. Leonard spends most of the time sitting in his chair watching television, or looking at Jody and not speaking. One night Jody goes into his room and counts his money, $246 from graduation presents and a little cash he has saved. Like EL, he leaves a note: *I won't be back for a while.* The only thing he takes besides a single change of clothes is a faded picture of his mother on the steps of the capitol building, holding him as a baby.

When he returns to the present, Jody walks through the house. Everything he touches brings back memories.

At the end of the hall he puts a hand on the door to his old room. The door is still closed. The knob feels almost electric. He tries to imagine what is inside, to think about all the things he wanted and dreamed about when he slept in that room. He stands like this for a minute, staring at the laminated wood, hollow in the center. Then finally, deliberately, Jody pulls his hand from the door, and slowly backs away.

CHAPTER 15

Late in the afternoon, Jody drives his father's truck toward town. As he passes the paper mill, tiny particles float in the air, pollution that makes the dusk more beautiful. He drives to the bridge, where the road turns and hooks back over the railroad track. He has barely slept since two nights before with Karen, who all of a sudden seems of another world. The fatigue is beginning to set into his body. Jody stops the truck at the edge of the bridge.

The track below crosses a service road. On the road stands a man with a bushy gray beard, wearing an orange vest and a white hardhat. He leans on a push broom as if to balance his enormous stomach and stares east down the tracks. When he looks up and sees Jody he smiles and begins to walk toward him, climbing partway up the hill.

"That's Leonard's truck, ain't it?" the man asks.

"Yes it is. I'm his son Jody."

"Peterson," the man answers. "What was I just talking about?"

"I don't know. I just drove up."

"Musta been talkin' to myself again. Well anyway, what's

happening fella?" He removes a glove, shifts the broom into his other hand. "Good to see you. Where you comin' from?"

"I just got into town. I'm coming from my father's house."

Peterson wipes the sweat from his forehead. "Well, where was you before that? I don't know you. I know everybody in this town. Or did, at one time anyway."

"I live in Chicago. Sounds like you know my father."

"All right, all right." Peterson throws his glove down, leans over on the broom. "My daughter lives way up north like that, up in Ohio or Iowa or something like that. I've seen it spelled both ways. So like I was telling you, her son, my littl'o grandson, goes to school and they cain't even bring nothing with peanuts in it to school! Can you believe that!"

"I've heard of things like that, Mr. Peterson. Food allergies. But you didn't tell me anything, remember? I just drove up."

"Oh yeah." He angrily shakes his head. "I told her, I said you tell them Yankee doodle-dandies your granddaddy was a peanut farmer, and they cain't take away your own son's rights like that! And on top of that they cain't have none of them uh, them big peanuts either, what do they call them?" He holds up a thumb and finger an inch apart. "You know, them big peanuts, uh, curvy-like?"

"Are you talking about cashews?"

"Yeah yeah that's it, them cat shoes. They cain't have no cat shoes at school either! 'Course I don't know why they call 'em cat shoes, I'm near about seventy years old and I ain't never seen no cat wear no shoes. Now maybe if I did see one wearin' shoes maybe I wouldn't hate them fluffy boogers s'much. Them highfalutin animals!"

Peterson cocks his head. "And if they did wear shoes how would they get 'em on? Now I guess if they had them Velcro things they could put shoes on, he could hook that Velcro with one of his littl'o claws and pull it on." He demonstrates by hooking a finger, pulling it toward himself.

"Or he could pull it on with them littl'o tiny teeth they've got—not the fangs mind you"—he demonstrates the fangs with two fingers held pointed down in front of his mouth—"but them littl'o tiny ones in between.

"My daughter, she's got a cat too. Up there in Ohio. Iowa. They let the boy bring the cat to school in a cage? For show and tell? But he cain't even bring any shoes? I'm telling you some things just don't make sense."

Peterson walks back down the hill, begins pushing the broom. "When I first saw you there I thought you was Leonard." Then he laughs. "About thirty years ago. I thought I had stepped back in time for a second."

Jody tries to place the man.

"Yeah. I worked with your daddy here for quite a few years. Don't worry, you prob'ly never knew me. I've never got out much except for work. I'm retired now but they let me come down here and sweep the stone off the tracks right here where it crosses. That way the train don't kick up into anybody's windshield."

"Well, that's nice of you, Mr. Peterson. I'm trying to remember you."

"Well." He leans on the top of the broom handle, which shifts to one side, and he begins to stumble, throws out his other hand to right himself. "It keeps me breathing. I mean, what else am I gonna do? Sit home and watch soap operas?" Peterson pokes his chest out, takes a few steps in an exaggeratedly prissy manner. "I mean those skinny little girls walking around with their plastic titties sticking out make Jezebel the whore of Babylon look like a *saint*, I'm telling you, a *saint*."

"I can't comment on the soap operas, Mr. Peterson. Wait a minute, now I know. Weren't you always making predictions about the future?"

Peterson leans on the broom again, exhales. "Yeah, that was me. Some of 'em I was right on too. Thirty years ago I told everybody that one day the kids'd be wearing overhalls for a fashion thing. Yep. But I never could've predicted city people'd like to eat this here *yogurt.* My mama never even kept that stuff, even she had the sense to throw out curdled milk. And she didn't throw out *nothing.* Well anyway, how's your daddy?"

"He's sick. Been in the hospital and they say he's not coming out."

Peterson finally shakes once, side to side.

"It was only in the last ten years Leonard and I started getting along. Where is he?"

"Here in Branden Parish."

"I'll have to stop and see him. Yeah, one day when we was both still working I saw him in the locker room and went up and told him a funny story I'd heard. We hadn't talked in forty years before that. But sometimes, you eventually just get tired of being mad at somebody."

"Mad about what?"

"Oh." Peterson breathes out again. "We fought. Me and your daddy. In high school."

"Over what?"

"Over your mother."

"Over my mother?"

"Oh yeah. A lot of boys wanted to fight Leonard over her. She was a real beauty, your mother. Damn shame she left us so young."

"I never knew about anything like that."

"Oh yeah. Leonard was a bulldog over her. But anyway, we moved on. Took a few years, but . . . How's Vernon?"

"I haven't seen him yet."

"Well, when you do, tell him hello for me."

"I will. Hey, I've got a question for you."

Peterson turns. "All right. I'm sure I've got an answer. Might be 'I don't know,' but go ahead."

"How far's the train go now, Mr. Peterson? Where's it headed when it leaves here?"

Peterson looks at Jody like he's crazy. "Same place as always, man. Lidem, Texas. Been goin' back and forth every day for eighty years now. Picks up the logs down there"—he points to a lumberyard half a mile away—"where they load 'em and takes 'em west."

"That's where my grandfather came here from. Lidem, Texas."

"Who, EL?"

"That's the one."

Peterson shakes his head. "Tough old coot he was. Tough on them boys."

"You said it. So the train's still running to Lidem, huh?"

"Yeah. Not too many of these small-town routes left." Peterson stands upright, then leans again on the end of his broom, crunches his entire face. "Years ago they tried to build more small-town routes but the union labor was too high, plus they could get these Mexicans to come over here and drive all this stuff on trucks for a dollar and two or three tamales a day. Next thing you know these small towns'll all be gone."

"You think so? Where's everybody going to live?"

Peterson scoffs. "Hell yes I think so. I *know* so. I been doing research on this. They're gonna make us all live in cities in these big buildings look like shoeboxes and you're sitting in your apartment and the guy next door goes in his toilet and you hear him grunting around in there and next thing you know the smell just *blossoms* all through your living room." Peterson shakes his head. "Those government idiotboxes!"

"Where do you come up with all this?"

"Aw. I like to surf the internet when I'm not sweeping. As a matter of fact, here's some *irony* for you: a lot of these places they go in and tear up the old railroad track so they can lay down internet cable, you can't take the cotton-pickin' train there no more but only the *virtual* train. You couldn't believe all the things going on out there, young man. But you can find out anything on that internet. I was just reading last night about these rich big-city folks, I mean these girls work as lawyers and bankers and models and making cups of coffee, when in the hell did people get to where Folgers ain't good enough for us anymore? Anyway, we're not talking regular down-home country girls that want to be barefoot and pregnant making chicken and dumplings in the kitchen, these rich big-city folks don't want to bother to have a baby and her get fat and him be hard up for nine months and next thing he's out there looking for some hooker and next thing she's got a pimp with a mouth full of gold teeth, beats the guy's face in and takes his Rolex watch and how's he gonna explain those black eyes and that Timex in his boardroom meeting? So they got these bands of gypsies coming over from Europe and going into the small towns and stealing babies. It happened just a few towns over from here, to a friend of mine's third cousin's sister-in-law, these gypsies came in and stole her baby."

"What! Bull! Where?"

Peterson hesitates, hawks and spits on the street, then spreads the gob of saliva with his broom until only a damp circle remains. "I can't remember just now the name of the town. But you can find out anything you want on the internet now. Right here in your own living room in old Branden. But like I say, before long they're gonna have all these small towns cleaned out and then the government will have all this wide open land to build these huge research stations and put fences around them thirty foot high and they'll have the spaceships come in and land at night and this alien creature'll come outta there with this big foot-long thingamabob flopping like a dead turkey's head and they'll have him mate with a human woman they've kidnapped and next thing you know we'll all have six eyes and three arms and be nine feet tall."

"Mr. Peterson, I've got an idea for you. Maybe you better get on that train. See where it goes. Get out of here for a little while. See the world a little bit."

Peterson turns and half looks at Jody. "Well, I know where it goes. Lidem, Texas. Just like it always has. Besides that, I can't go nowhere. I've got too much sweepin' to do. What are you, crazy? That sounds like something Leonard would have said to me."

"Is that right?"

"Leonard used to say that kind of thing to me all the time way back. Maybe you are Leonard. Maybe my time machine has worked after all. Praise God! It's 1971 again."

The train whistle sounds. "Ooh. Here it comes now." Peterson leans once more on his broom, takes in a deep breath. "Smell that, huh? Aahhh. See, some fellows like to drink. Me, I get drunk on the smell of cellulose." Peterson's hand flutters in the air. "It's like a fine wine." He breathes in. "Aah. Only difference is, the best vintage is from trees that was cut today. Only one better is them cut tomorrow."

The train approaches, blowing, then goes under the bridge and comes out the other side. Jody takes in the scent of iron, the burning tracks, the dewy smell of fresh-cut hardwood. The train whistle slowly fades as it heads toward the next towns over in Texas. Jody wonders, if things had been different for EL when he was a boy, if he ever would have left his home. He wants to use Peterson's time machine and get on that train and go to Texas, see if little boy EL is still there in some imaginary place, be friends with him, see if he can make anything any different. But of course he knows he can never make anything any different from the way it is and the way it has been. He watches the train run until the two tracks in the distance become one, and though he is so tired, he feels, as he watches the train, a shift inside himself, like the shift in an engine when it finally gets warm, and then runs so smoothly. The evening light is disappearing, slowly sinking back into the ground, and with it the red fading glow of the train as it moves onto a track he can no longer see.

CHAPTER 16

Jody makes himself comfortable in the house, spreads his things out on the kitchen table. Each day he calls Lurleen at the hospital, asks about his father, and each day she tries to beckon him back. He spends most of the week alone in his former home, thinking, remembering. Periodically he rises and goes outside, surveys the yard, walks up and down the old roads he once traveled looking for his brother. He doesn't return to the back of the house, and the door to his old bedroom remains closed. Shirts hang on hangers from the doorknob of the living room closet. The closet is filled with Leonard's boxes and thirty-year-old rarely worn coats. Laundry begins to pile in another corner. Jody fills the washing machine, pours in soap, paddles his hand in the froth before adding his clothes.

He drives into town in the truck through a dull gray morning, knee-high clumps of weeds that line the ditches still wet from morning dew. Ahead a flock of buzzards tears apart the remains of a dog at the edge of the pavement. The birds scatter into the heavy air. The stacks of the paper mill spit out clouds of pungent white steam, which the low, heavy ceiling pushes back down to the dirty ground. He opens the truck's window as he passes, hears the groan of the machines through the deepening fog.

At the strip mall beyond, a few storekeepers sweep the sidewalks out front, though most of the stores are dark, permanently empty. He passes through an area the locals call the bottom, a dip in the road that in his youth was spanned by the longest stretch of unbroken sidewalk in the United States. On the sidewalk a man rides a gelding, old Mr. Vick, someone Jody hasn't thought about in years. Mr. Vick used to say his great-grandfather had ridden into Branden on his own horse years before, and the younger man didn't see any reason to change a thing that didn't need to be changed. Jody stops at a light and watches as Mr. Vick, now a bent old man himself, walks the horse into the parking lot of SuperValu, gets down, hitches the animal's reins to a column in front of the store.

Leonard is awake and looks better than he did on Jody's previous visit. He has scrounged up some scraps somewhere for John David, who alternately licks his plate with gusto and chases it around the room when he licks it too hard. Leonard has changed into a clean blue tee shirt and shaved, though random spots of whiskers still dot his face. He sighs when he sees Jody. They stare at each other. Neither addresses their last meeting.

"Well, Jody. Son. What's it look like? How's the place?" Even these few words take all his breath.

"Pretty good. You've kept it up all these years."

"Grass prob'ly needs cutting, huh?"

"Yes it does."

"I'll have to find somebody to do it. Hate to come home to a mess." Leonard sinks into the bed.

"I could probably take care of it."

"You? No. I'll get it taken care of. You've got your own things to worry about now. I'm just thankful you came back to see me." Leonard begins to sigh now, great gasps of air. He seems ready to say more, instead settles for a doleful smile. He holds Jody's gaze.

"Lurleen told me you've been calling to check on me. These last few days."

"I have."

Leonard appears ready to say something but doesn't.

"So what have you been doing all these years, Jody?"

"I was working for the army. I tried to join. It just didn't work out. But I ended up working for them anyway. As a civilian."

"What did you do? You worked on a base?"

"Several of them. We moved around a lot. Art and I."

"Who?"

"My boss. Guy I still work for. A project we were doing."

"Mmm."

"It's a long story. Big research project. It's kind of hard to explain."

"I bet you've had some good times."

"I have. I've been lucky. I've enjoyed traveling around. Seeing different things."

"I knew you'd do something like that. Get away from here. I knew you would."

"Did you? I didn't really plan it that way."

"Yeah. I knew you would. I always knew it."

"Well, you could've told me."

"You figured it out just fine. By yourself."

"Maybe."

"But you didn't have to stay gone so long."

"Maybe not."

"Anyway." Leonard blows out. "How long you been in Chicago?"

"Just since last fall. I like it."

"So what are you doing now? Same type of thing?"

"I work for a paper company."

Leonard smiles, tries not to laugh. He holds on to his chest.

"What?"

Leonard wheezes, recovers. "You didn't have to go all the way up there to work for a paper company."

"I never thought about it like that. But I've got a good life."

Leonard tries to sit up. "What's your girlfriend's name?"

"Karen."

"That was your grandmother's name. Your mother's mother."

"That's right. I forgot about that. I never knew her."

"Y'all plan to be married? Have kids?"

Jody opens the window. At the edge of the playground a man stands in a knee-deep hole, swings an ax at the roots of a stump.

"We haven't got that far. We're a ways from that yet."

"Well, I recommend it."

"Okay."

"Y'all gonna stay up there?"

"Well. Karen's not a Louisiana girl."

"One of those, huh?"

"I guess you could say that."

"You love her?"

Jody watches as the man on the playground rocks the stump back and forth. He clenches his teeth and pulls. The stump separates from the roots around it with a ripping crack. The man twists the stump, jams a board under it, begins to lift it slowly from the ground.

"I think so." Jody turns back to his father, who tries a weak smile. Leonard settles himself into the bed. Jody moves closer. Sleep closes in on Leonard.

"I've got one more question for you, Jody."

"Yes?"

"What does it look like out there? All the places you've been."

"What does it look like?"

"Yeah. The whole big world. You seen anything out there looks like Branden?"

"Sure. It looks a lot like this. Just the details are different." Then Jody hears his father's breathing. Leonard sleeps, the faintest touch of a smile on his face.

At the reception desk, Lurleen shuffles papers. "Lurleen?"

She licks her finger, turns a page. "Yeah, baby?"

"Does this town have an internet café?"

Lurleen leans back, laughs. Her weight makes the springs of the chair squeak. She dips her fingers into an open jar of pickles, pulls one out, takes a bite, leans the open jar toward Jody. He refuses. She shakes the half-eaten pickle at him, crunches her face against the vinegar, swallows.

"Down where Ward's pharmacy used to be. You remember where that is?"

"I think so."

"At the end of Main Street. 'Course nobody in this little town could make any money on something like that, so a group of Christian kids started it. Better look out, one of them might try to make a Holy Roller out of you."

Jody starts toward the door. "I'll find it. And I'd like to see them try."

In town, Jody hears his name before he is fully stopped. Gary Wayne, the taxi driver, is in his car parked down the block. He sits sideways with the door open, his knees bent and extending out the opening. Jody approaches.

"What's happening, buddy?" Jody asks.

"How 'boutcha?" Gary Wayne answers. He stares at the storefront closest to him, never looks at Jody. "I hadn't been down here in a couple years, but seeing you the other day got me kinda fired up again. I thought I'd pay my old pal another visit."

"Who's that?"

Gary Wayne jumps up. "Well, speak of the devil. There he is right now." He bounds past Jody and runs up the three steps to the elevated sidewalk of downtown Branden. Another man stands in the entrance to an office, holding the door open and talking to someone inside. A State Farm insurance logo is painted on the door.

Gary Wayne stands nose to nose with the man. He tries to walk around but Gary Wayne blocks his way.

"Leave me alone, Gary Wayne." He puts out his right hand to push the taxi driver aside.

Gary Wayne holds his position. "When you gonna do what's right, Clem Mathews?"

Mathews finally brushes past, pushes him to the side, begins walking down the sidewalk.

"When are you going to get a life, Gary Wayne?"

Gary Wayne turns on his heels and chases after Clem. He moves himself in front, turns and walks backward as Mathews scurries down the sidewalk.

"I'm goin' to have some lunch, man. Just leave me alone, huh?"

"Oh, I'll leave you alone. I'll leave you alone. Just like I've been doin' all these years. After you give me my credit. I just want what's mine."

Mathews draws up, huffs out a long breath. "Are you still talking about that *stupid* basketball game? Is that all you've got, man?"

"'Course I am. You got all the credit and I never did get mine. And I ain't leavin' you alone until I get it. I want to see that story in the *Branden Independent* this week. And even better yet in the Shreveport paper. You got all the credit and now look at you. Everything goes your way now. And I didn't get nothing."

Mathews looks up at him again, stands rattling the coins in his pocket. "You're crazy, Gary Wayne. And I'm tired of you bothering me about this. Just let it go, huh? That was twenty-five years ago." Mathews brushes past Gary Wayne again and opens the door to Chevy's, the only restaurant downtown, a 1957 Chevy painted in pink and black on the storefront glass.

Mathews turns back. "Look. If you promise to be good I'll buy you some lunch. Come on in with me. Let's just have some lunch and talk about old times."

"I want what's mine," Gary Wayne says.

Mathews shakes his head. "Just forget it, man. Just forget it. Just go on." He ducks inside and doesn't look back.

Gary Wayne opens the door and starts inside, then seems to reconsider and returns to his car.

"I'm gonna get this straight once and for all." He gets in, rolls down the window, starts it, and begins to back out.

"Looks like it might rain. Say, did your daddy plant any of them tomatoes 'fore he went into the hospital?"

CHAPTER 17

He digs through cupboards, moves plates and cups and dishes to the side, reorganizes things. He finds pork and beans with faded labels, yellow corn. He dumps the contents into pans, heats them on the stove until the mixtures begin to bubble. He reads a month-old newspaper while he eats, then goes back to the recliner, leans the chair back, lets the silence of the country sink into him.

The sound of crunching gravel wakes him from a brief nap as a truck turns into the driveway. The truck stops and a man gets out. Then John David slumps out and tears across the yard. Jody goes outside.

"Hey, Jody buddy." The two embrace awkwardly.

"Vernon. How you doing?"

"Your daddy told me you were here. I told him I'd bring the dog over to run around some." Vernon claps his hands and points upward. "Get that squirrel." The dog takes off again toward a sweet gum tree full of squirrels, stands at the base clawing the roots, circling the tree and barking.

"So how you been?"

"Pretty good. Trying to get used to being here again."

Vernon grabs a pencil from his dashboard, uses it to scratch his neck. "What you doing up north?"

"I work for a family-owned company. Basically I manage the office. They call me 'human resources director.' But it's just a fancy title."

"I never could've worked inside. They couldn't have paid me enough. So what kind of company is it?"

"It's a distribution company."

"What do you distribute?"

"Paper. We inventory different kinds of paper and sell it to stationery stores, book manufacturers, artists."

"Well, that's kind of funny."

"Yeah, I know. I've been thinking the same thing. Same thing Daddy said."

"You go halfway around the world to end up working with paper like me and your daddy and just about everybody else around here."

"Yeah, I know. It's one of life's little mysteries."

"Well, it's hard to get away from what you know, I hear. I've never tried to myself, but that's what I've heard."

"I've been away a long time, Vernon. A long time."

Vernon leans back to face the clouds, pink and purple striations in the sunset sky. "You kind'ly skipped out on us, didn't you?"

Jody rubs his forehead. John David yelps, hooks his toenails in the bark, climbs a few feet up the tree before falling back in a pile. "Maybe so. Felt like the right thing to do at the time. But I know that's how my father sees it."

Vernon scratches his neck again with the pencil. "So let me get this straight. We make the paper down here and you sell it up there?"

"I guess it goes something like that. Some of it may very well start out here in Branden Parish."

"Well, what happens in between? There's a lot of steps in between."

"I haven't really thought about it."

Vernon eyes the squirrels in their nest, snaps his fingers at the dog, who takes a run at the tree this time. "I used to know. I used to know every step in the process. From planting the seedling to the tree growing year after year to the loggers cutting it down in their flannel shirts to trucking it to the mill to making it into paper, and eventually to kids all over the world sitting down at their desks writing on it. I used to be a lot more curious about things like that. But . . ." He shrugs. "It's like a lot of things. You quit thinking about it, it just goes out of your head."

"Unless it's a number, right?"

"Right. Unless it's a number. Or a pattern of some sort."

"You want something to drink?"

"Yeah, sure." He moves toward the house. Jody follows. Vernon surveys the yard.

"Place isn't looking up to Leonard's usual standards, I have to say."

"I told him I'd cut the grass here in the next few days."

"Well, I can help you."

Jody hears a sound like grass being ripped from the ground and turns to see John David coming at him like a freight train, his floppy ears back and his eyes wide. A gigantic black-and-yellow cat closes in on him and leaps for the dog's back as the men look on. The animals fight, John David baying and the funny-looking cat scrowling. They roll around, interlocked, three times before John David stands back on his feet with the cat in his mouth, jerks his head and throws it as far as he can. The cat tears away and John David lopes toward the door.

"Good dog."

Inside, Jody is glad for the company. Vernon sits at the table with his work boots still on while Jody boils water, strains the teabags, fills two glasses with ice and pours the steaming liquid in.

Jody takes a drink. Vernon covers the opening of the glass with his hand, swirls the tea around. A blanket of steam passes through and rises from the cracks between his fingers.

"You forgot something."

"What?"

"Sugar."

"Oh yeah. How could I forget. It's not legal to drink tea in Louisiana without sugar." He finds the sugar dish. Vernon heaps in several piles of it. The two drink in silence for a minute until John David starts scratching on the door.

"Thank you for calling me, Uncle Vernon. You were right, I wanted to know about this. About Daddy."

Vernon opens the door to let the dog exit, stands in the opening looking out at the yard.

"Well, your brother's gone, and I figured if Leonard was lucky enough to still have somebody alive to look after him, well . . ."

"Anyway, I'm glad you called me. You don't ever expect these things."

"No you don't. No you don't." Vernon takes off his hat, holds it in his hand. "Me and your daddy, we haven't kept up like we should have. I make no excuses for it. But still, it's unexpected."

Vernon returns to the kitchen table, sits down. "First memory I have of your daddy he was pulling a fishhook out of my finger. I guess I was three, four years old. Screaming and hollering. Seems like just last week." He blows out a long breath. "But I guess we've had our chances. Me and your daddy, we're not that old. But I guess his time is up. Nobody'll say he died too young. Look at me, I'm supposed to be retiring in six more weeks. I keep saying, wait, I'm not done, I can't be getting old."

"You're not getting old, Vernon."

He puts his hat back on. "That's kind of you, Jody. But it's not true."

"Sure it is. Of course it is."

"No. I'm old."

"Well. I have another question for you. Daddy asked me to do something. I wondered if you could help me."

"Sir?"

"He asked me to bring Scooter back here to see him. Have you got any idea where he is? I mean, you found me."

Vernon returns to the doorway and looks out at the yard, at the fading light. The dog stands at the base of the tree now, perfectly still, silent. He seems to be hoping the squirrels won't notice him if he doesn't move, will lead themselves directly into his waiting maw.

"I hear things. I'm not surprised Leonard asked you that. You were the only one could ever talk any sense into your brother. Waste of time, you ask me. But you didn't ask me."

Jody feels suddenly exhausted. "I'm gonna ask you to tell me what you know later, okay?"

"Sure." Vernon fills his glass again, walks over to sit in the other chair. The two chat for a minute about happenings in Louisiana. Corrupt state government. Indentured local officials. Financial scandals.

Vernon goes briefly to his truck, then comes back in. Jody relaxes in the chair.

"Hey, I've got another question for you, Vernon."

"Yessir?"

"They still play *Hee Haw* on Saturdays?"

Vernon twists his face at his nephew. "You're behind the times, Jody. Went off seven, eight years ago now. Maybe longer. You can't even find reruns anymore. Besides, that was always on Saturday, not Friday. Today's Friday."

"Oh, I know. Just sitting in this chair made me think about it. So it's gone, huh?"

Vernon picks up his iced tea again, takes a long drink. "Yep. Long gone. Like a lot of things."

"That's too bad."

"Well. It is what it is. So, Jody."

"Yes?"

"You just made thirty, huh?"

"Last Saturday."

"Your cousin would have made thirty later this month. In fact he was supposed to be born the same day you were. But you were a week early, and he was two weeks late. I remember me and your daddy talking about it at work. Made a five-dollar bet on who would have a son first."

"I guess he took your money then."

"No. Wouldn't take it. He told me to get a little present for you with the money."

"Is that right? I guess I don't remember. What'd you get me?"

"Just a, a . . ." Vernon holds up his hands. "A stuffed lion. A little stuffed animal to play with when you was a baby."

"I remember that lion."

"Yep. When I'd see him at work your daddy always said you loved it."

"I did. I remember."

"Well . . . That was from me."

"Well, thank you, Vernon. I never knew."

"Oh. You're welcome. That was a long time ago."

They talk for a few minutes more as the sunlight coming in the window fades to gray. Then Vernon sets his glass down, leans over on Leonard's old sofa and starts to doze. With his work boots still on.

CHAPTER 18

Outside, Jody lies in the grass, looks up at the sky. Vernon should be home now, pulling up his long driveway, making his way to the door. Jody waits until the coolness of the grass begins to sink into his shirt, thinks of the many times early that spring he and Karen passed hours in the grass of the park next to her apartment, Jody under the blanket, Karen on top of her half.

As Jody loses himself in the sky, his uncle's face is all he can see. Pearl was a stargazer. He and Dot never had any kids of their own, and Pearl spent many an afternoon and evening at the Davidson house. Though he was often described as a younger, just-as-mean version of his father, Jody never knew Pearl to be anything but a kind and gentle man.

Pearl kept a pile of books in his truck, and Jody and Scooter often found him reading one of them in the driver's seat when they got back home on the school bus. He never finished high school, but Pearl knew things about the workings of the universe few others seemed to know. He loved to read about the oceans and weather systems, of the evolution of animals—he maintained this was the final straw in his break with the

Baptist church—of anything to do with stars. Though he was a small man feared by many in Branden, at home with his family Pearl was unassuming, kind, and devoted. Many nights, after supper, he gave Scooter and Jody, and Leonard if he cared to hear it, a lesson about a star or constellation, then took them outside to point out the very thing. When the boys were a little older he liked to stand between them with his hands on their heads and, later, with his arms around them. But when they were small he picked them up, gave them rides on his shoulders, held on to their legs with one hand, pointed up at the sky with the other.

But the reputation that followed him was well earned. Pearl never talked about this himself, but according to Leonard, in addition to beating both of them regularly, EL sometimes had the men who worked for him bring their boys over to fight Pearl, in the horse corral he had specially built behind their barn. The men were rough and their boys were too, and rarely did a father or son refuse the offer. Refusal meant the fathers lost their jobs, and the sons what little place they had begun to have in the community. The boys, without fail, were older and bigger than Pearl. According to Leonard, Pearl preceded each fight with the same instruction for his brothers: *Watch if you want, but don't try to help. Save yourselves for your own fights. They'll be coming.*

EL claimed he wanted his boys to learn to take care of themselves. Leonard liked to say he was never sure why EL only did this to Pearl and not him, though the spinoff from these Sunday afternoon events meant many brawls for Leonard and Vernon in the weeks that followed, which led to more fights for Pearl as he looked after his brothers.

Many years passed before Pearl began to learn to control his temper. And with the disgust for Texas drilled into him from birth, when he was a boy all anybody had to do was call him Tex if they wanted a fight. Pearl was short and wiry, kept his hair in a bowl haircut, and a lot of guys were fooled by that. They didn't figure out how fooled they were until they were shouting for help under a barrage of his punches.

He tried to work for his father when he was old enough, running parts or fixing machines, but what the company really needed him for was his smarts, of which he had plenty. But he didn't have the patience to work inside. And as protective as he was of his brothers, he wasn't one to hold his tongue for a customer or a supplier or anybody who wasn't family. And in some cases, his fists. Eventually Pearl figured out he was most happy being outside, out where he could just do his job and keep his mind clear. And not have EL on his back telling him what to do all the time.

Pearl Davidson was jumpy. Jody rarely saw him look relaxed. Unless he had had a drink or two, and he only did that when it was just close family around. All the rest of the time he felt like he had to be on guard in some way. He was a great man to have as an uncle, and Jody always felt Pearl's love for him, as rough as it was. But he was never soft in any way with anyone, not even with children. Pearl was always play-fighting or wrestling with everyone, with Jody and Scooter too.

Pearl was fun to be with in bursts. He loved to play or jab with Jody, but by the time Jody recognized jovial Uncle Pearl, he was back to the other Pearl, the one standing on guard. Especially if there were other people around. Pearl never went anywhere without a short-billed, high-crowned train engineer's cap on his head. The cap was such a part of him that Dot had to remind him to take it off in the shower sometimes. Anytime anybody asked him a question he would stand there kind of bouncing on his feet, just waiting for the question to end so he could answer and get it over with. When he started to respond he would yank that cap off his head and then slowly replace it, trying it on and pulling it off again several times, smoothing back his hair until it was perfect, as he came to the end of his answer.

When Jody was eight—Pearl was not even fifty at the time—Pearl got into a disagreement with somebody at work. By that time he operated machinery on a logging crew full time. Not his father's crew. Any machine made, he could work it or fix it. Pearl called himself a top hand, like in the old days when a cowboy wouldn't work on the ground but only on top of his horse. Pearl had lost half his left foot to a falling tree in his twenties and preferred to work on top of one of the machines after that.

One of the guys who worked on Pearl's crew was a local roughneck named Tommy Nash. Tommy had a habit of revving one of the skidders before Pearl thought it was properly warmed up, and Pearl had talked to Tommy about this a number of times. This particular day Pearl was operating the other skidder when Tommy revved his up too early. Pearl saw red and started yelling at him from the chair of his own machine. Then just slumped over the controls.

After that his doctor told Pearl he had to control his temper better or he would have another stroke. And the only way he knew how to do that was by drinking. The drinking never got to be a problem, if anything it helped. Pearl was just like Jody's father. He was a happy drunk. Putting a little liquor in him was like putting a key in a lock and turning it. But Pearl was careful with his drink, and still often, especially at work, tried to control his temper by will. When he couldn't do it, he just got madder, and everything got worse.

A few months after EL and Hazel died was the last time Jody saw his uncle healthy. He was almost sixty then and had taken early retirement from his job as equipment manager for Alexander's Construction. He said the arthritis in his back and knees finally got the best of him. That and one of Mr.

Alexander's sons had recently taken over the company, and he knew he was bound to "stomp that little sucker's ass," as he said it. He had stopped by the house on a Sunday. Jody was inside washing dishes and Scooter and Leonard were out in the yard.

The two of them took up lawn chairs and sat down when Pearl hobbled out of his truck. Jody waved through the window at him, but something about the lightness on his uncle's face drew Jody outside.

Pearl shook each of their hands with his powerful grip, pulled them in toward himself to slap their backs. "I got something to tell y'all," he said. They all sat down. Pearl took off his cap and ran a hand over his hair. For the first time Jody noticed he was wearing something other than his engineer's cap. A John Deere cap. Jody grabbed his chest, pointed at Pearl's head; the others murmured in agreement.

Pearl took off the cap, held it in front of him. He didn't say anything, just giggled.

"So what you got to tell us, Pearl?" Leonard asked.

"Just something that happened. Thought y'all might think it was funny."

Leonard shifted in his chair. "Well, what is it?"

"Aw, just a funny story. Something funny that happened. Maybe we oughta call Vernon."

"Call Vernon?"

"Yeah, call Vernon. Get him up here so I can tell all y'all at the same time."

"Tell us what at the same time? Vernon lives a hour from here, what are you talking about?"

"Aw, nothing, just something funny that happened." Pearl always talked this way. He liked to tell stories but wanted to make sure absolutely everybody was listening before he started. And he knew exactly when to begin before anybody's attention drifted away.

"Dad gummit, Pearl, what is it? We're all ears."

Pearl looked up to the top of the oak tree in the front yard. He took off his cap again, turned it around in his hands, stared at the bill. "John Deere," he said out loud. "Mmm mmm. Good tractors."

Leonard stood up. He had heard these drawn-out presentations from Pearl all his life.

"All right, all right," Pearl finally said. "Hold your horses, son. It ain't every day a old man gets to tell a story like this." Leonard stared at his brother dubiously, sat back down.

"A story like *what*?"

"Like what happened to me yesterday. Something kinda, you know, unusual. Not something that happens every day."

"Last chance, Pearl," Leonard said, and stood back up.

Pearl put his hands out, palms down, in a slow-down signal. Then began.

"I went in Mikey's store yesterday afternoon to get me a cold six-pack. They got a kid working there now, no kin to Mikey far as I can tell. Indian kid I believe. Not one of them 'merican Indians—one of them other Indians." Jody looked over at his father, whose head was dropped straight back and was looking at the sky, mouth open. Even Jody knew Mikey had not owned that store in thirty years.

Pearl saw Leonard and got the point. "Anyway, Jimmy's the kid's name. Well, I don't think that's his real name, he's got thirteen or fourteen letters in his real name and most of 'em's vowels. He wrote down his real name for me one time and after that I started calling him Vowel Boy. But his nametag says Jimmy. Tall kid, about six foot four? Got hair down to here?" He tapped two fingers onto a shoulder. "Pretty hair too, for a boy. Well, I looked around at the candy some, thought I'd get me a Reese's. I like that chocolate and peanut butter mixed together." Pearl swirled his finger as if mixing an imaginary concoction. "Then I picked up a bag of pork rinds. But the last time I eat them they give me the heartburn so I figured I'd just stick with the plan. Y'all know sometimes that's the best way to go. Make a plan, stick with the plan." Pearl flipped one palm faceup, looked at it, then followed suit with the other. "So I went back and grabbed a six of Old Milwaukee. Hey, that reminds me of something, Leonard, you remember when they used to put it in them fourteen-ounce cans?"

"Yeah, I remember. 'Course I remember. What the hell's that got to do with anything?"

"Oh, I was just thinking. About the good old days."

"Don't start all that bull crap, Pearl! Just tell us what happened! We're settin' here waiting!"

"All right, all right. But you've gotta admit it ain't like it used to be."

"Pearl! When I get finished, you ain't gonna be like you used to be neither! Don't make me open up a can of whoopass on you!"

"Psssh! Son, you ain't got a can opener that big!"

Leonard looked down at the ground.

"So I grabbed me a six of Old Milwaukee and set it down on the counter. Jimmy said, 'Hey, Mr. Pearl,' just like he always does. You know them jackasses are charging three dollars and something for a six of Old Milwaukee now? *Three dollars and something!*" He shook his head. "I'd gripe to Jimmy about it, but it wouldn't do no good. Like I say, he ain't even no kin to Mikey. Probably doesn't even make that much an hour."

Leonard began to slowly stand up again.

"So I put the beer down and was thinking about that first cold drop. Hawwwwww!" He leaned back in his chair, tipped an imaginary can of beer. Then he stopped and looked at Jody and Scooter, remembering where he was. "Now you boys know my doctor told me I's supposed to drink some beers every day, right? Y'all remember that. I know they tell y'all in church not to."

"Pearl!" Leonard shouted.

Pearl put his hands out again, palms down. "I slapped that twenty down on the counter. Jimmy took it and put it in the cash register. Then he, you know, he went to get my change. Now see I've been in a lot of stores and most of your cashiers, they'll just take that roll of coins and slap it on the corner of the countertop to break it." Pearl demonstrated. "But not Jimmy. He uses a *scissors*." Pearl did a scissors motion with two fingers. "He didn't have enough pennies in there so he got a roll out and cut it open with the scissors. For a, you know, a Indian he's a very neat young man. So he counted up the change and put the change in my hand. Now what's interesting about it"—that was an expression Pearl always used, *what's interesting about it*—"is that I stuck out my left hand? For the change? 'Cause I always take the change in my right hand and put it straight in my wallet? But for some reason I stuck out my left hand."

At that point Pearl paused and looked around again. There was a family of crows in the top of the oak tree, and they were squawking and carrying on and he turned and looked up at them, then held his hands up like an air gun and pretended to shoot. Leonard exhaled loudly, and Pearl turned back, took his hat off, and turned it around in his hands again but didn't say anything.

"I guess I had me a little mini blackout as I was standing there because I didn't see him coming. I was thinking about that first cold drop and all, and I guess Jimmy had been looking at the *Playboys* because that plastic shield? They put over the front of them? That shield was off, good God, have y'all seen the *cojones* on Miss May? Hell, I'd like to get a closer look at her!"

"Seen the what?" Leonard said. "'Cojones' means testicles, Pearl! Where'd you hear that word?"

Pearl looked heart shot. "Nosir," Pearl said. He set down his Dr Pepper, cupped his hands to form breasts. "These here."

Leonard was exasperated. "Just tell us the story, Pearl."

"Anyway, she's got a pair on her." Then he mumbled, looking to the side. "Like to get a closer look at them."

"Hot dammit, Pearl!" Leonard snatched off his own hat and threw it down on the ground. "You couldn't do nothing with her if you did get closer to her, you dried-up old coot! You may as well be a hundred and thirty-six years old up next to that girl!" He stomped on his hat. "Now what happened?"

"Oh, yeah," Pearl said calmly. "And you're right, I couldn't do nothing with her because I'm a married man. Thirty-eight years now, boys," he said, looking to Jody and Scooter.

Leonard rubbed his temple, lowered his voice. "You didn't see who coming?"

"See who?"

"Who didn't you see coming? When you were looking at the, the cojones on that girl?"

"Oh, that. Yeah, uhhh, the kid. Kid just walked in the door and grabbed the money in my hand. Couldn't have been no older than Scooter. White little son of a butt kisser." Then he took a long sip of Dr Pepper and smirked when the fizz hit his tongue, like he was just talking about fishing.

Leonard sat up straight. "He grabbed your money?"

"Psssh," Pearl said. "Tried to. But when he did I grabbed his hand." He raised his right hand in the air and snapped his fingers back in a gesture of dismissal, then took another sip of the Dr Pepper and winced.

"Whoa!" Leonard shouted. "Now we're finally getting somewhere! Then what happened?"

"What happened. Let's see, what happened." Pearl leaned his head back to the sky.

Leonard stood up and threw his chair across the yard.

Pearl put his hands back up, motioned for Leonard to slow down. "Well, at that point I figured he just wanted to get away.

He was trying to get his hand loose from my hand and next thing I knew I popped him one."

Scooter jumped up. "You popped him one?"

Pearl put his fist to the right side of his own face and pushed, demonstrating how he had punched the kid. Then he jerked his head back hard and opened his eyes wide, as if in terror. Finally, he hung his head all the way forward, closed his eyes, and tried to look dead. Or unconscious at least.

"Yeah, I popped him one." Pearl pulled his fist back like an arrow in a bow, then released it and punched the air with a loud *ha-ka!* "And that little sucker went down like Cooter Brown! Damnation! Laid out there on the floor of Mikey's store cold as a hammer!"

Leonard started laughing then, great gasps of air spilling out. "Cooter Brown went down because he was drunk, Pearl. Anyway, then what'd you do?"

"Well, the way this fool acted he mighta been drunk." Pearl threw his hand in the air again. "Who knows. But I didn't mean to kill him or anything, so I felt of his chest to see if he was still breathin'. Then I picked up sixteen dollars and thirteen cents off the floor. Still had a quarter in my hand. By that time Jimmy had came around the counter. 'You want me to call the police, Mr. Pearl?' He asked me."

"What'd you tell him?"

Pearl looked up at the crows again, held up his pretend gun, said, "Caw caw caw," then refocused for the end of his story. "Naw, I told him, don't worry about it. I've done took care of him. But I'm gon' tell y'all right now. People just keep getting crazier. People're crazier than anybody."

He was full of stories, Pearl was. But listening to him, being around him, he always seemed like he was just one step ahead of something. Like he was always waiting for the next big blow to come. Pearl was so unable to relax, he sat so close to the edge of his chair, his legs shook from the effort. He didn't take it well when EL died, and then Mama Hazel just two weeks later; after that he kind of seemed lost, like an old dog. He had been stopping after work to see them several times a week for years. Then after they died, for a while he stopped by Leonard's house every day after work. One day he pulled up just after Jody and Scooter got off the bus, and a little puppy Labrador jumped down from the cab of his truck.

"That's John David," he told them. "Old boy at work had some puppies he didn't know what to do with, so I told him I'd take care of one. He looks like he'll be a pretty good old dog."

Not long after, he got another blow. He called Leonard late one afternoon about six months after EL and Hazel died to say he had walked in and found Aunt Dot passed away in their recliner chair. Pearl said the snap-open cigarette case she was never seen without was open on her lap and her lighter was in her hand. She had a beautiful smile on her face. Not a month later, Pearl had another big stroke that left him paralyzed on one side and landed him in the nursing home.

There he remained, as belligerent as ever, in a way even worse, since he wasn't in a good position to even protect himself anymore.

The last time Jody saw him they had stopped by the nursing home one Sunday afternoon to visit and watch the Superbowl with him. Pearl was completely confused. They all sat down in the television room with him and some of the other residents, and through slurred speech he kept saying something about LSU. Another man was in the room, older than Pearl but in better shape physically, and the man kept telling Pearl to shut up, let it go. Jody was on the opposite end of the room and saw his father glance over a couple times. Finally Jody understood what Pearl was saying. "LSU is going to play the winner of the Superbowl!" His family knew that Pearl knew college teams don't play professional teams. No one was sure what to say to him; instead they all looked at Pearl with pity. Jody still pictures the hurt look Pearl had on his face. At that he tried to jump out of his chair and shout it out, in broken speech. "LSU is gonna play the winner of the Superbowl!" Before Jody saw what was happening, the other man jumped on Pearl and punched him several times in the face before Leonard pulled the man off and helped Pearl up.

The staff of the nursing home said he never left his room after that, just sat in his bed with the curtain drawn between him and his roommate, holding a mirror with his good hand, studying his two black eyes. Five days later one of the nurses came in and found him lying there dead with his eyes open, the mirror a jumble of pieces on the floor.

CHAPTER 19

Safe at home, Vernon throws down three quick belts of whiskey, then takes another shot mixed with the mustard into his chair. He switches on the television, turns the volume all the way down, loses himself in the azure glow. An old Western movie he has seen several times is playing, though he can't remember the name. In the movie a sheriff's deputy on a horse chases a gunman into a canyon. The gunman fires his pistol backward, over his shoulder. The camera moves in on the face of the deputy as he is struck by the bullet. The footage is old, grainy. Vernon studies the face of the lawman, his fierce, determined eyes. The lawman's eyes fade. He falls from his horse.

Vernon switches off the television, reaches for the framed photograph of his son that sits on his coffee table. In the picture the boy is fifteen. He stands beside his truck, a '78 Ford, blue and white, which his father had bought him for his birthday. The truck is newer than Vernon's own, though it doesn't have the shine Vernon's does. Vernon thinks back to their conversation that day.

"You're a third my age now, Billy. You're catching up to me."

Billy shared his father's penchant for numbers. "And when

I'm thirty, I'll be half your age. If we both live long enough, eventually there won't be any real difference. Statistically, I mean. Like parallel train tracks. In the distance they come together." Vernon beamed. His son made him so proud.

In his chair, Vernon lifts his drink, swirls the oily mixture around in the glass. Then raises it in the direction of Billy's picture. "Thirty," he says. "Happy birthday, son. You're about to be thirty. Half my age finally." Then Vernon takes a long, hard drink, chokes on the bitterness he takes into his body.

Vernon and Misty were married seven years before their son was finally born. They had been good years but hard years, filled with the disappointments of half a dozen miscarriages. Yet the two of them had, somehow, made it through, on the strength of the feelings they held for one another. And on the strength of the hope that, one day, their greatest dream would come true.

Vernon for sure had had his doubts, but Misty did not allow such feelings into her life. She always said and always believed that, one day, God would bless them with the child they were intended to have. Though Vernon grew up in a church, he never had really understood the things they prayed about every week, the faiths people claimed to have that things were going to work out the way they should. He just went to church because that's the thing people did.

But the years of waiting changed him. When he and Misty were finally rewarded with a healthy, beautiful boy, Vernon felt himself move into another world. Just being married had taken him to a place he never expected to be, had lent him a point of view he never expected to have. But when the baby finally came, after all the years of waiting, heartbreak, and disappointments, Vernon experienced a whole new change. Afterward, when he thought through the sum of the changes, from his beginning as a skinny, self-conscious, yearning boy to his transformation into a married man with a family, no longer all alone, he could only come up with one word to describe it. The change was a miracle.

Vernon couldn't stop holding the baby. Nearly every moment the two of them were together, Billy lay cradled in his arms. EL talked to him about it. Leonard talked to him about it. Pearl talked to him about it. They told him to set the baby down, let him roam, let him learn to walk, wrestle with him. But what did they know. Vernon reaches for a pillow, squeezes it tight. Fact is they were lucky. His love for his son was the only thing in all those years that allowed him to even tolerate EL, who only wanted to poke the baby, to try and hold up Billy's little hands and make him punch the air.

Once Vernon and Misty had Billy, they only wanted more. But what followed their son's birth was another six years of disappointments and three more miscarriages. This turn of events affected the two of them in different ways; Vernon remained oddly hopeful, while Misty turned uncharacteristically sour. Eventually, they grew apart.

The two of them remained friends, and did a pretty good job of parenting their son together, if in two different homes. In the end only Vernon continued with just one child; with her new husband, Misty had two more boys when she was forty and forty-one. Billy lived most of the time with his mother and stepfather, and as hard as it was for him, Vernon swallowed his pride and agreed to the plan. And put his faith for his son's future in God's hands.

As Billy grew, he and his father spent many days together fishing, hunting, and sometimes sitting at home, just talking. Even as he remembers it now, Vernon marvels at how much different Billy turned out from himself. When the fishing was good, Billy was happy. When it wasn't, he felt the same. When he brought down a teal, his smile was no bigger than it was when he missed. Vernon was awed by the way his beautiful son kept his head level, how easily he forgave himself and others, how slowly he rose to anger and frustration at others or, more importantly, as his father did, at himself.

From a young age, Billy Davidson loved to go to church, to shake hands with everyone, talk it up, press the flesh. When Billy came to stay with Vernon on weekends, the two of them never missed a Sunday morning sermon. They were such a part of the community that eventually Vernon was invited to be a deacon. That day was one of the proudest of his life, the day he stood before the congregation and accepted the role, then sat back down to see his son baptized, dunked under the water in his long white robe at the ripe old age of nine.

And *sing*. Billy remembered the words to every hymn they ever sang in church, even if they only sang it once. Billy did have a favorite, something about God's hands. *God our father, hold us in your hands.* When they sang that song in church, Vernon just stared at his son. The face Billy showed the world reflected nothing of the way Vernon felt about God when he was a boy. For the first time in his life, Vernon understood the meaning of the words. For the first time in his life Vernon became comfortable in his suits and ties. For once he understood that, maybe, somehow, someone up there was watching out for them after all, was looking at Vernon and his little family as if they sat, cradled, in the palm of God's hands.

There was another time that stands out. Billy was fourteen, maybe fifteen then. He went to the altar, sang a song in front of the church. One of these popular songs, a modern gospel piece, played in the background on a cassette player. Billy had a rich tenor voice by then, wore a suit and tie, a curl of brown hair hanging down on his forehead. Vernon sat, looking on, his heart filled to bursting.

Later, they waited in line for lunch in the fellowship hall. Vernon stood behind his son, hands on Billy's shoulders, which then were still lower than his own. In that moment, he felt so proud of his boy he couldn't speak. He tried and tried but nothing came out. With his hands on Billy's shoulders he scanned the room, smiled at everyone he saw, fought back the tears pooling in his eyes, shuffled forward in the lunch line. And asked himself, again and again and again. How had he, how had Vernon Davidson, son of EL, become father to such an amazing boy? How did it happen?

Eventually they filled their plates, found seats at an empty table. Reverend DuBois approached, Vernon's onetime father-in-law, retired from the church, now long dead. Vernon stood to greet him. Reverend DuBois put his hands on Vernon's shoulders, turned to look at Billy, offered his congratulations, told the boy how proud he was. Billy beamed. The reverend turned to Vernon, smiled, and told Vernon how proud he was of *both* of them. For a moment Vernon felt like a boy himself, as if he were growing out of his clothes.

Billy's love and admiration for his father never waned. For Vernon, living with his son had been so easy when Billy was just a boy, when the problems he faced were skinned knees and needing help with homework. But as he grew, he needed more. After the boy went to live with his mother, Vernon looked forward to his visits like a boy himself. Though their time together was not as easy as Vernon hoped, each time, it would be.

Billy came back to live with his father when he was still in high school. In his chair Vernon considers the story again, for perhaps the ten thousandth time. He wonders, as he always does, if maybe this time the ending will be different, if maybe, just maybe, he will stand up from his chair in a whole other world and shake the hand of his handsome blue-eyed son. Only this time, if he does, he'll pull Billy in close, like he did when his son was just a little boy.

Billy was seventeen then, in his last year of high school, and his stepfather's attempts to rule him had begun to get the best of the young man. Vernon was so excited when he moved back in. But living with his son as a young adult proved harder than Vernon expected. The boy had changed so much over the years; he was no longer that child getting out of bed to come and sit in his father's lap, smelling of bad breath and rayon pajamas, telling Vernon how much he loved him, how he was the best daddy in the whole wide world, reaching his little arms around Vernon's chest and back.

The first thing Billy wanted was to build a loft in his room. Vernon agreed to it, but complained bitterly about the cost, the noise, the dust. Billy was still working on the loft that spring when his birthday came. He asked Vernon if he could have some other boys over on his birthday, under the guise that he needed some help with the loft he was building. And then he added that, since they would be over anyway, would it be all right if they had a few beers to help him celebrate his birthday. Build a fire outside, have some beers, just camp out in the yard. Everybody would be better off if they just camped out in the yard. Billy was the last of his friends to turn eighteen and they all wanted to be there and see him finally become a man for real.

And Vernon Davidson, deacon of the First Baptist Church, had told his son no. Which is what Vernon thought he was supposed to do. Billy never had been like the other kids, sneaking around and drinking with his friends. What kind of a kid had Vernon raised? Billy had always told him everything, had always craved the love from his father that was sitting right there for him to take. Which worried Vernon more than anything. For one, that his son put so much stock in him. For another, that he couldn't just reach out and take it. Vernon felt he had to do anything, *anything*, to hang on to his beautiful son's innocence. Anything to keep from losing him to the sadnesses of the world.

"No," Vernon said, "we don't drink. I don't want any beer

here and I don't want you to drink or even be tempted to. And you know that, son. I'm a deacon in the church and you know we don't drink. And besides that, you've got better things to do with your life. Nothing but trouble comes from alcohol."

But Billy was unfazed. Somehow, Vernon had no idea how, his incredible son had never learned to be fazed.

"Couple of beers, Dad, come on. Eric and them will bring a cooler over, we'll make some hamburgers and just sit out back, camp out. Be safer for everybody."

In a bathrobe in his chair, Vernon mouths the words again that he said a dozen years before. "My mind's made up, son. It's against our religion."

Our religion, Vernon thinks again. *Those do-gooder fools!* They put all of that crap in his head. A few beers! What was the harm? Vernon struggles up, stumbles into the kitchen, makes another drink. He imagines all those boys sitting around the fire in his backyard, being young, just having fun. Vernon wishes with every cell in his body he could just get up, walk over to the door, open it and tell them all to keep it down, to keep the party outside. Vernon wishes with everything he has that he could just hold Billy's hand again.

The loft still stands, unfinished, in Billy's room. For the millionth time Vernon wishes, as he does about so many things, that he had handled that differently too. That he had never complained about the noise, the dust, the cost. That he could just go back and change something, anything; he would change absolutely anything if he could just make something different. But complaining had been all he knew how to do, and no had been all he knew how to say.

Vernon wishes he had been a completely different person, wishes he had never held his son or had an honest conversation with him. He stumbles back to his chair. He wishes he had just beat the tar out of Billy, like EL did to Leonard and Pearl, or ignored him, as EL did to him. Wishes he had done anything different that could change something that would bring his son back to him. He would do anything.

One way or another, he can find a way to live with anything that has happened. He can drown the sorrow, keep his clothes clean, go to work every day, keep letting his former friends know how much he hates everything about the god they still worship.

But the thing that still worries him, that's always there no matter what, is the thought that nags him in the middle of the night, when he turns over in his sleep to see that daylight is still so, so far away. Did Billy know how much his father loved him? Did he ever really know? Did Vernon at least do that much right? If only there were some way he could be sure. If he couldn't have his beautiful boy anymore, could he at least have that? Vernon would give anything, absolutely anything. His own life even. Just to know that Billy knew. Just to know that he had done at least one thing right in his life.

Vernon picks up his glass and stares at it. He looks out the window. He's sure he sees a campfire out there, some flicker of orange light. Then he hears a knock at the door. He tries to stand, falls back. That man, that preacher from the church, is standing there in his living room, looking down at him.

"Do you hear it?" Vernon asks.

"Hear what, Vernon?"

"Amazing grace, how sweet the sound." Vernon sings the words. "They're singing it out there. Out there in the backyard. Can't you hear it? Tell them to keep the party outside. Will you?"

"Vernon?"

"It's such a pretty song. *That saved a wretch like me.*"

"I wanted to see you again, Mr. Vernon. See how you're doing."

"I once was lost, but now I'm found . . ."

David Adams moves in closer. Vernon, badly drunk, trembles. He looks up at a spot to the reverend's side.

"So why did he die, David Adams? Billy was sweet. Good natured. Perfect. You want to know how I am? That's how I am." The words come out all at once.

"I can't answer that, Vernon."

"Was blind but now I see."

The minister moves over to Vernon's chair. The half-filled glass is ready to tip over in Vernon's lap. Adams takes it from his hand, dumps the liquid out in the sink. He goes back to Vernon's side. Vernon's eyes are closing.

David Adams reaches for the handle of the chair, pulls it back until Vernon is horizontal. Vernon continues to sing. The preacher bends down, close to the older man's ear.

"Vernon?"

"Sir?"

"You know it's almost Easter. Another chance to be reborn."

"Reborn."

"Another chance for you. For all of us."

"Another chance."

Adams wants to say more, but he knows his work, for the moment, is done. He picks up a small blue blanket, spreads it over Vernon's legs. Then he puts his hand on Vernon's forehead, closes Vernon's eyes, walks back over and opens the door.

"Tell 'em to keep it down out there. Do you hear it? Can you hear the singing?"

"Sure I hear it, Vernon. I hear the singing. The music all around us is beautiful. If only we take the time to hear it."

"No, wait a minute. Don't say anything. Just let 'em sing."

Adams, assessing things, turns to leave. "You want me to lock this door?"

"No sir. No sir. Don't lock it. Don't close it. Leave it open."

"Open?"

"Yessir. Leave it wide open." David Adams opens the door.

"I'm just gon' go on to sleep. But leave that door open. They're singing so pretty. So pretty. Just leave that door open. Such pretty music. Just let it on in."

CHAPTER 20

By the end of the week, the road from his father's house into town is familiar again. Things haven't changed much since he lived there before. Sidewalks are still broken. Most of downtown remains shuttered, a continuation of the process that started many years before. Buildings that have stood abandoned for long enough are swallowed by vines, creeper and kudzu that barely stop for winter in the tropical Louisiana heat. What stands out most is the time; the emptiness of all the time around him with no job to do, spent in a place both familiar and not.

Each day, as he leaves the house in Leonard's old truck, Jody has a question on his mind, something he wants to ask his father about. Maybe a story about their family, maybe something Leonard said or did once long ago. Perhaps a question about his mother. But each day as he drives, the fields and sights and sounds of the town and all the other cars go by, and pictures remembered from the past are superimposed on the scenes from the present and everything, for the moment, seems okay. By the time he parks and walks inside, by the time Lurleen waves hello, Jody's thoughts have returned to the present.

"I miss him," Leonard says. Jody stands by his father's bed. He opens the window to welcome the sultry air hovering just above the earth, the smoky scent of wetness mixed with chalky dust. A thunderhead bursts. Children playing on the swing set scatter, shouting.

"You know he's just like your mother was. Out there on his own."

"Well, Dad. You know I don't remember her much."

Lightning strikes again. Leonard reaches to the floor to pat John David, who is cowering under the bed. The dog whimpers, licks his lips again and again.

"You know your mama was the one that loved to garden. She's where I learned all I know about tomatoes."

"I didn't know that."

"Oh yeah. EL, he couldn't grow a pine tree. He never taught us much about plants. How to cut 'em down with a chainsaw, maybe. But your mother. She could make anything grow."

"I never knew that. Y'all liked to work in the garden together?"

"She taught me all I know. And she was so proud of her tomatoes. I can grow 'em but I haven't made one in my life that tasted like hers. Nothing could get her out of that garden."

"And Scooter? What's the similarity?"

"Neither one of them had the sense to come in out of the rain." Leonard turns away, looks backward. By now the dog has come out from under the bed, whimpers repeatedly while covering his head with both forepaws.

"I remember one time she was out tending her plants. Big storm blew up, out of nowhere really. It was a hot day and then, bam, these clouds come racing across. Early, like now, maybe May, late April. That lightning was coming closer. The rain was coming down in buckets. I was looking at her out the kitchen window, waiting for her to come in. She never moved. Finally I ran out there, it was raining so hard I was soaked before the door even slammed behind me. Grabbed her up. I had my arms on her shoulders. She stood up, smiled at me. Water pouring off her face. Those *eyes*." Leonard stops, gives himself a moment with the memory. "You know what she said to me?"

"What?"

"'Thanks for coming, Leonard,' your mama said. 'I've been waiting for you.' I said, 'Baby, what are you doing? That lightning's coming!' Just then it hit again, not a quarter mile away. I felt the hair on my arms raise up.

"'I've been waiting for you. To come stand in the rain with me.'"

"That's a pretty picture."

"And I said, I said, 'Well, here I am.' And she took my hand and we went on in the house together."

A nurse walks in and puts the blood pressure cuff on Leonard. The nurse is short and round, her face so fat her eyes close when she smiles. Leonard clinches his teeth when she pumps it tight. Neither says a word until she leaves.

"Has it been good for you, being away?"

"It's been good to see the world."

"I wish I'd got a chance to see it." Leonard turns toward the quickening sunlight.

The sky has begun to clear and now a man is pushing a child on the swing set. The boy is yelling, "Higher, higher."

"I asked 'em for this room. I was two rooms down and I could always hear kids screaming outside. I asked one of the nurses what it was and she wheeled me down here to show me. The room was empty so I asked if I could move."

"You wanted to be closer to screaming children?"

"I just wanted to watch them having fun I guess. Once Doc Spencer told me how bad it was"—he taps his chest, over his heart—"I just wanted to see people happy. That's all I wanted to see. Jody?"

"Yes?"

"There's a couple things I have left to do. You know you get to laying down in a bed like this all day and you think about things you never did before."

"I imagine."

Leonard blows out. "Maybe I should have got married again for you boys. I don't know."

"Doesn't matter now, Daddy."

"Well. You're the only one ever could talk any sense into your brother. Will you see if you can find him for me?" He reaches out for Jody's hand. "Please."

"You know I never could get through to him. You know that, right? I just cleaned up some messes, brought him home sometimes."

"I know. And I appreciate all you did do for him. I just need you to get his body here. That's all I'm asking."

"Vernon says he knows where Scooter is. I don't know how he knows it, but."

"Your uncle has special talents of his own, that's how. But Jody. I don't have much time left. I can feel my old heart slowing down every day." Leonard gasps for breath.

"Just see what you can do."

John David wags his tail and barks at everything on the drive back to the house. When Jody pulls into the driveway the dog doesn't even wait for the truck to stop, instead leaps out the window and bounds across the yard toward the pond, jumps in and begins to swim. Later, he is running around with another dog when Jody gets in the truck to drive back to town, and doesn't want to go for a ride.

Jody drives straight to the mill, waves at Peterson out there holding court by the railroad track with some other old man, leaning on his broom. Peterson removes a glove and waves. Jody parks his father's truck next to Vernon's, which he finds sitting with one other at the edge of the lot. He waits a few minutes for the shift whistle to blow, and Vernon shuffles out.

"I didn't expect to see you here." Vernon looks white, more jittery than usual. Behind him the stacks belch more steam, which drifts into the sky. The whole place smells of sulfur, the scent clawing through the humid atmosphere.

"He's going fast now, Uncle Vernon. He asked me about my brother again. Could you stop by there with me to see him?"

"Okay. I'll follow you."

"Hey. What's the deal with you and this other truck? You're the only ones parked way out here."

Vernon turns toward the shiny, jacked-up truck with the rebel flag in the window, spits on the ground.

"Don't ask." He sits down in his own vehicle. "I'll follow you."

They park at the hospital, get out. Vernon doesn't look so jittery when they get there but he smells of whiskey.

"You all right, Vernon? You don't look too steady."

"Good as ever. Let's go on in."

The two walk together to room 314. Leonard has an old *Bonanza* playing on television. Ben Cartwright goes down from a shot to the shoulder as they enter the room.

Leonard switches the television off. "Don't worry, Ben'll live. Must've been shot two hundred times by now." Vernon sits on the windowsill. Jody hears the swing set creak from the weight of a child as Vernon mutters to himself.

Leonard seems to be feeling better. His face doesn't have the gravity Jody has witnessed in prior visits. Instead he wears one of the faces Jody remembers well. The jovial one. Vernon, though, is pensive, continues looking out the window.

"How you think he stands it up there, Vernon? Living up

there in Yankeeland?" Leonard laughs after he asks the question—*tssh tssh tssh*—and Vernon turns inward again.

"I'll be the last Davidson in Louisiana," Vernon says, after a long silence.

"What's that?"

Vernon wheels back into the room. "You heard me, Leonard. I'll be the last Davidson in Louisiana. Except for your brother." He nods his head at Jody.

Leonard sighs. "You always was kind of by yourself, weren't you? With me and Pearl being older, you always was kind of by yourself."

"Yeah, well this time it's sho-nuff."

"Scooter will come around. Jody's going to get him as soon as you can help him figure out how to find his brother. Gonna bring him back up here in the next few days. Get him straightened out. Gonna help him some."

Vernon scoffs. "Hunh. Well, good luck, Jody. I called down there to New Orleans, Leonard, where I thought he was the same day I called your sensible son. And one of them boys that answered the phone said he wasn't around. Haven't heard from him yet."

"Well, you know where he is. Jody's gonna go get him."

"I hope he does. I hope he does. Look, brother. Scooter ain't never been a part of this family. He's always done what he wanted to do. And he broke your heart. Don't forget it."

"Don't you blame him for that. It's my own fault and you know it is! He never did have a mother!"

"Well, hell, we never did have a mother! Or much of a daddy either! We had 'em but they wasn't much good! That boy's gonna do what he wants to do and you may as well give up on him. Make your peace with it now."

Leonard points his finger accusingly. "Don't say that, Vernon! Scooter's a good boy! Jody came back to see me and Scooter's coming too!"

Dr. Spencer enters the room. "Gent'men, let's let the patient rest, okay? Come back a little later. Maybe tomorrow. Let's let him rest."

Vernon is already at the door. Jody follows. Neither says a word as they walk out to the parking lot. Vernon goes to his truck, opens a cooler, squeezes some mustard into a glass and fills the rest with whiskey.

"What are you doing, Vernon?"

He looks up. "I'm minding my own business, Jody. I didn't call you back down here so you could mind it for me."

He sucks down half his drink, looks inside the glass. "I apologize, Jody. Don't mean to talk to you like that."

"Forget about it."

"I just can't get over this, that's all. I just can't believe it. I don't know when all this happened." He looks inside his glass again, dumps out the dregs, and throws the glass onto the seat of his truck.

"Seems like just last week your daddy was teaching me how to shoot squirrels."

"I believe it."

Vernon stares at his boots. "Well anyway, I've got to drive on home. I've got a favor to ask you. Come down and see me tomorrow, would you? I'd really appreciate it."

"All right. I'll come by here in the morning and then head down around lunchtime."

Vernon nods, slides his key in the ignition.

"Vernon?"

"Yessir?"

"If I'm going to find my brother I better not wait any longer."

"Yeah, I know. Come on down. I'll make you a bologna-and-cheese sandwich and tell you what I know. Maybe you could go on Sunday." Vernon tips his cap at Jody, fires up the truck, and drives away.

. . .

He starts the drive back. He wishes again for the speed and comfort of the Mustang instead of the large, slow, clunky truck, imagines the sights flying by. He settles his thoughts with the reminder that, soon enough, the car will be his. The early spring light is just fine. The evening smells of pine and, with the afternoon showers, coolness. He leans forward, cranks down the window. Jody reaches out into the space and tries to catch the air, stuff it into his mouth, his nose, into himself.

Halfway home he turns back, heads toward the mostly abandoned downtown. Gary Wayne sits in his taxi cab in front of the State Farm office, reads a magazine. He looks up as Jody passes by, motions for him to pull over. But Jody just waves and keeps going.

He drives past the liquor store and remembers a joke. One of the Catholic kids from school told Jody the joke in seventh grade. What is the difference between Catholics and Baptists? When Catholics go to the liquor store, they go in the front door. Somewhere along the way, Leonard figured out a little beer wasn't going to hurt him and became one of those back-door customers.

Once he finally got the hang of it, his drinking turned into a Saturday night habit. Leonard was what you'd call a happy drunk. Jody himself has known men who can't so much as take the cap off a bottle without clenching their hands into fists. But not Leonard. He liked to drive to the beer store, as he called it, about five o'clock on Saturday, after all the work that needed to be done was done. Then he'd drive straight home and empty a can or two in the ten-minute trip.

Sometimes Jody or Scooter made the drive with him. The ride was short, but always fun, one of the times their father was sure to be happy. They took it at the end of the day when everything was quiet. In the truck they rolled in the twilight or in the dark hearing nothing but the groan and periodic shift of the old Ford engine, the whispering buzz of the radio turned down low. Then Leonard got his cold beers and the boys headed back, eager to cook up the TV dinners they liked to eat on Saturday night and watch their show.

Jody drives and thinks back to a Saturday night when he was twelve. Scooter was at Uncle Pearl's house that day, so just he and his father went into town. At five o'clock they set out for the short trip. It was almost dark, light barely hanging on to the December evening. Though not particularly cold, a steady drizzle had been falling all afternoon, and by evening the sky was low and the temperature was dropping. Leonard made his purchase and went back to the truck.

He shivered in his seat. "Son. It's colder now than when we left the house. This is one ugly day." Leonard eased back onto the highway, pulled his coat around his neck. A dark black cloud sat low between the town and their house. They were headed straight for it.

"Who you think's gonna be singing tonight?" Jody asked his father.

"Singing?" Leonard cracked open his first beer, took a drink, wiped his mouth with his wrist. "I think Merle may be on there. Not sure." He took another long drink and let out a satisfied breath. "Aahhh. Nothing like a cold Miller. I wish I'd started drinking a long time ago. Now that I know I'm not gonna turn into a drunkard or anything. Listen to most of what you learn in church, son, but don't listen to everything."

Jody didn't say a word, just basked in his father's advice. Then Leonard reached for the radio, cranked it.

"Hawwwwww!" He roared in a falsetto voice. "Listen to that! Sing it, Bobby!" Leonard joined in with his whiny baritone, matching Bobby Benjamin's down-home voice word for word, twelve-bar blues shaking the cheap speakers in the doors of the truck.

Well the train from Oklahoma's comin'
down the line
And the orange settin' sun's about to make
me blind
Boys and men are shoutin' up and down
the track
Hopin' that old train'll soon be comin' back
And mamas cooking supper, bakin' up a
pie
Shuffle through the kitchen as the train
goes by

When they entered the cloud at the top of the hill they saw the first snowflakes, which elevated the mood even further. Jody's father looked over at him and didn't say a word. He just looked happy. He rolled down his window and stuck his left arm out into the snow, out the same truck window Jody sticks his hand out of now. Leonard steered with the last two fingers of his right hand, which held the can of Miller in the other three, and didn't miss a word in the song or a perfectly timed sip of his beer.

I got the freight train blues
From my head to my shoes
Every time I hear that whistle as the train
rolls past
I get that lonesome feelin' and it just might
last
I've got the freight train blues

They pulled into the driveway just as the song was ending, a thin sheen of white beginning to form on the grass, the roof, on everything. Scooter had come home while they were gone, and the three of them cooked up their dinners, gathered around the television, and settled in. Nothing bad ever happened on Saturday night. Unless you count the gobs of snow and ice the three of them stuffed down one another's shirts after dinner. And it wasn't Merle that played on *Hee Haw* that night, it was Waylon Jennings. And boy, did he ever put on a show.

CHAPTER 21

He mainly drinks at home, when he is alone. His friends don't enjoy his company as much anymore, when he says the things he says, tells the same old stories from school, high school, college. His girlfriend too, more and more, needs a break, and he knows better than to begrudge her this; to keep himself drinking, he has had to learn the delicate balance of giving and receiving. And lately, with Jody gone, with the place to himself, he puts in more and more time in that chair, blowing hard, blowing softly, just blowing.

Tonight he's feeling vigorous. His horn and his bottle have rendered him most comfortable prone, at a three-quarter angle on the sofa. He gives himself a few more sips, now a few more scales and his guest is there, Robert's there, in the doorway. His brother is grown now, and looks like Art, the first fine lines appearing around the nose, the mouth, the squinty road map of his temples. His cardigan no longer reflects the style of the ten-year-old, rather that of the man on television who speaks kindly to children, and the first few specks of gray dance in the light reflected from his perfectly combed hair.

Robert at first doesn't speak, and Art follows his brother

with weight-lidded eyes as he enters the room, sits across from the sofa, and smiles.

"Listen to this," Art thinks he says, he can't be sure, and he blows his horn in phrases as he reaches for the high note.

Robert beams, never says a word, and Art begins to glow inside as he reaches ever higher. He hits the C, the D, the E, perhaps the F, possibly even the G, he can't be sure how high he goes but what he hears sounds good. He takes another sip, raises again the horn to his lips. The last thing he remembers is his brother's eyes, looking right through him but at him and in him and all around him at the same time, filled with a love brought with him from his new home, it can't be that bad of a place, the one where Robert lives now, that place in that whole other world where we'll all one day go and be free.

CHAPTER 22

"Come on in." Jody cracks open the door of his uncle's house late the next morning. Vernon speaks as he rises from a worn leather chair that he had the last time Jody was there.

"Jody, son. Thanks for coming by. How's your daddy today?"

He falls into what used to be a couch, blows out a big breath. "He's holding steady. Still talking, griping at the nurses."

"Leonard," Vernon mutters. "Leonard. I always thought I'd be next. Hoped I would. I guess it ain't my time, though. You hungry? Want me to make you a fried bologna-and-cheese sandwich?"

Jody smiles. As far back as he can remember, all Vernon ever ate was fried bologna-and-processed-cheese sandwiches. Leonard said many times that, even when they were kids, Vernon fried up a bologna-and-cheese sandwich at least once a day.

"I've got a better idea. Is there somewhere we can go eat?"

"It's been a few years since you've been to Talton's. Why don't you let me take you over there for some lunch?"

"There's got to be someplace nicer than that dump. You name it. I'm paying."

"Naw. Everything else is too expensive. Save your money. Let's just drive over there. You may like it."

"Okay. If you insist, I'll go over there with you. Hey, speaking of those sandwiches, how many have you eaten now?"

"I'd have to look it up. Probably twenty-five thousand or so."

"I just have one question for you, Vernon. Why?"

"Oh. I like them."

"Sounds like a real opportunity. But I'd really like to get a taste of the local food again. I've been eating canned beans for a week. I'll try Talton's if there's nowhere else you can think of."

Vernon opens his refrigerator, takes out bologna, cheese, bread, shows them to Jody, resists weakly for a few more seconds, then agrees to go. They drive in Leonard's truck over to the crossroads. The lot is nearly empty so they park by the front door of a plain cinderblock building. So much paint has peeled from the walls that it's not clear whether the building is supposed to be gray or the bright yellow peeking out all over. To the right of the front door, in a shaky hand, is written the name of the place, Taltons', although the apostrophe is in the wrong place. Jody turns toward his uncle, scowls.

Vernon shrugs.

Before they are out of the truck the smell surrounds Jody—the pulled pork, the smoke from the ribs, hot links stewing in a long, shallow pan. Jody remembers the barbecue man was once a member of Vernon's church.

"I haven't been here in a year or more myself," Vernon says as they stand up from the truck. A short, round man moves into the doorway as they approach. Vernon turns, goes back, rolls his window all the way down so John David can get some air.

"Hoddy, Vernon," the man says, steps toward them.

"Talton Thibodaux." He extends his short arm to Jody.

"What do you say, fella," Vernon responds.

"I'm Jody." The two men shake hands.

Thibodaux waddles over and sticks his head in the window of the truck, begins to talk to John David. The dog responds to his attention and licks him all over the face.

"There you go, that's a good dog, that's a sweet doggie." John David whimpers and kisses the fat man some more. Then Talton's eyes grow wide. He reaches into the truck and pushes the dog back from the window, looks underneath him. He jumps back from the window.

"Good night!" he exclaims. "This is a boy dog kissin' all over me." He wipes the slime from his face with a handkerchief. Then he sticks his hand in and shakes John David's paw. "Nice to meet you, I'm Talton. What's your name?"

John David whimpers louder, runs in place on the seat.

"Stay here, dog. We'll bring you something to eat."

The three go in. Jody scans the trays behind the counter. Chicken, brisket, a steaming pile of ribs Talton says he has just laid down. Next to those is a tray of white hamburger buns and then about a ten-gallon vat of beans, bean juice permanently etched in the outside of the pot. On one wall hangs an LSU banner in purple and gold, and a black-and-gold Saints fleur-de-lis hangs cockeyed on the other wall, duct-taped at the corners. Jody relaxes into the familiarity of the place.

Thibodaux waddles around the counter, stands to face Vernon and Jody. Across the front of his apron is a bloodstain made with his left hand, then a swath of barbecue sauce made with his right. The lunch crowd has cleared out, and there are empty trays, plates, and cups all over the place. He draws in a big breath. "Sorry about the mess y'all, *Aprile*!" he hollers. "Where are you girl?" Another big breath. "I got to get me new girl, prob'ly on the damn phone somewhere." Breath. "Y'all know women, cain't make a phone call without making another call first to make sure it's all right." Breath. "So what y'all want? Fish and chips? Chicken fangers?" Each time he draws in a breath the effort itself exhausts him, and he expels most of it before beginning to speak.

"Charlene got the day off, Talton?" Vernon asks. "I don't remember y'all ever having any help besides just the two of you."

Thibodaux looks away for a moment, then turns back to Vernon. "Aw hell, Vernon, I may as well tell you, she took off the day after Christmas."

"Charlene left?"

"Yeah. She's been gone four months and something."

"Well, I'm sorry, Talton," Vernon replies, and Jody echoes his uncle's sentiment. "I never heard. What in the world happened?"

Talton shrugs. "Who knows. Twenty-seven years and I still don't understand that woman any more than a pan of beans. She said she needed something to make her feel *alive*. I tried to stop her, I said, 'Baby, I've got a hundred fifty pullets, twenty cases of pork, and four sides of beef in the freezer back there.'" He cocks his thumb over a shoulder, looks Jody in the eye, then immediately turns his face away. Jody wants to reach out, touch the man, but doesn't.

"I said, 'Baby, tell me something. What could make you feel more alive than being around *that* much dead meat?'" Thibodaux takes another big breath. "She didn't see it that way, I guess. I tell y'all what, though." He nods exaggeratedly. "She'll start missin' my bobba-cue and I'll see her in that door any day. Aprile, she's pretty good help when I can keep her off the cotton-pickin' phone. Had another girl come in here applyin' for the job before Aprile, y'all shoulda seen her."

"How's that?"

"Psssh." Thibodaux wipes crumbs off the counter with his hand, sweeps them into the vat of beans. He picks up the ladle and stirs the crumbs in. "I mean, I like a woman that can make some intelligent conversation, all the time we spend together. Y'all know, politics, uh, NASCAR, other interesting subjects.

But this one, she's about as smart as that picture frame." He points to a yellowed newspaper clipping thumbtacked to the wall. Jody shrugs at him.

"Igzackly," he says, then quickly looks away again. "Anyway, she come in here one day and said, 'I'd like to apply for the job.' I said, 'All right, girl, what's it look like?'"

"Yeah? What'd she say?"

Thibodaux snorts. "She said, 'What's *what* look like?' Well, strike one. I decided I'd overlook that, but then she started talking about everything she wanted to change about the place. Said we should paint the place orange, said orange makes you *hungry*. Like I'm gon' sit all day up inside a orange room. I told her, I said, 'Woman, standing over this hot fire all these years has already made me half-crazy, I need to hang on to what little sanity I got left.' *Orange room!* On top of that I told her orange'd make people think about punkin pie, and you don't have to have no dayum psychology degree from no LSU to know punkin pie don't go with bobba-cue! Psssh. I told her to just get on outta here, she's too skinny anyway. Make it look like my food ain't no good."

"Well, I'm sorry, Talton. I didn't know about Charlene."

Talton shrugs. "Yeah, what can you do? Can't live with 'em, can't keep 'em on a leash."

Vernon shrugs. Talton's eyes are wide, stunned. "What y'all want to eat?"

"I'll have me a bologna-and-cheese sandwich if you got any," Vernon says.

Talton turns back to Jody, smacks his gum, then looks away once again. "You funny, Vernon. Hey, who is this, you ain't took in a drifter, have you?"

"It has been a while, Mr. Thibodaux. I'm Jody, Vernon's nephew."

"Oh yeah. It has been a while I guess."

"I've been here with Vernon before, years ago. The decorations look about the same." Jody looks around the room. His eyes settle on something colorful hanging on the wall, under the LSU banner.

Thibodaux sees Jody looking, lights up. "That's my disguise," he says. Nearly all of his words are expressed with a big, happy face. But all of a sudden Thibodaux switches to the most disgusted face a person could muster.

"Y'all not gonna believe this." He pulls an empty chair on his side of the counter over, puts his foot on it. "I've been hearing lately, from diff'rent people. Said that Davis's—that and a black-owned joint south of Natchitoches, they call it Junior Boy's or Senior Boy's or Daddy Boy's or Sonny Boy's—something Boy's—I distinctly remember it had the word 'boy' in it. Or maybe it was 'girl.' Well anyway, they been putting spicy sauce in their ribs and chicken." He draws his breath and adjusts his disgusted face. "I'm not talking just the hot links—I'm talking about the sweet meat. I got me that clown suit and went in to both of 'em one day last week to see if it was true."

"What happened?" Vernon asks. He seems genuinely baffled.

"They both recognized me. Kicked me out."

"Well, you get 'em, Talton," Vernon says.

"I aim to."

"What should we eat, Vernon?" Jody asks. "I'm hungry."

Thibodaux snorts. "Well, see, that's your problem. See, you ought not to eat when you're hungry. You should eat so you don't get hungry. It works for me. I haven't been hungry in years."

Vernon takes off his cap and sticks it in his pocket. "Just give me some ribs I guess. Jody here says he's payin', I don't want to eat up all his money."

"Money? What's that?" Talton throws his hands up. "Oh yeah, what I owe my ex-wife a ton of. Hell, I'm so broke I cain't pay attention." Talton rhythmically wipes his hands on the apron. One of his teeth is missing on the left side of his mouth, and anytime he's not speaking he keeps sticking his tongue in the hole and making a sucking sound.

"Naw, listen, y'all the two millionth and two million and oneth customers." He picks up a little bell off the counter, rings it over his head. "Everything's free today. Don't argy with me."

"No, no, no. We're paying, Mr. Talton. Maybe you wouldn't be so broke if you quit giving your food away. Just give me a four way and . . ."

"All right, four ways for both of y'all. Y'all want Dr Pepper or tea? And don't you contradict me!"

Vernon and Jody both ask for tea. Thibodaux lays two melamine plates on the countertop and begins to fill them with meat. In the sunken area on one side he piles beans. Then he turns and puts the plates in front of them, throws knives and forks down on the counter. He moves almost spastically as he works. Music plays in the background, turned down low, and his head jerks along with the bass beats. As the song ends he begins to shake from side to side.

Thibodaux moves to the wall and turns up the stereo. "Listen to this, y'all. This here's some *music*!" He cranks the volume. He sings along, loud, a slow, ballady blues, grabs a bottle of Tabasco sauce for a microphone.

My baby has left me
For the very last time
I gave her my love
And I treated her fine
But now there's another man
She says his name is Joe
He sits in my chair
And he eats all my gumbo
He's makin' me look like a fool
Yeah I've got the ol' Cajun blues

When the song ends, Talton turns the music back down. "MMM—HMM! That's Tommy Boudreaux. The Cajun bluesman. That'll keep the haints off, I'll tell you."

"That's good music, Mr. Talton, I agree with you."

"Yeah boy, it is. I'm related to him in some kinda way on my daddy's side. All us Cajuns is related really, even them like me with a lot of redneck blood. 'Course my granddaddy and his brother *related* to every Cajun woman they could. Both black and white. Prob'ly Daddy too. And stayed married they whole lives. An' look at me, never even turned my head for any woman but my Charlene. Look where it got me." He hangs his head pitifully. Jody feels his hand reach out, and this time he squeezes Talton's shoulder.

"Well anyway, that's the past. So where you been, Jody? Been gone so long? I know you ain't been around these parts and kept outta my bobba-cue joint."

"I live in Chicago."

"Chicago, Illinois? They got any good bobba-cue up there?"

Jody bites into a rib. "Not like this. Not half this good and they'd charge twenty-five dollars a plate."

"HHHHNNNNGGGG!" Thibodaux throws up his shoulders and exclaims with a noise that sounds like a cross between a laughing mouse from a cartoon show and a truck tire popping. He follows with a lengthy snort.

"Dang, Vernon, maybe we oughta go to Chicago!" Then he thinks about it for a minute, puts his disgusted face back on. "Naw, maybe not. I doubt I could rent a single-wide trailer *and the lot*"—he taps hard on the counter with two fingers—"for seventy-five dollars a month."

Vernon agrees.

"Well anyway, y'all enjoy." He steps back, stirs his beans, adjusts the hot links in the pan. "Y'all know what, I'm getting a little bit hungry too, wouldn't want that. Maybe I'll eat with y'all. I got me a tofu samwich in the back. Won't need these."

With that he leans forward and, with a motion like a sneeze, spits his teeth into his hand. Then he stands back up and flashes a gum smile.

"What y'all think? Ain't that somethin'? Removable teeth! Just got them suckers last month." Both men are speechless.

"How come you got one tooth missing?" Jody asks. "If you have dentures?"

Talton nods in an exaggerated way. "I'll tell you why. Now I want to look good." He rubs his fingernails back and forth on his chest. "But I don't need to look too good. I don't need ever' woman in Natchitoches what thinks she needs a lover man puttin' her hands on me, just 'cause I'm single again. That's why."

He stirs the beans, holding his teeth in the empty hand, appears to reminisce. "Naw. I miss her, Vernon. I do. Bein' here helps me feel better, though. And hey. I've still got my hot links. But speaking of removable body parts, only thing better'd be if I could get 'em to make me a removable pecker so I could drink all the beer I wanted and wouldn't have to get up and tee-tee at night." The disgusted face. "I hate wakin' up when I'm dreamin'."

"Do you still dream about Brooke Shields?" Jody asks. He hasn't even thought about Talton Thibodaux since the last time he sat in the barbecue joint, but back in his presence a memory reappears.

"Yeah I do. How'd you know that?" For an instant Talton looks stumped.

"You used to talk about it years ago. I just happened to remember just this minute."

"Hunh. Dadgum, I believe you're right. I have dreamed about her off and on for years. It ain't adultery if it's just in your dreams. Must be something about drinkin' a case of beer that gets me dreamin' about her, 'cause seems like every time I drink one she shows up that night. And just about the time"—he slams his hand on the countertop, the hand holding the teeth, and they go skeetering off—"I get her down to her bra and panties is when I have to wake up to tee-tee. Actually I got one side of her bra off one night but that's as far as I've ever got with her."

He waddles around the counter, picks up his teeth, blows on them, then leans forward and pops them back into place. He reaches for a plate and piles it high, comes around and sets it at an empty place at the counter next to Vernon. He sits down as they begin to eat and tears into his own plate.

"Hey, Vernon, I got a joke for you." He drops his fork noisily in his plate. "Tell me if you've ever heard thissun. This man goes on a date with a Baptist lady. Takes her out to eat at a nice restaurant. A catfish place."

"Uh huh."

"So he's havin' a pretty good time, thinks she's looking pretty good. He finally gets his nerve up and asks her if she wants to have a drink with him. With their dinner."

"What'd she say?"

"'Heck no,' she said. 'I'm Baptist. I don't drink that demon liquor.'"

"I can see where this is going."

"So he felt a little put off, but he kept on eating. Still had some, had some hush puppies left on his plate. That and a little piece of fish. When he finally gets done he pulls out a cigarette and lights it up. 'Want one?' he asks her, and holds the pack out to her."

"Did she smoke it?"

"Of course not! 'I'm a Baptist,' she says. 'I don't smoke.' So the man's feeling shot down but he's had himself a couple cold beers by then so he figures what the hell."

"'You wanna go get a motel room with me?' he asks her. Just figuring she'd say, 'Take me home and go see the devil at his house you *fiend*. You dirty rascal. You *cad*.' Something like that. But he's getting liquored up, so he don't really care."

"And did she?"

"*Naw!* She thought about it a minute and looked up at him and said, 'Let's go!' So they go to the motel room and next thing they're stuck together like two cockleburs! And this lady is passionate, I'm tellin' you. She's moaning and hollering! Throws him around so hard they fall down on the floor and shake the whole motel!" Talton bangs his hand on the countertop, sends Jody's plate toward the edge until he grabs it. "Finally after a couple hours he cain't do it no more and he falls asleep. Then a few hours later he wakes up."

"Let me guess. She's gone."

"Naw she ain't gone! She's the one woke him up! Wants to play hide the hot link again! But he could only do it one more time and then he told her he had to take her home. He was flat wore out. Shriveled up like a empty pod! And here she was still wrapped around him like the dayum I-R-S! But she needed to get home anyway, it was Sunday morning and she had to get ready to teach her Sunday school class."

"She taught Sunday school!"

"Oh yeah she did. This was a fine upstanding Baptist lady! So he gets her back to her house, now he's feeling a little bit sheepish at this point, wondering what she's thinking. He can't think of anything else to say. So finally he asks her a question."

"Yeah?"

"Said, 'What're you gonna talk to your Sunday school class about?'"

"Yeah?"

"She said, 'I'm gonna tell the kids what I always tell them. You don't have to drink and smoke to have a good time!'"

Talton Thibodaux leans back on his stool and laughs as hard as a human being can laugh, with both hands on his enormous belly. After a minute of this he scrambles forward and grabs the counter to keep from falling on the floor.

"That's a good one, Talton," Vernon gets out through his

own giggles. "That's a good one. You don't hear good stories like that anymore."

"Hawwwwww! We can still laugh, can't we, Vernon? When we don't have nothing else, we can still do that. Can keep on telling our stories." He reaches out and claps Vernon mightily on the back.

"Hey, speaking of Baptists, guess who was in here the other day."

"Who?"

"That Staples boy, I can't remember his first name. Remember what a fop he was? He was a friend of Billy's, wasn't he?"

Vernon looks down. "Yes he was. Richie Staples. That was his name."

"That's right. Well, I'll tell you, he's still a nice dresser but ain't got that pretty head of hair no more. Matter of fact he's as bald as I am. Said he was living out in Dallas. Kinda looked like a city slicker."

Talton picks his fork up and drops it back down again. "Hey, I had me a idea the other day, tell me what y'all think about it."

"Go ahead."

"I'm trying to find me a way to get the profits up, you know? Come up with somethin' they'll sell on one of them shopping channels? What y'all think about me selling little knickknacks outta here? Little gewgaws?"

"Such as?"

"Well, the only one I've come up with so far is plastic bobba-cue. You know like them plastic apples and oranges and bananers some people keep? But I think a steaming pile of ribs would look even better on a coffee table."

"Not a bad idea," Jody says. Thibodaux twists his mouth into a pucker.

"Only problem is the steam. How to make it look like it's

steam coming off of 'em. Only thing I can come up with is this little clear screen with some cloudy on it, I can stick it out of one of the ribs with a clear plastic toothpick." He throws his hands up. "I'm still working on it."

"Well, it sounds like a good idea."

"Worth a try."

Talton goes back to his food. Jody hears him rooting around in his dish, breathing loudly through his nose. Periodically he expels a pleased-sounding sigh and, once, a whistle of a fart. Then he lays into the beans, tapping the plate loudly and slurping with each dip of the spoon.

"Beats the devil out of a bloney-and-cheese sandwich," Talton says as he chews, spits a spray of food. "Dawg, y'all." He wipes gently at his mouth with a paper napkin. "That's good." He pulls the napkin away to show a face full of barbecue sauce, sauce covering one earlobe, on the bridge of his nose, and even a brown daub of it above his eye. He drops his fork into his plate and leans back into his chair. He sighs again and reaches his hands out to rub his stomach.

"That's another thing. I keep eatin' like this, before long I ain't gonna be able to rub my ol' belly anymore. I talked to a doctor last week, I told him I want him to cut my hands off right there"—Thibodaux makes a sawing motion with his index fingers just above each wrist—"put a piece of bone in there, then sew my hands back on. Make my arms six-eight inches longer. I told him, doc, don't worry about the bone, I got all kinds of bones layin' around here."

Then Thibodaux picks up the napkin again and wipes daintily at the corners of his mouth. He leans back in his chair, belches, sighs, and begins poking his tongue through the hole in his teeth and making that sucking sound again.

CHAPTER 23

Jody never cared about football but Scooter loved it. By the time the two were teenagers, Jody began to look forward to Sunday afternoons in the fall himself, just to see the transformation in his brother. In front of the television watching the Saints play football, Scooter was at home with himself in a rare way. Sunday afternoons in the fall were the few times Jody could count on his brother not to go off somewhere by himself. Something about the guys out there on the field together, the way they beat each other, hugged each other, drew Scooter into the screen and at the same time pulled him out of the closed-off world he inhabited most of the time.

Jody points the truck to New Orleans, switches on the radio, searches for a station. As the sun comes up he's been on the road two hours already, is almost halfway there. The old radio is worthless, staticky, so he switches it off and returns to his memories.

One year the Saints made the playoffs. Nobody ever expected something like this to happen, but as the weeks went by and they kept on winning, a wild card game and then two more rounds, a buzz began to be heard in the state of Louisiana like nothing Saints fans had ever known. It was a fluke really; the team had always been bad and then that year they got a new coach who was a known drunk and gambler. They managed to put together an 8–8 season and squeak into the playoffs by taking huge risks on the field and running an offense whose general strategy was razzle-dazzle.

On the day before the Superbowl, Leonard had to work. He told the boys when he left in the morning to spend their day breaking up a new plot of soil he intended to use for his vegetable garden. But then Scooter disappeared and Jody spent most of the day looking for him, and the two didn't get anything done.

On Sunday after church their father told them, Superbowl or no Superbowl, they were going to break that ground up. Jody griped about it a bit, but not Scooter. Somehow Scooter knew exactly where to draw the line. And the look on their father's face told them both it needed to get done. They watched the opening kickoff, then got straight to work.

It was a mild January day that felt like early spring. Jody propped open the door that led into the living room and turned the television sideways, so they could hear and see what was going on without having to take off their muddy boots and go inside. The two took turns running up to the house to check the progress of the game. Scooter never slowed down, didn't want to stop for lunch or anything. All afternoon the game stayed close and they kept working—digging, raking, breaking up clods of dirt with their hands. Once in a while Jody looked at his younger brother to see if he wanted to take a break or something, just go in and sit down for a little while. For all his flakiness, Scooter had an uncanny sense of how long things took. Each time Scooter just shook his head and kept working.

The Saints were down by three when the game reached the two-minute warning. The boys walked into the house during the commercial, sat down in time to watch the Saints drive the ball from their own twenty to the other team's twenty-five-yard line with three seconds left. They set up for a field goal and the brothers waited nervously on the edge of the sofa. The opponents called a time out to ice the kicker, and the game went to another commercial break.

When the broadcast returned, Scooter leaned back in his seat and said just the kind of thing Scooter said. "Watch this." The kicker lined up, took two steps up to the holder, then stopped and pulled his helmet off. The play clock was still ticking. Then Chartrand—that was the kicker's name—squatted down to tie his shoe. He stood and looked at the shoe, then called his own time out, reached down to pull it off, and hobbled over toward the Saints' bench.

Chartrand was nuts and was always doing things like that. He kicked his final field goal for the Saints when he was fifty-three years old, and he only quit then because a linebacker from the Bucs came in to block the kick but missed and piled on Chartrand and broke his leg so badly he never walked straight again. But Chartrand was just a kid then, only forty-five or forty-six, and he limped over to the bench, one foot bare. He got a new shoestring, laced it in, and put the shoe back on.

The camera followed his trip up the sideline. Chartrand said something to Daniels, the coach, who held his cowboy hat in his hand; out of respect he removed it for indoor games. Chartrand checked his watch, took it off, shook it, held it up to his ear, put it back on. Then the camera zoomed in for a close up as Chartrand picked up a can of Dr Pepper, cracked it open, and poured it down his gullet like a bullfrog in a rainstorm until it was gone, then crushed the can and threw it down on the ground. He walked back out to the line of scrimmage and stood there jumping up and down until you could tell by the look on his face that he had belched. Then he put his helmet back on and lined up to kick.

The center snapped the ball, and the holder threw his hands up to catch it. Chartrand took two steps forward and snatched the ball in mid-air, then hauled it left to right with a rookie running back named Planchard flanking for him. Planchard was a short fireplug of a kid just over from LSU who could outrun a motorcycle. At the fifteen-yard line Planchard split the other way and Chartrand did a funny little move like a hook shot—two guys the size of gorillas were closing in on him, and he reached the ball out like a basketball and hook-shot it over his shoulder to Planchard, who took the pitch in his soft hands like it was nothing and loped the last fifteen yards into the end zone. Scooter sat still on the sofa smacking his gum. Like he knew what was going to happen.

Jody reaches the outskirts of New Orleans, starts into the long spillway bridge. He glances down to the seat at Vernon's directions. Vernon knows somebody that knows somebody—for as much of a recluse as he has become he still knows people all over the place—who knows where Jody's brother is. As Vernon told it, Scooter found some group on the internet that's a bunch of people who never had one or both of their parents. They've got communities all over the country, and people go and live there in these big houses with one another and older adults who live in each house and pretend to be mothers to the residents. Or fathers.

Jody pulls into the city, follows Carrollton to the Mississippi, then sidles along the river until he reaches the Marigny. It's only ten thirty, but he is hungry and stops at a neighborhood restaurant for lunch. The place is tiny, little more than the front room of an old house, but the four-dollar bowl of gumbo is absolutely fine. Jody stands from the table, sated, asks the waiter for directions to the address on North Rampart.

"Hold on a minute. Angel lives down there."

A man comes out of the kitchen, short and thin, with tattoos down to his fingertips and peeking out of his shirt collar. He gives Jody directions in passable English. Jody drives that way until the house numbers narrow in on his target. Ahead of him a large green van pulls to the side of the street. When the side door opens, people pour out. Five are on the sidewalk and the van is still shaking, so Jody sits and watches as three more get out. He drives slowly past and continues to check the house numbers until he realizes he's passed it. At the next intersection he turns around and drives back in the opposite direction.

The van is parked in front of the house he's looking for. He stops on the other side of the street and leaves the engine running, sits and looks at the house. It is a huge house, four stories tall, that may have been nice at one time but hasn't been painted in many years. The porch is obviously slanted and two of the front steps are just thrown-down planks that may not even be nailed in place. Two people are on the porch, one sitting in the other's lap, and the one on top looks in his direction.

Jody makes it to the sidewalk in front of the house when he hears Scooter's voice.

"Happy Easter, brother."

Jody looks up to the porch. Scooter is the one on top. In his hand he holds a can of Delaware Punch, his same old drink, and rests it on the other person's knee. His hair hangs onto his chest. Underneath him is a round, middle-aged woman in a rocking chair, and she slowly continues to rock the chair. Both of them look on at Jody.

"You're looking good."

"You, you look good yourself, Scooter." Jody stands in the yard, hands at his sides. Scooter looks much older, even more handsome than before. Through the thin beard Jody can see his face is hard, the jaw rigid, as if he's been carved out of stone.

"Me? Naw, hell, I look like the north end of a southbound mule. Or either the south end of a northbound mule."

Jody laughs, stays on the sidewalk. In response Scooter laughs himself.

"I'm glad to hear somebody is still amused by me." Scooter flashes his beautiful smile, then giggles as if at something inward. He leans his head into the woman's neck. She lifts her flabby arm higher around his shoulder and squeezes him. "Nobody here gets my humor."

"They're not family, I guess."

He sighs. "No, they're most certainly not. Emmie here"—he leans into her again—"she should have been a Davidson." Underneath him the fat woman shakes and Jody guesses she is laughing, though he can't hear a sound.

"So you heard about Daddy?"

"Vernon left a message, said he was sick. So what's new?"

"What do you mean?"

"He's always been sick. In his mind anyway. So it's finally moved into his body. Eventually that's what happens. We all fall apart, if we don't keep ourselves together. Down here"—he gestures toward the house—"we try to learn that we can make ourselves better. No matter what ails us. For a while we can at least."

Scooter lifts the can of Delaware Punch and takes a long drink. He settles himself farther into the woman's lap, smiles at her.

"They still make that Delaware Punch, huh?"

Scooter lowers the can, looks at it, turns it in his hand. "Yeah, there's a few things left from the good old days. Not many, but a few."

Jody steps up toward the porch. Scooter still doesn't get up. The second step squeaks but doesn't give.

"Daddy's gonna die, Scooter. That's why I came back to Louisiana."

"Back from your travels, eh?"

The woman whispers, "Scooter?" Then she tickles him, he jumps.

"He's dying, no doubt about it. His heart could go any minute. It could be any day, probably won't be more than a couple weeks. He begged me to come and bring you back to see him. Begged me." Scooter seems so much older, seems like a hundred-year-old wise man.

"So sad. It didn't have to happen this way."

"He begged me, Scooter. He says he just wants us to be together again."

Finally, Scooter stands from the woman's lap and walks over to his brother. Jody takes the last three steps up to the porch and Scooter meets him at the top. Scooter takes Jody's shoulders in his arms and shakes his brother a little. Then he smiles—his warm, disarming smile—and pulls Jody close.

"I knew you'd be coming," Scooter whispers. "You always did. Just let me get some things together."

Scooter is quiet as they pull away from the large house. A few blocks away he opens his window and waves at another man walking down the sidewalk carrying an overstuffed backpack. The guy looks up but shows no response.

"Hey, stop here a minute." Jody pulls over to the curb. Scooter opens his window again and points at some older men sitting and drinking beer on a porch.

"What you got there, Mr. Richard?"

"My lunch," the white-haired man answers in a gravelly voice, lifts his can of beer to drink. The other two men shout their laughter.

"You boys want a drank?" Mr. Richard hollers back. "We don't mind drankin' with white boys. Come on." He motions them over.

"No, thank you. I quit that a long time ago, Mr. Richard. I don't drink anymore."

The old man considers. "I've tried to quit myself. But I just get so thirsty."

. . .

"How did you find this place you live?" The truck travels again across the spillway.

He shrugs. "People just find each other."

"You really live there with this big group?"

"Yep. There's about ten of us."

"I guess you like it there? Should I be worried about you? Is it some kind of a cult or something?"

He shrugs again. "I like it. I guess. It's not the Ritz. It's not even as nice as living at home. But man. What are you talking about? You haven't worried about me in so long."

"You don't know that."

"I'd say it's a good guess."

Jody considers a thousand things he wants to say but doesn't say any. "You like it down here?"

"It's all right. I'm staying busy. In the house we've got to keep all these rules, how we do things. Different stuff. Not really my game."

"You've been there a few years?"

"Like I say, it's all right. I'm a free man again. Sometimes . . . I don't know. Some of 'em are a bit gung ho for my tastes. Always want to have group meetings, expect the rest of us to talk too much. Talk talk talk. Like that's going to change anything. I haven't found anything better yet, so . . ."

"You're planning to stay there?"

"How do I know? Till I find something better I am. They're good people."

"You know I've been up in Chicago?"

"No. I didn't know that. Last I heard you went to the army. I guess we left home at the same time."

"Yeah. I guess we did."

"Hey. You all right driving? You want me to drive?"

"No. I'm okay for now."

"All right. I'm gonna take a little nap." Scooter opens his

duffel, pulls out a sweatshirt, folds it into a pillow. He leans his head against the window.

"So why'd you leave, Jody?"

"Say again?"

He shuffles in his seat. "You heard me. Why'd you leave?"

"I guess I couldn't see staying."

"I guess I couldn't either."

"Hmm."

"So. What've you found out there in the world?"

"Plenty. Good job. I'm liking it."

Jody turns toward his brother. Scooter settles into the seat. Then he nods and doesn't speak again.

Leonard opens his eyes when his sons walk into the room. The two roll away the tray that once again holds a pile of gelled-over mashed potatoes with a plastic fork buried in it. Scooter doesn't say anything but stands by the bed, looking puzzled. He reaches out to touch their father on the arm.

Leonard begins to stir. Scooter reaches back and squeezes his ponytail. Jody managed to convince him to stop by the house and shower, but Scooter refused his brother's offer of a haircut. James the orderly comes into the room, acknowledges Jody when their eyes meet, takes the tray and rolls it out. Leonard's face turns on like a light when he sees his younger son. Scooter still looks puzzled, as if he expected something different.

"Well well. The prodigal son has returned," Leonard says. He raises a hand as best he can toward heaven.

"Go kill the fatted calf," Scooter answers. Leonard pulls his younger son down, holds him cheek to cheek.

For the next several hours the men sit in the room together, a cottony breeze and the voices of screaming children coming in through the window. They tell the same old stories they've always told, of days at home and family reunions and Uncle Pearl and EL Finally, Leonard begins to fade, asks his sons if they will return to see him tomorrow.

"Where's your harmonica, Scooter?" Leonard comes to life as the boys are walking out. "Can you play me a little tune before you go?"

Scooter appears wistful in a way Jody has never seen his brother.

"Sorry, Daddy, I don't have it. I don't play that thing anymore."

The two drive in silence, except for the groan of the truck's engine, back to the house. They roll through town, past the high school and the paper mill, over the train track that leads all the way to Texas. Inside, Scooter begins to cook and refuses any help from Jody, who rests in the recliner. He reaches into the cabinets, pulls down bottles of oils and sauces. Before long a savory smell pours into the room.

"I'm not used to people cooking for me. Certainly not what I expected from you."

"I can cook."

"You never used to cook."

"What? I cooked all the time."

Scooter heaps two plates full of rice and a stir-fried concoction, carries them over to the living room. He hands both plates to Jody, then goes and takes two TV trays from the closet, sets them up, and puts the plates on them. The food steams. Scooter goes back into the kitchen, gets utensils and two cups of water, and comes back to sit on the sofa.

"You think *Hee Haw*'s on?"

Jody laughs. "Too late, brother."

"How about *The Dukes of Hazzard*?"

"Ditto."

"Oh well. Have to settle for one of these reality shows."

"Hey, maybe we should check into making a show about your house."

"Sounds good. I could be a star."

The two sit back, satisfied. Jody turns the television to the local news.

Scooter stands. "Let's go catch some fish."

Jody turns down the volume. "Excuse me?"

"Let's go catch some fish. For old times' sake."

"Yeah, sounds like fun. It's a little dark, don't you think?"

"That's the best time. Come on, let's fish. We can put them back or you can keep them for yourself."

"I've got a better idea. Let's hit it first thing. I can't sleep past daylight anyway, and it's too early to go back to the hospital."

"Naw, let's go now. Hey, you never know what's going to happen." He raises one hand toward heaven. "The good Lord may come back tonight."

"Okay, okay. I'll do anything to keep you from preaching to me." They gather their things—nothing more than the old Walmart rods with push-button casting reels and a few spinning lures. They pull out lawn chairs and set them on the floor of the carport, tie on the lures.

"So you do know how to take care of your own equipment, huh?" Jody asks. "I seem to remember I was always the one taking care of all the details."

"Yeah. I can tie a fishing lure. What are you talking about?"

"Just how I always took care of things like this."

"Hnn. If you say so. I don't remember it that way." Scooter rubs his jaw, seems to be thinking.

"Well. Just forget it. Let's go." They take a few steps toward the pond and then stop. "We forgot the flashlight." Jody turns back toward the house.

Scooter grabs his brother's arm. "I believe we know this place well enough, don't you think? Besides, look up."

Jody looks up for the first time to see a full moon and a smattering of stars. Only then does he notice how visible everything is. He can see the shapes of birds flitting in the trees, hear crickets screeching and bullfrogs pumping. At the edge of the pond, Scooter casts first.

Before Jody's line is in the water he hears a pop, and Scooter is at it again. His rod is bent double. Jody stands, watches.

"Son, look at that!" Scooter shouts. He keeps the line taut. Still, the fish pulls out more. The reel being pulled in reverse gives a screech.

In a moment everything comes back. "Play him, play him!" Jody shouts. Scooter leans into the rod and then bends back, reeling. The reel screeches again and the fish runs farther away. Five minutes later a good-size bass lies panting on the bank, its gills flapping at the air, shattering moonlight as Jody's brother gently reaches into the fish's mouth and pulls out the hook.

He picks it up and tries to look it in the face. The fish doesn't squirm, continues flapping its gills in the refracted moonlight and working its mouth open and closed.

"You want to keep it? I'm a vegetarian now, like I said."

Jody touches the fish, runs his fingers down the bony spine. "It's a beauty," he says. "A real beauty. Too dark to take a good picture."

"We could take it up on the porch."

"No. That's all right. Put it back. That fish belongs in the water."

The two catch six more fish that night, one for Jody and the rest for his brother. Finally they have enough and go into the house. They both take showers and lie in front of the television, Jody in the recliner and Scooter on the sofa, the air conditioner humming them to sleep.

Jody sleeps all night in the chair. When he wakes up the

television is still on. Scooter is no longer on the sofa, so Jody goes back to the toilet and then looks through the rest of the house for him. Posted to the door of his old room Jody sees the note.

> *I should have asked you brother, you don't have to tell me that. All you had was $45 and as you can see I am just doing what I can to make it. I have no other money to get back home. You're going to get the house and everything. That was fun fishing last night. I see I still have my talent. You know, I was thinking. It's too bad the things that come easy to me are things I never did care about. But still, it was fun. We haven't done that in quite a while.*
>
> *I'm sorry I just took the money. Thanks for coming to get me. Your brother, Scooter.*

On the kitchen table Jody's wallet is open, and sure enough it is empty. He doesn't spot the keys to the truck, and walks outside to see if it is gone. But there it sits. In the carport another piece of paper is on the floor, held in place by a rock. The rods and reels lie next to it, and the tips of both of them rest on the note. The ends of both lines are empty, spinning lures missing. Jody doesn't remember taking them off. Then he reads the message.

> *Hope it's okay, I took these too. S*

CHAPTER 24

Vernon has a hard time waking up on Easter Sunday. A low-pressure system has moved in overnight, and when he reaches over from his bed to part the curtain he sees a morning that's heavy, gray. He feels a dull ache in his chest that pins him against the musty mattress. Vernon lies there half-awake. Over and over he dreams he's getting up, swinging his legs over the side of the bed, putting his feet on the cold floor. After nearly an hour of this, a thunderhead rolls in and spits out a sizzling bolt of lightning, followed by a crash so loud it rattles his windows. Vernon sits straight up at the sound but still feels a lightness in his head and has to fight to keep himself from lying back down.

From the living room window Vernon watches the church camp. He takes note again of his new view. Vernon removed a cypress tree over the winter, which means now he has a full view of the covered picnic area from his living room, and that they have an even better view of him from there. Before, everyone had to walk out into the playground to get a good glimpse of him. And he knew they came and looked, even the ones who would say they never did.

Vernon sets up his first drink and sucks it down. He opens the refrigerator, takes out bacon, eggs, butter, carries them to the counter, and suddenly he's lightheaded again. His vision goes black. Vernon stands still with his hands on the counter. It feels like a gas bubble is working its way up his chest, into his throat, head, ears. He waits for the pressure to clear. A plastic jar of mustard catches his eye, and suddenly he's daydreaming again about something Pearl and Leonard used to tell him. He raises two fingers to tap against his temple, a reminder to ask Leonard about it. Next time he sees him.

They used to tell him he came from another family. The older boys loved to tease Vernon with these stories. Pearl did the telling, Leonard just nodded along or added comments for emphasis. The two told Vernon that their mother had found him as a baby in the woods and brought him home. That EL had agreed to keep him and made Leonard and Pearl promise to help take care of him. But that EL himself didn't care one way or the other about Vernon. Whether he lived or died.

"But you're lucky," Pearl told Vernon once. "Daddy don't hit you like he does us."

"Why does he hit y'all?" Little Vernon asked. Nearly sixty years later he still can feel the little boy's confusion.

"Just does," Leonard chimed in. "He don't never say why. We do something he don't like and he just hits us."

"That's what daddies do, I guess," Pearl added.

"But at least he didn't put mustard in our milk."

Vernon didn't understand. "What do you mean?"

"Daddy ain't never beat you but when you was a baby he used to put mustard in your milk and mix it up real good. He said it would be good for you. He never let Mommy see him do it."

"Why? I don't remember that."

"'Course you don't. You was just a little titty baby. But that's what daddies do. They're mean."

. . .

Maybe they had made the whole story up. Vernon may never know. He stares at the bottle of mustard on the counter, picks it up, and squeezes a heap of it into his glass, half fills it with Jack. *Screw you, EL,* he thinks to himself, *I drink mustard now because I like it.* He downs the drink and just feels more foggy.

He opens the coffee can and finds it empty. He curses at himself, then goes into his room and picks some dirty clothes out of the pile to wear to the store. He knows better than to let something little like this throw him off his game. He has an important job to do.

He rides down to Deke Howard's minimarket next to Thibodaux's barbecue. Deke stands behind the cash register, counting coins. He doesn't look up when Vernon comes in.

Vernon walks the aisle toward the coffee, grabs a can, and goes back to the register. Approaching, he hears Deke barking at someone. Vernon sees his old neighbor Gerald Sampson waiting at the register, looking down. Gerald's son Jimmy is down on all fours patting his hand on the floor. Vernon knows that the boy, man really, has some sort of disability, and he's just looking for his Coke-bottle glasses while the old man shouts at him to get up. Then Gerald kicks his son in the butt, pushes him over onto the floor.

Vernon goes over and picks up the glasses, squats down to put them back on Jimmy's face. He has witnessed scenes like this before.

"Why don't you make yourself useful, Sampson," Vernon says as he helps Jimmy up.

"Mind your own business, Davidson," Gerald Sampson snorts in his mean-drunk voice. Vernon pounces. In an instant he has Gerald Sampson bent backward across the counter. He leans over the man, inches from his face, nearly spitting.

"He's your son, you pitiful fool. He needs your help, not your abuse."

Sampson pushes back but Vernon doesn't let him go. Vernon feels the tightening in his arms, feels the other man's helplessness against his strength. Finally Sampson squirms out from under him, falls in a heap on the floor.

"Mind your own business, Davidson," Gerald Sampson says again.

"Take it outside you two," Deke shouts. He reaches behind the cash register and pulls out a club, slaps it on the corner of the counter. Vernon pulls Sampson up, tosses him back to the floor. Jimmy laughs when he sees his father sprawled out.

"Keep your coffee, Deke," Vernon says as he leaves the store. He throws the can down on the counter. "Plenty of other places to shop." Deke doesn't respond, continues tapping that club on the countertop.

Driving home, Vernon steams. "What a bunch of crap," he says aloud. Gerald Sampson's son is perfectly healthy, yet the old man treats him worse than a dog. Sure, the boy's about as smart as a mule, but what does that matter? These low-down people still have their kids. Treat them like crap and still, there they are.

He goes home and eats his breakfast without any coffee. Then he remembers the clothes, goes into the bedroom, gathers them up, and takes them out to the porch to sort them. He goes back in the house, fills a five-gallon bucket with hot water from the utility room sink, carries it out, and divides it equally among the three waiting basins. Then he fills the remainder of the basins with cold water from the hose, pours in soap, puts all the clothes where they belong, removes his tee shirt and underwear, and sinks them too.

He figures he still has a couple hours before anybody starts showing up at the camp, so he walks around the yard a bit for practice. He feels strange being outside and naked again. This time something feels different, though he is at a loss to name it. He goes back into the house, mixes up another drink, and walks to the edge of his yard to survey the situation again.

Something still doesn't feel right and he knows it. It makes him angry, when he stops to think about it. What in the world is going on? Somewhere in his mind is the nagging feeling that he shouldn't do it this year. What with Leonard dying and everything, maybe he should have some more respect or something. As he thinks about it further, he gets more and more steamed. Just screw 'em. Screw 'em all. Why should he show them any respect? Did those people show any respect to Vernon? Did they help him raise his son in a good, decent home? Or did they just encourage him to be part of something that would end up getting the boy killed? It was all that crap they taught him in church. Just a bunch of crap. They deserve to have to watch Vernon run around his yard naked. That and a whole lot more.

He still has plenty of time, so he begins washing his clothes. First he does the work shirts, and then the pants, finally making his way down to the socks and underwear. He holds up one of the shirts and tries to work a stain out of it, just under the left pocket, like the one on the sheriff's shirt when he came by that night. It doesn't come at first, so he goes in the house, gets a brush and scrubs it for half a minute until he begins to sweat. The stain makes him angry, really, and his fingers are starting to hurt. It still doesn't budge, and then he stops and looks at the stain. *I'm almost done with these anyway,* he tells himself. Finally he drops the brush, dunks the shirt in the two basins of rinse water, squeezes it, and hangs it on the line. The sun begins to peek out, and he finishes the rest of the wash this way, hangs it all on the line. There is still nobody there next door, so he goes back in for another drink.

The washing machine was on its side that night when Sheriff Norm came by. Vernon and Norm had been friends for many years, went to church together, so when Vernon hollered out at the knock and Sheriff Norm walked into his house, Vernon was nonplussed. He had just dug that penny out from under the agitator, and the realization that the machine was ruined had not yet sunk in. Norm came in, stood there with his hat in his hand. "Just give me a minute, Norm, I'll set this machine back up and get that stain off your shirt." The sheriff looked at him then, pursed his lips. Vernon stood, stared at Norm's shirt, remembered as if in an instant all of the days of his life, felt the rage begin to bubble.

"Just tell me, Norm. Just tell me."

As he opens the bottle in the kitchen, Vernon stares out the window. Donnie Lyles and Jerry Reeves stand under the picnic roof. They are looking toward his house, and then Donnie points, he guesses, at the hole where the cypress tree used to be. Jerry shakes his head at this, and Vernon feels his excitement. When he lifts the bottle and pours it, though, the fumes of the whiskey hit him in the wrong way and he suddenly feels sick.

He puts the bottle down and walks out to the edge of his carport. The two men are watching him, and he stands there, naked, looking back. After a minute they leave, and when they don't return for a little while he goes back inside and waits.

He tries to take another drink. Each time he lifts the glass Vernon feels an ache in his stomach, and with it an unnamable dread he has long forgotten. He walks back out into the yard and checks on the clothes. He must have been cheap on the pins today, and a few shirts hang lopsided from the breeze, a pair of underwear lies in the grass. He adds pins to the shirts, picks up the underwear and hangs it again.

Vernon hears voices from below and turns to see a throng of Baptists walking into the picnic area. On instinct he bolts for the house. He stands behind the closed door for a moment, feels his eyes wide and his heart beating. "What is happening?" he says aloud. "What is happening?" He walks back over to his glass.

He still can't drink it. He stands naked by the window. They all are sitting down for their picnic and nobody even looks up in his direction. He opens the window all the way to hear what they are saying. Then the people stop what they are doing and only the minister is speaking. Donnie Lyles puts his hands on the shoulders of his seated wife, Cheryl. Looks like she's in a wheelchair now. When did that happen?

Vernon remembers when she got the diagnosis. He was still a deacon in the church then, when the doctors told Cheryl she had multiple sclerosis. She and Donnie had a boy just a little older than Billy, and Cheryl had always been fond of Vernon's son.

Vernon slumps down to the floor, shakes his head against the confusion raging through him. Billy was a big part of Vernon's life in that church, even after the divorce, when Misty moved to Alexandria and took Billy with her. Sunday mornings the boy went to church with his mother, but Sunday nights were Vernon's. That was part of the deal the two of them had worked out. At the services, as he got a little older, Billy always wanted to sit with his friends, including the Lyles boy. This had hurt him at first, he felt he had such little time with his son and wanted to be next to him every minute, just like when Billy had been small. But eventually he relented, and Billy sat with his friends.

Vernon worried so much about that boy. For a dozen years it must have been, that's all he can remember doing. He can't remember his work, his church life, or anything else he had done, just years of worrying about his son. But as the little boy grew up and wanted to spend more time with his friends, Vernon got a chance to look at his son in a different way. Many Sunday nights he had marveled, stealing glances at Billy as he stood by the door and ushered in the people, at what a happy young man his little boy had become. His handsome Billy, laughing and having fun with his friends. Until the service started. Once business was started, Billy was the one to help quiet all the other boys down. Billy was such a reverent child. Where that came from Vernon had no idea. How many times had Vernon looked over at that boy, that happy young man, when he had his own doubts, when everything just became too much? That was all it took. Just a few stolen glances at his own little god incarnate.

Vernon slides up the wall. Halfway there he stops, slumps back to the floor. He has never felt so tired. He just wants to sleep. Finally he stands, gets his binoculars, and goes back to the window. All the people are going through the line, picking up chicken and potato salad, sitting down to eat. They all are happy, smiling, joking, slapping backs. Some of the children are running around the tables, stopping by their parents' spots for a bite, and running around some more. A few times someone glances up his way, but mostly they just go about their picnic.

Through the open door Vernon hears the sound of splashing in the creek. He throws open the screen door, looks down the hill of his backyard to the water. What he sees behind his house gives him such a chill that he jumps back inside and lets the door slam. Only when he hears his name being called does he step back into the doorframe.

David Adams, the young minister who won't leave Vernon alone, stands in the creek looking up at him. He calls out Vernon's name. The heavy rain from the week before has swollen the creek so much that Vernon is astounded the man can keep his feet. The water, normally just a trickle, is almost waist deep. Yet there David Adams stands in his clothes, stock steady in the stream, smiling. It takes Vernon a minute to see what the man holds in his arms. In the crook of one elbow, with its back turned to Vernon, sits a little naked baby. Whether a boy or a girl, Vernon can't see. The baby kicks its legs, and over the roar of the water Vernon hears its happy shouts. Puckers dot the baby fat of its little butt. As Vernon takes in the spectacle, bewildered, David Adams pushes the kicking baby into his other arm. Then he spreads the free arm out toward Vernon in a gesture of welcome. Vernon's and the young man's eyes interlock. Then David Adams brings his extended arm back toward himself. He folds both arms around the squealing baby, then rocks it from side to side and holds his gaze on Vernon as he squeezes the little creature tight and smiles proudly, as only a father could. He and Vernon stare at one another until, finally, David Adams bends his head to kiss the little naked baby on its cheek.

CHAPTER 25

Later, in the night, Vernon dreams. He is driving to work in that first muffled light when amorphous gray shapes change from general to particular in front of his passing eyes, to trees and houses with porch lights on and fields of grass with steam rising from them. He switches off the radio, opens the window of his truck just a bit, enough to hear the roar of the old six-cylinder, the shifting of the gears. Then, perhaps for the ten thousandth time, his truck rounds Dead Man's Curve, the engine downshifts, slows, groans its way around the bend. Cool air hisses through the cracked-open window. The road straightens, the truck picks up speed. Ahead, on the left, is the turnoff to Big Boar Lake, a spot where he and EL and his brothers used to fish. Pearl and Leonard claimed when they were boys that they had seen boar there, lapping at the water's edge, their long white tusks, or "tushes" as the locals called them, buried beneath the surface.

Vernon takes the turn and follows the rutted dirt road down to the lake. He stops his truck and looks out at the water. On the edge stand a man and two boys; though he can't see their faces, he somehow knows they are EL, Pearl, and Leonard.

The three of them cast their worms out into the water. The lake is flat, but in the dream Vernon can see below, down into the turmoil under the surface of the water, the fish darting about, searching for food, the permanent quest for survival. Dodson, the old sheepdog the three boys shared over fifty years ago, lies splayed on his stomach on the bed of EL's flatbed truck. Waiting.

When Vernon wakes he doesn't move. He opens his eyes, looks up at the darkened ceiling, lets the pins and needles of sleep work their way through his body. He hears a voice, his own voice, some sound from the dream, an unfinished exclamation. In the real world, everything is quiet. Even the bullfrogs are sleeping.

Those were some times, they were, with his daddy and his two big brothers. Some good times when everybody was happy, when even Vernon at four and five and six years old was expected to be dead quiet and just work the water. And if one of them happened to catch a fish, that was all well and good as long as he kept it quiet and got the fish onto the bank. If it was a good day, EL would let them ride in the back of the truck and shout and holler all they wanted on the way home. Something to look forward to.

All those years ago. As sleep begins to leave him, Vernon tries to compute in his head all the time he has spent in the company of Leonard in his life. Say four hours a day, three hundred some days a year until Vernon was about thirteen, then much less but still a lot of time. Thousands and thousands of hours. And since those days when they were out there fishing, all this time had passed and they had all gone on and lived their own lives and had kids of their own and now everybody was moving on.

Vernon shifts his position as he re-enters the world, hears his breathing. What had they talked about all that time? He tries and tries to remember. How many times in the last thirty years has he driven within half a mile of his brother's house and thought maybe he'd just pop in and say hello? Something on his mind. Something he was thinking about and thought he'd see if Leonard had anything to say about it. Here his nephew has been back for just a week or two and Jody and Leonard were talking about all kinds of things. And all the time Vernon had had, all the time when they were boys, all the time he could have had with his brother for most of his life, even in that time they did spend together, what did they talk about? Fish? The price of paper? After all this time Jody and Leonard were having conversations about all kinds of stuff. But what about Vernon? When would he have his conversation?

Vernon checks the clock, sees that daylight is still far away. He lies in the darkness and wonders. How was he, now, supposed to deal with the fact that EL had been a terrible father? And with everything that happened after that? What could he, what could sixty-one-year-old Vernon Davidson, do about it now?

And what was it that Adams said? Right on cue, he had come over yesterday after the picnic. He even had the baby with him. But what was it he said? That he had suffered too? That he had killed his own brother in an accident when they were boys? That he wouldn't give up on Vernon? That God's plan is a mystery?

Vernon only had one answer. It's not the only mystery.

CHAPTER 26

Jody is watching the movement on the wall when the phone rings. Just one of those things he has forgotten about, the way the streetlight from across the country road shines on the white oak tree in front of the house, casts its cool, gray shadow on the wall above the fireplace when the curtain is open. He lies on the sofa, cozy, daydreams that the tree is standing proud and waving at a group of children congregated on the front lawn.

"Mr. Davidson? This is Gary Spencer."

"Dr. Spencer."

"We've had some complications this morning. The nurses called me in about four thirty. We just can't get the fluid out of his lungs. He can barely breathe. Your daddy didn't ask me to call you but I figured I better."

The light around him closes in. "How much time are we talking about?"

"Probably tonight. Maybe tomorrow morning. He never did want any machines or anything."

"You're sure about this."

"Yessir. Yes I am."

"Thank you."

Jody quickly dresses, then, when he can't find a coffee cup with a lid, pours it into a large plastic tumbler. He backs the truck out of the driveway, begins the slow drive toward town. He pulls into the parking lot, drives over, and waits by Vernon's spot.

By the time his coffee is gone Vernon is there. He looks puzzled at first, and then Jody watches his face sink with the realization. He gets out and walks to the driver's side of the truck.

Vernon puts his hands on the sill of the window. "Jody, son."

"Sir."

"You know, sitting there you look just like one of us."

"Like one of who?"

"Like any one of us that works at the mill. Like your daddy and me, like Pearl did for a little while, like your brother even did for a few months. Did you know that? Your brother worked here for a few months after he got out. Leonard got him on."

"No, I didn't. I can't see it."

"Didn't last. He wasn't cut out for working hard. You, though, you look just like one of us."

"Well, I'll take that as a compliment, Uncle Vernon. As long as you've worked here, you ought to know what one looks like."

"Now I don't know if you would have liked it, a traveling man like yourself. On the other hand, you never was afraid of work."

"That's true."

As they talk, another truck tears into the lot and pulls into the parking spot on the other side of Vernon's. Music blares out through the black-tinted windows. The door of the truck flies open and a huge man sits staring at Vernon, nodding to the music, his eyes covered with reflective sunglasses. Then he cuts the engine. The giant gets out and walks straight toward Vernon, walks right into him and shoves Jody's uncle against the side of Leonard's truck. Vernon's arm thrusts into the driver's seat on top of his nephew.

"Watch it, kid," Jody hears him say.

"Oh sorry, Vernon. I didn't see you there."

"Yeah I bet you didn't."

"I mean it, Vernon. It was like you was invisible."

Vernon rights himself. Jody can't see his face, but feels the heat rising from his uncle's back.

"Time to go to work, kid," Vernon says.

Without another word the giant walks away. Vernon stares after him until the guy turns his head and keeps looking back even after he is well past them.

"One of your pals, Vernon?"

Vernon still looks after him, shakes his head. "Just a kid that works here. Just a big, dumb kid."

"Nice fellow."

"Yeah, well. He ain't worth messing with. Just wants to play games with me. But I'm not interested. I'm too old for games. Anyway, sorry for the rude interruption."

"Don't worry about it. Hey, Vernon, the tree's looking good."

Vernon points at the sugar maple. "This one?"

"Yeah. I hadn't thought about it in a long time. But it's looking good."

"What do you know about it?"

"What do you mean? We planted that tree."

"Who did?"

"Me and Daddy and Scooter. Daddy said we were planting it by your parking spot so you'd have something to remind you of Billy when you went to work."

Vernon pulls off his cap and stands there wide eyed. "Leonard planted that tree?"

"Yes, and we helped him. You never knew? I figured he had told you."

"No, but it was there all by itself next to where I parked when I came back to work after his funeral. I just started watering it and taking care of it and called it Billy's tree."

"I can't believe he never told you. That's exactly what he said you would do. But he never said it was some kind of a secret or anything."

"You know, it all makes sense now. I always thought the city workers planted it since it's here next to the street; on the other hand it never made any sense for those idiots to do anything constructive. But I'll be. Right up to the end my brother surprises me."

"I can't believe all these years you never knew. Well anyway, that's a good-looking tree. Now that I think about it I'm not sure I've ever planted another one. But it's looking good. Strong."

Vernon puts his cap back on, then takes it off again and holds it in his hand. He walks over and puts his hand on the tree, then moves back toward the window next to Jody and stands upright, so Jody can't see his face.

"So is this it, Jody? Did the doctor call you?"

"Yes he did. I wanted to stop by, figured you might have missed Dr. Spencer's call."

"Must have called after I left. What'd he say?"

"Said it'd probably be today."

Vernon sighs. "Listen, thanks for coming by. Why don't you go on ahead, I'll just go in and tell them I'll have to miss today. I'll see you up there."

"I'll be glad to wait. We can go together."

He considers this a minute. "Sure, why not. I'll just leave my truck right here in my parking space. Just give me a minute." He walks back to his vehicle, around to the passenger side. Vernon ducks his head and goes out of sight. Then he stands again, shivers as if to clean out cobwebs, and starts toward the office.

CHAPTER 27

The men walk down the endless corridor to Leonard's room. A doctor in the hall looks at his pager, then bolts in the other direction. Lurleen whispers hello when she exits the elevator as they pass. James the orderly meets them pushing his cart of freshly laundered sheets, the smell of soap powder and heat still rising off them. Even at the early hour, televisions mumble, and moans from patients spill into the hall.

Vernon removes his short-billed cap and carries it over his heart. His blue work shirt is wrinkled in a way that doesn't fit the Vernon Jody knows. The button is missing from one side of his overalls, suspender held in place by a safety pin. His stare is blank, breathing ragged, as if he could pass away himself. When they finally reach the room, Vernon stops outside.

"I'll be right in. Just give me a minute." Jody walks in alone. Leonard lies on the bed, blanket neatly wrapped over his legs. No tray of food is waiting for him to eat. His eyes are closed and he struggles to breathe. A nurse stands at his side, checking the dial on his IV drip. She hurriedly finishes, then turns to walk out, squeezes Jody's arm as she passes him.

Vernon walks in. He passes his brother and goes straight

to the window. Outside a man and two boys throw a baseball back and forth. Vernon cracks the window enough to hear the leather of their gloves pop each time one of them catches the ball. At the edge of the playground is another man. He stands next to a waist-high tree stump and has excavated a moat all the way around it, filled in the hole he made when he took out the other stump with the soil from this one. Jody joins Vernon at the window.

"Daddy used to have these contests with me and Scooter. Contests to dig stumps out. He used to stand over to the side and shout at us. He must have cut down a hundred trees when we first moved out to that place. 'Get those roots out,' he'd shout at us. 'Get down in that soil.'"

"EL did the same thing with us. I was faster than your daddy or Pearl, even though I was the youngest. They probably let me win. I don't know. You have to know where to chop the roots. And then to get enough soil off so you can lift it up out of the hole. I haven't dug one out in years. But that Louisiana soil is hard to get off. I remember that much."

Leonard begins to stir. "Vernon?"

"I'm right here."

"Where's Pearl?"

"Pearl's gone, Leonard. He's gone."

"I . . . was dreaming. About Pearl fighting them boys."

"Is that right? Did Pearl take care of them?"

"We were standing there watching . . . cheering for him."

A swelling of tears pours onto Vernon's face. "Leonard?"

Leonard opens his eyes.

"I have a question for you, Leonard."

"That one boy got Pearl down. Son, he was big."

"Just one question, Leonard. About something y'all used to tell me."

"That boy was as big as a grown man."

"Just one question, Leonard."

"But Pearl got back up."

Vernon begins to sob now, bites his lip, brings the flat side of his fist down in slow motion over and over on Leonard's bed.

"Leonard? Leonard?"

Then Leonard Davidson closes his eyes and does not open them again. Vernon and Jody stay in the room the rest of the morning and the afternoon. They take turns sitting on the one chair in the room as doctors and nurses come in and out, talking to themselves. They both are still there late in the evening when Dr. Spencer comes into the room, announces the time, expresses his condolences.

"You want to come and stay at the house so you don't have to drive back tonight?" The two men talk in the parking lot. Vernon is completely white, looks tired beyond exhaustion. He has pulled Leonard's tailgate down and sits on it. Jody wishes he could smoke a cigarette.

"No thank you, Jody. I've got to get on back. I've got to work the day shift tomorrow."

"I'm sure you could get a couple days off. Come on over and I'll make us some sandwiches like you like and we can think about it all in the morning."

"I'd rather just go and work. Best to keep myself busy. Can't do nothing about it now. All we need to do is arrange the funeral and make some phone calls."

"Well, you're more than welcome. Who do we need to call?"

"I can get it around the mill tomorrow, other than that you can just tell all the neighbors. BF ain't too well and I doubt if he can travel over here, but I'll call him and Eddie and let them pass it around to the Texas family."

"I guess we'll need a funeral?"

"I'll call Mike Toler first thing in the morning, your daddy had a burial policy with them, he told me. We'll set the viewing for Wednesday evening and then the funeral Thursday."

"I'll call the neighbors in the morning then."

"Just drop me off at my truck, would you?"

The two drive back to the mill, stop next to Vernon's truck, which sits all alone. Vernon slides in behind the wheel. Workers are coming in for the night shift, slamming car and truck doors and chatting jovially. The giant paper machines roar, expel sulfur and ash into the night sky.

"Jody. I'm real sorry about your daddy, son. I'm real sorry."

"Me too, Vernon. He got more time than some get. And I guess he did okay for himself with it."

"Leonard, he did okay. I'm going to tell you something. This is not something you can understand because you don't have any children. But after your mother died, those were some hard times for him. Some hard times."

"I believe you."

"You better believe it. Two boys all by himself was a handful. Especially when one of them has as many problems as your brother did. But it's tough. Trying to raise y'all right. Trying to teach you something. If you stop and think about it too much you'll never know if you're doing it right. And being an only parent he didn't have time to stop and think about it anyway. He just done what he knew how to do and figured y'all would turn out how you was going to turn out."

"There's a lot of wisdom in what you're saying, Vernon. That's one thing I took from the work I did for the army. You study people and what you see is that mostly they just are who they are."

Vernon reaches a hand out to his nephew. "Well, you turned out all right. Your cousin Billy would have been like you. Hard working. Full of energy."

"I know he would have been a fine fellow."

"Your brother, though. I don't know. There's just so much we can't understand. The two of y'all were raised in exactly the same situation, yet you turned out so different. It's like you went out one door, and he went out the other."

"I always wanted to help him . . ."

"You did, Jody. You did what you could for him. And look at you, you're still doing it. And he's still just as lost."

"When Daddy was talking in there. About the fights. I never have known exactly what happened."

Vernon stands, reaches into the bed of his truck, grabs a stob from a tree limb, holds it in one hand and rubs it with the other. "EL used to have some of the men that worked for him bring their boys over to fight Pearl. Daddy built a corral around next to the barn, kind of like a fighting ring." Vernon shakes his head as if to dislodge the memory. "EL said he wanted to toughen Pearl up. He said he wanted us boys to learn to take care of ourselves. And Pearl was our example."

"I just don't get it, Vernon. That's a terrible thing to do. This was the same EL I used to know? My grandfather?"

Vernon goes to the back of the truck, opens the tailgate, raises one foot up onto it. He slams the stob onto the tailgate. "Oh, it was terrible. EL was terrible. Just plain cruel. When he was young. You knew EL the old man. But Pearl, he knew he couldn't do anything about it. So he took it like a man."

"You were there? You remember what it was like?"

"You're dadgum right I remember. I still dream about it sometimes. Pearl always told us they were his fights, told us not to get in there and try to help. He told us not to get messed up in it."

"I bet y'all did anyway."

"Oh." Vernon rubs the stick in his hand again. "Sometimes your daddy did, if one of them boys got Pearl down, started hurting him too bad. I was too little I guess. I don't know."

"You couldn't have helped him, Vernon."

"I know, you're right. I wasn't but seven, eight years old. But he always told us not to get messed up in it.

"The only thing any good that came of it was after the

fights. When Pearl leaned on us. On your daddy mostly. Pearl didn't too much lean on anybody in his life."

"I remember that about him."

"But we'd walk back up to the house, after the fights. Pearl would be beat up pretty bad. We'd try to help get him home. He was so tired, he'd lean on us, let me and your daddy help him. Let us help him walk back up to the house. After the fights. He'd let us help carry him home."

Vernon slumps down to the tailgate, slaps his hand on his knee. "He'd say it again, too, as we were walking."

"Say what?"

"He'd say, 'I told y'all not to get messed up in it.'"

"And what would you say?"

"Not me. Your daddy. He'd tell him, he'd say, 'Pearl. We can't help but be messed up in it. We're brothers. We're one flesh.'"

CHAPTER 28

Jody wakes well into the morning, oddly rested, as a full complement of sunshine bears into the living room. He lies looking up at the ceiling, too overwhelmed to do anything. He will have to find Scooter again and make a plan for the house, the dog, for all their father's things. The telephone rings but it will just be something else to do something about, so Jody remains glued to the sofa and lets it ring.

Finally, he begins to move about. His only real obligation for the day is the viewing at five o'clock, and as he makes a pot of coffee and picks up the telephone, Jody feels a blooming of time that puts him in mind of earlier days. He dials. The message, of course, is from Art. He wants to talk things over some more, to hear how Jody is, to make a new plan, put their heads together and see what they can figure out. At the end of his message Art plays a few plaintive notes on his horn, some jazz number Jody has heard many times before.

He spends the day walking the property, looking through things, making lists. The task is hard, but Jody slogs through a job he knows has to be done. As he moves into the different rooms of the house, into the various areas of the storage shed, as he pulls back the tarps covering and opens boxes holding the things his father has gleaned and collected over the years, Jody surveys all the goods. But when he reaches out his hand and touches the things, they come to life in a different way, tell their own histories and memories, through the contact, right into Jody's skin. Tools Leonard had since before Jody was born. Pictures of Leonard with Pearl and Vernon when he was a boy. Boxes of Jody's mother's decaying clothes he never saw her wear.

Late in the afternoon he drives past the paper mill to Toler's funeral home. The afternoon sun has taken on, by then, much of its slant. Mike Toler shakes Jody's hand as he opens the door.

"Haven't seen you in many years."

"Well. I'm sorry you have to see me here now. But anyway, it's nice to see you again, Mr. Toler."

"I understand what you're saying. I know exactly the sentiment you express. Everybody loves to see ol' Mike down at Walmart or Chevy's restaurant or at a ball game. But here, it's a different story. Well anyway, we're glad we can be here for you and your family at this time. Your daddy was a good man, a real good man. I'm sorry to see him go. Too early."

"You know, Mike. Is it all right if I call you Mike?"

Toler claps Jody on the back. "Sure. Of course it is."

"You know, I kind of, well. I kind of fell out with my father, my whole family. After that deal with my brother."

"I understand, Jody. I know what you're talking about. I see a lot of people in exactly that situation. Coming home to deal with things when they finally have to be dealt with. Wishing they had done it a long time ago."

"I've been gone a long time."

"Did you get a chance to see him before he went on?"

Jody forces a smile. "Yes. Yes I did. I've been back in town for the last couple weeks. Like I say, I've been gone a long time but my Uncle Vernon tracked me down. Do you know my Uncle Vernon? Daddy's brother?"

"Sure I do. Speak of the devil." Toler points with his head over Jody's shoulder as Vernon parks across the street. Vernon has changed into his respectable clothes, one of his old suits from his days as deacon of the church. Though out of style, the clothes are immaculate. Vernon's hair and beard are combed perfectly, as always. He bends and checks himself in the side-view mirror, straightens his necktie.

"Mike," Vernon says as he approaches, shakes hands with Toler, goes into the building.

"So how does this work?"

"They'll start showing up in a few more minutes. There's some coffee and little sandwiches in there if you want. Your daddy had a lot of friends, even if he didn't have a big family. Lots of people around here will miss him."

"And what if they can't make it?"

"Them that don't get a chance to come see him this evening can pay their respects at the service. After that we'll drive out to Mt. Olive for the burial, then back here for an early supper prepared by the ladies from y'all's church."

Toler turns to speak to a couple Jody doesn't recognize as they come in the door. Jody goes into the viewing area. He looks at Leonard's preserved body, feels at once a numbness and a sort of dread that gnaws a hole in his stomach. In the few minutes he stands there the guests begin to arrive for real. By the time he turns toward someone calling his name the place is mostly full, buzzing with conversation.

"Hey, Jody."

Jody does a double take. Standing next to him is Goon, Jody's large classmate from high school. He still stands six foot six but doesn't have the frame of a basketball player anymore.

Jody shakes his hand. "Didn't know I'd find you here."

"Yeah, I been back quite a while. Played basketball a year

at East Texas Baptist"—he puts both hands over his head as if he is shooting a basketball—"but I didn't like it, so I quit and been back ever since. Couldn't stand to be away from the most beautiful place on earth. God's country." At that he spreads his arms wide.

Jody laughs. "That's one way to describe it."

"Hey, I'm sorry about your daddy. What got him?"

"Heart. I hadn't been back since, well . . . My uncle called me a couple weeks ago and told me he was going. And here we are. His heart just wore out on him."

By now, the room is full. Jody recognizes a few faces. "Hey, do they still call you Goon?"

The large man laughs so hard his gut jiggles. "Naw, it's back to Keith now. Once I got married and had kids and all. But I guess a few still do." Then he turns and yells to someone across the room. "Hey, Goober." He waves with his arm. "C'mere."

The man approaches, springy on his toes. Jody doesn't recognize him until he gets close enough for Jody to see the tiny black lines under his eyes. The man is just as short but a lot thicker than he used to be. Apparently Goon has lost his high school nickname, and Dewayne has gained one.

"Hey, Jody. Sorry about your daddy."

"Yeah, thanks, Dewayne. How's those eyes?"

He breaks into a smile, shows a large chip in one of his incisors. Then he touches his face. "These are permanent, thanks to you. I don't hardly think about it anymore." Dewayne was the second baseman in high school, and Jody played shortstop. One day during practice the two butted heads going for a ground ball up the middle. At the time everybody said Jody got the worst of it, as he had to be carried off the field unconscious. But the top of his head had smacked Dewayne in the face, causing him two black eyes that swelled so badly the bruises never completely went away.

"Hey, come out and play some ball with us and I'll get you back for this." He points to his face.

Goon—Keith—looks at him. "Hey! Goober! You're a genius, son!" He claps Dewayne on the back. "That ain't a bad idea! Hey Jody, what are you doing later? Me and Goober may be short one man on our softball team tonight—we play at eight. How 'bout you come out and play some ball with us?"

"I haven't hit a ball in many years. I might strike out."

"Aw, c'mon," Goober says, "you'd have to be blind not to be able to hit this ball. When's the last time you looked at a softball? Sucker's big as a watermelon."

"Near as big as a basketball," Goon adds, and reaches up and does the shooting motion again.

"Thanks for the invitation, guys. Let me get back to this thing. One of y'all got a glove for me? I've still got a glove, but it's somewhere up in Chicago."

"Chicago? You live up there? I never would've pictured you up in Yankeeland."

"You never know what's gonna happen. Anyway, let me think about it. I appreciate it."

"Yeah," Keith says. He turns to Dewayne. "Be fun to see if ol' Jody can still hit the ball like he used to could."

"I doubt it," Dewayne says. "He'll prob'ly strike out."

All of the neighbors come to visit, and the preacher that calls himself Brother Herb from Leonard's church. People Jody doesn't know shake his hand, say his father talked about him all the time, said what a fine son he was, how he served the country and wasn't afraid of anything. At each of these comments Jody laughs and smiles, says, "I don't know about that," thanks them for coming and for being a part of his father's life.

By seven the crowd has dwindled and Mike Toler is sweeping the floor. Goon and Goober approach Jody one more time.

"You know where the field is, right? We got to get on over

there, get the team ready and everything. But it'd be fun to have you play."

"You know what. I may just do it. I've got some old clothes and some tennis shoes in Daddy's truck, I'd just have to borrow a glove."

"We can take care of you. Come on. If you can."

Jody waves at them and they go out the door. The Tolers continue cleaning up and Vernon is talking to a small group of people in chairs. Jody walks over and they all look up.

"This is Jody, Leonard's son," Vernon tells the group of men. Four of them are there, all Vernon's age or older. They smile at Jody, nod, say, "Nice to meet you." All except one, a man in overalls. Jody recognizes him from the railroad track.

"He ain't a Communist is he, Vernon?" Peterson says.

Vernon backhands the man across the chest. "No he ain't no Communist, Peterson, this here's a red-blooded American. He . . . Well, he was in the army for a little while."

"Oh," Peterson says. He stands partway up and reaches for Jody's hand. "Good to see you again. We shared quite a few interesting views the other day, but we never did get to politics." When they were boys Leonard helped Peterson with his schoolwork and, in trade, Peterson helped Leonard with his chores, even looked out for him when Pearl wasn't around. As Leonard told it, Vernon never did care for the man, who, though two years older, was in Vernon's class at school. Vernon considered him an overgrown dummy, too stupid to keep from getting himself stuck in his desk at school, which was way too small for such a huge kid. And, as things in the present appear to Jody, nothing has changed.

Peterson turns back to Vernon. "But you've got to admit it, Vernon, a lot of these young people these days, the way they act, they's just Communists. Now they may call it freedom of speech or something, but what it really is, is freedom of *certain kinds* of speech." Peterson leans back, raises a finger like a philosopher. "Take that there rap music, for instance. It's all, N-word this, N-word that. I mean, just listen to the way I'm talking! Things has got so bad I can't even bring myself to say the word anymore, not even with a group of old friends! Used to be we was the only ones could say that word, now they can say it and we can't! If that's not a, a upheaval in the social order, I don't know what is! This used to be a free dang country! I'm telling you, it's Communism. It's all around us."

Vernon looks at him, smirks, and backhands him again. "He ain't no Communist, Peterson. I've been telling you for thirty-something years Communists is nothing to worry about anymore anyhow. On top of that, have some respect for the dead." Vernon backhands him once more. "And quit trying to use words you ain't smart enough to use. You just read that bull crap on the internet somewhere."

"I'm telling you, Vernon, you're kidding yourself! I mean, we better watch out for that Putin. He's the devil, Vernon! Remember how they always used to say in church the devil speaks with a forked tongue? Remember that?" Now Peterson backhands Vernon across *his* chest. "Now this was back before going to church was all about *peace* and *love* and all that Commie bull crap. Same thing them long-haired Commie girly boys liked to preach about. But that Putin, he's the real thing! Trying to pass himself off as an economic reformer! And besides that why would you trust anybody named after something comes out your hind end?"

Vernon scoffs. "Peterson! They speak another language over there, son. 'Putin' just means something else in Russian than it does in English."

"You're wrong, Vernon!" Peterson bares his teeth. "It ain't another language, it's English! I've seen it wrote on paper, it's just a old version of English, some of the letters look different, and they spell some words different is all!"

"Bull corn it is, you knuckklehead! It's Russian!"

"It's English, Vernon!" Peterson slams his fist on his knee. "I've seen it wrote down! It's English! Not Chinese or some old scratch like chickens trying to dig up a fat grub worm in a god dang chicken yard!"

Vernon throws his hand up. "Peterson. You've lost your mind. What little you had."

"No, Vernon." He points toward Leonard's body, lying in his casket. "Me and Leonard talked about this! He felt the same way I did!"

Vernon backhands him yet again. "You ain't talked to Leonard in years."

"Well, that's true, but Leonard was a good old boy! I know he felt the same way I did! I know he did!"

Vernon sighs. "Peterson, let it go, huh? My nephew ain't a Communist."

"Well, you never know," Peterson says. "Good book says you never know what's going to happen. They's a *antichrist* around every corner!"

Vernon scoffs. "No it does not! I haven't read that book in a dozen years and even I know it doesn't say anything like that. Peterson!"

"Well, it might as well. They's always somebody out to get us." Peterson throws his hands up.

Vernon stops, hangs his head. Blows out a huge breath. "Peterson, I've told you my nephew's not a Communist. Nobody around here is a Communist. By god, you sure haven't changed. Never did know when to shut up." He raises a fist, shakes it in Peterson's direction. "I ought to beat you senseless like I used to."

"What!" Peterson exclaims. "I won every fight we ever fought!"

Vernon snorts. "I tell you what, partner. You remember things any way you want to, son. I guess there are a few advantages to getting old after all."

“Beats the alternative,” Peterson says. Jody turns to go.

“You cain’t ever be too careful.” Peterson stands, picks up his hardhat from under his chair. “And as much as I’d like to continue this informative conversation, I’ve got to get down and do my sweeping.”

Jody aims the truck toward home. The night is warm, and he opens the windows to let in air. In town he stops at the railroad crossing again. There is no train but he sits and looks at the tracks, tries to think about something. His mind is unusually blank, though he suddenly doesn’t want to go back to the house. He makes a U-turn, drives back through town to the softball field.

Dewayne/Goober and Keith/Goon are throwing a ball back and forth when he drives up, as are a few other guys in green shirts alongside them. They both wave at him when he gets out of the truck.

“He’s number nine,” Goober says.

“Let me just go to the dressing room,” Jody shouts out, and proceeds to change his clothes standing right there by the truck. Just like old times.

When Jody sees the lineup he goes to Keith. “You’re batting me ninth? And got me in right field?”

Keith pulls one side of his mouth open, sticks in a wad of tobacco, tongues it around for a minute, then spits a wad of juice in the other direction. “You said you haven’t played in years. Plus I didn’t know if you were coming.”

Keith looks up at Jody’s cap, spits again in the other direction. “’Sides that, you’re lucky I let you play at all. I hate the Cubs.”

“I’m kidding you, man. I just hope I can hit the ball.”

“Game time, boys.”

The other team bats first. A short guy that looks familiar hits first and swats a ball into left center all the way to the fence. He isn't very fast and makes it to third base standing up. The next guy takes a pitch and then swings and misses, and on the third offering he hits a scorcher back to the mound so fast Goon can barely get his glove up. The ball bounces off the back of his mitt and flies, still a heated line drive, into the hand of the third baseman, who catches it. Even with the deflection the play happens so fast the runner is doubled off third. Then the next batter lofts a high fly ball to right center. Jody races over and is closing in on it when the lanky center fielder cuts in front of him and carries it home.

The home team scores two in the bottom of the first on a mammoth home run by Goober, then holds the opponents again in the second. In the bottom of the second Jody gets a turn to bat. He is scheduled to hit third, in the hole. The center fielder, a tall black guy named Arthur, waits in the on-deck circle, and the first batter rips a single the opposite way. Arthur drops the donut off his bat and walks into the box. "Hot Rod" is on the back of Arthur's shirt. As soon as he steps out of the dugout, Jody can feel his heart begins to race.

And that's when it all comes back. He picks up the donut and slips it over the end of his own bat, begins loosening up. The pitcher has a backspin on all his pitches, and watching from the on-deck circle, Jody hates him immediately, his old instinct returning. Arthur stands with the bat on his shoulder and takes a couple of high pitches, then fouls off the pitcher's attempt at a curveball.

Keith/Goon stands in the coach's box at third. "Come on, Hot Rod," he shouts. He claps his hands together, looks over at the dugout. "Let's hear it, y'all," he shouts. At once the dugout erupts in a smattering of cheers, a chorus of baseball chatter.

"Light 'em up, Hot Rod," Goober shouts, and climbs halfway up the fence. "Light 'em up, light 'em up!"

"Put it to it, Hot Rod!"

"He ain't got nothin', Hot Rod!"

"Put the hammer to the nail!"

"Knock the crap out of it!"

The next pitch comes in. Arthur rips it right back at the pitcher and off his ankle. He bolts for first as the ball caroms into the space between the first and second basemen. The runner on first tears for second and never even slows down. By the time the second baseman picks up the ball in short right, the runner from first is standing up going into third and Arthur is completing a pop-up slide into second base. The pitcher limps back to the mound with his glove up, asking for the ball.

Jody drops the donut and looks at the runners as he walks into the box. He feels his heart racing, feels it all coming back. The pitcher bends down, places his glove with the ball in it on the ground at his feet and ties his shoe, then looks at the bruise on his leg and rubs it before standing back up.

"Come on, Hank," Goon shouts out from the coach's box. A nickname Jody hasn't heard since ninth grade. That was the year all the players took their grandfather's name as their nickname. Jody still doesn't know why. They had a Hugh, an Iry. Jody's choices were EL or Hank. Jody went with Hank so he wouldn't be confused with Dewayne, whose grandfather's name was LE.

"How 'bout you, son? Put a pop on it like you done that night in Choudrant!"

Jody steps back out of the box, knocks the dirt off his shoes with the bat. Goon is standing on his tiptoes looking into the distance, shading his eyes with one hand as if to see something far away.

Choudrant was Branden's rival school in both baseball and basketball. Like many of the country schools, their sports programs operated on a near-zero budget, which meant the players did all the maintenance on the baseball field while the coach borrowed a tractor from somebody in the community to rake and level the field at the beginning of the season. While most of the high school fields had some sort of fence, even if it was only hog wire stretched straight across center field to save on materials, Choudrant used the elementary school building as a left field fence. And as sure as he was standing there, Jody suddenly pictured a ball he hit onto the roof of that building one windy night his senior year.

"Come on everybody, let's hear it for Hank!" Goon shouts at the dugout. Then the whole dugout is chattering, talking it up.

"Let's see what you've got, Hank!"

"He ain't hit a ball in years," Goon shouts. "Probably gonna strike out!"

"Hey, pretend the ball is Goon!" someone shouts. "He stole your girlfriend and he just got out the back of the truck with her!"

After that, Jody doesn't hear anything else. He watches the first two pitches come in. They are pretty good to hit, but he just looks at them. The umpire calls strike one, and then strike two. Jody steps back out of the box. Goober yells at him from over in the on-deck circle.

"Like this," he shouts, and swings his bat at the air. "Like this. You've got to swing it. You musta forgot."

Jody steps back into the box, then steps out again, sticks a finger at Goober in the on-deck circle. He steps back to the plate in the bottom of the second inning in a beer-league softball game between two teams he doesn't know anything about, representing a team that a few hours before he had never even heard of. But the next pitch means everything. The pitcher stands on the mound shaking off signals, which is just a joke, then backs off again, sets down his glove with the ball in it, and ties his other shoe. He comes in with his next offering. Which is just the same as the first two. Jody opens up with a mighty hack and hears the ping of aluminum on cowhide, smells the rising puff of dust and burning leather. The ball rockets toward the sky in right center field. Jody tears for first, rounds toward second, watches as the ball flies into the fence and then falls down, and turns for third. Goon waves both hands toward the ground. Jody hasn't seen that motion in many years but its meaning comes right back to him. He hits the ground head-first and beats the tag. The third baseman tosses the ball back to the pitcher, who stands nonchalantly on the mound. "Nice stroke," he says. Goober bats next and lines the first pitch over the third baseman's head, and Jody trots toward home.

Goon is there to shake his hand at the dugout. "Dang, son, maybe I oughta take a few years off. I haven't hit a ball that hard in a long time."

"Well, it's a big ball, you know. Easy to see."

"Yeah, if you've got the vision."

"Hey, Jody. I want to talk to you." Jody stands by his truck, knocking the dirt off his shoes. Goon drives over to Jody. He cuts the engine but leaves his radio on, turned low.

"What are you doing now, Jody? Up there in Chicago?"

"I'll tell you, but you're just going to laugh like everybody else does. I work for a paper company."

"Now that's original." He pulls out his tobacco plug and throws it across the grass. "Well, how long you staying down here? You've got to take care of your daddy's house and everything? Your brother's not back here, is he?"

"I don't know how long. Scooter's down in New Orleans."

"Well, here's my number, if you want to play again let me know, we need some more guys that can hit like that."

"Thanks Goon, I mean Keith."

The big man spits on the ground again. "Naw, you know what. I been thinking about it all game. The hell with it. Call me Goon. My wife hates it, but dad gummit, a man can't let her take everything away from him, you know? I mean, she's got the checkbook, got keys to my truck whenever she wants to drive it. My son Charlie said the other day, he said, 'Daddy, I know one thing girls can't have that we have.' I told him, 'Son, once you get married she's got that too.'" Goon snorts at his joke.

"You gonna let your kids call you Goon too?"

"Aw, they'd love it. Beats what they'll be calling me in a few years, you know? Like what we used to call our daddies. Anyway, I'll see you at the funeral."

"I'll see you there."

He begins to pull away, then stops and backs up until his window is even with Jody again. He shuts off the engine.

"I've been meaning to say something to you." Jody takes a step closer to him.

"So . . . Well . . ."

"I know what you mean."

"I'm real sorry about that, Jody."

"Thanks, buddy."

"You know, you've probably thought about it more, but I've thought about that night a hundred thousand times since then. And wondered at least that many times if I could have done something to stop it or change it some kinda way. You know that thing could have gone a completely different direction."

"Yes, it could have."

"You're damn right it could have. Darrell could have put a slug in you and Scooter and Tammy too. 'Course that slut would have deserved it. She's still around here. Still trashy as hell."

Goon pulls off his cap, covers his eyes as if thinking. "Never expected ol' Scooter to save your tail, did you?"

"You got that right."

"'Course he was the one brought all that on in the first place. I guess if it had gone that other way I'd be standing here talking to myself right now."

"That's true."

"Well." Goon reaches down, turns up his radio. "I'm glad it didn't happen that way. I know I ain't seen you in years, but I'm glad to know you're still standing."

"Me too."

"You and me, we go way back. We was just little pistols together. Remember that time we got in a fight with the third grade?"

"You mean when we were in the second grade?"

"Mmm-hmm. Good thing them boys were a bunch of pansies or they probably would have killed us. But anyway, who would've thought we'd still be playing together when we was thirty?"

"Not me."

"But Scooter. He never did know where he was going, did he?"

"No. He didn't. I just saw him the other day. Far as I can tell he still doesn't. But I don't think he ever intended to go the route he did."

"I imagine not. Not everybody gets lucky, I guess."

"This is true."

On the ride back, Jody rolls through town. In front of Chevy's restaurant again sits Gary Wayne, sideways on the driver's side seat of his car with the door open. His legs extend from the car and he's looking at a magazine.

As Jody turns into a parking space, Gary Wayne jumps up from his seat and approaches a couple on the sidewalk. Jody cuts the motor and gets out, hears Gary Wayne shouting.

Clem Mathews is walking down the elevated sidewalk holding hands with his wife. He turns toward the yellow taxi and moves his body between her and Gary Wayne. Then she reaches out and grabs the boy and girl on the sidewalk with them.

"I want to see that story!" Gary Wayne shouts. "I want

to read it in the *Branden Independent* this week! I know you know James Wallace, he can get the story right in for you! He'll print it right away!"

Clem's wife squeezes herself around him to shout at Gary Wayne. Clem extends an arm, tries to hold her back. She forces her head under her husband's arm, still holding on to the children's hands. They lurch forward into the back of their father.

"Why don't you just go away, Gary Wayne Walker! Leave my husband alone! Get back in your taxi and go give somebody a ride or something!"

"I want the credit I deserve!" Gary Wayne shouts.

Clem Mathews turns away from Gary Wayne, puts one hand on his wife's shoulder and his other hand on his son's. The boy reaches out to his sister. The four of them form a circle on the sidewalk. She looks up to speak. He shakes his head and loudly says, "No." He points down the sidewalk toward a parked white Cadillac. Mrs. Mathews grabs the children and marches them down the sidewalk, shouting as she does.

"Get a life, Gary Wayne!"

Then, slowly, Clem Mathews walks toward the taxi, steps down off the elevated sidewalk. Clem wears a windbreaker jacket with the State Farm insurance logo on one side. Gary Wayne follows him back to the taxi.

"What the devil do you want, Gary Wayne?"

"You know what I want. I want credit for what I did."

"So let me get this straight. You want me to say we cheated? To win that basketball game?"

"No! No! Don't say we cheated. I just want you to tell the truth. That I saved that ball for you and it wasn't you diving into the seats that saved it."

Clem Mathews pauses, collects himself. "Let me ask you a question. Were you one of the five players on the floor when that play took place?"

"No. 'Course not. I was the bench boy."

"Were you even on the team? Were you wearing a uniform?"

"'Course not. You know what I did."

Clem Mathews hangs his head. Stops a minute. "Gary Wayne, you've been telling this story so long even I'm starting to believe it. But think about it. What you're saying is we cheated. What you want me to tell everybody is that Branden cheated to win the state basketball championship in 1979. And you want everybody to know you helped us cheat to win."

"No! I just want the credit I deserve!"

"How does that make you a hero, Gary Wayne?"

"I just want some credit. I just want what's due to me."

"If your story is true it doesn't make you look like a hero. It makes us all look like jerks. Including you." Clem jostles Gary Wayne with his hand.

"That was, what, twenty-six years ago? I liked you then and I like you now, Gary Wayne. But you've got to move on. Just get on with your life."

Gary Wayne starts to respond but Clem holds up his hand. "Just get on with it, Gary Wayne." Clem turns and moves toward his family, waiting in the car. They drive away heading east. Gary Wayne, west.

CHAPTER 29

He stands outside the house before going in. The evening is cool, with a tickler of a breeze working its way through the trees in front. Crickets riot in a deafening chirp from every direction. Suddenly, for a moment, there is silence.

Then, as if waiting their turn, begin the bullfrogs. From the bank of the pond, for the first time since he has returned, comes the pure country sound of croaking bullfrogs. Almost on cue the crickets begin again. A hooting owl joins in like the periodic crash of cymbals in an animal symphony.

Jody goes inside.

At the end of the hall, the door to his old bedroom still stands closed. He walks toward it with his good clothes from the funeral home in his arms. Jody puts his hand on the doorknob. His entire past stands right behind that door. Everything Jody ever wanted or thought about when he lived there in that house with his father and brother.

He opens the door and goes inside. Though he hasn't been in the room in years, he walks straight to the opposite wall, where the light switch was mistakenly placed when the house was built.

Jody switches on the light, stands breathing the years-old smell of sheets, books, and boxes of baseball cards, none of which has been moved since the day he left. A poster of a girl in a bikini, a calendar from 1992. The same old toys, pictures of his mother, shelves full of baseballs, bats, and gloves. Jody surmises by the lack of dust that his father has been in the room. His body is flooded by a feeling so strong he has to sit down on the bed.

On the nightstand he finds an old school yearbook, which is packed in a plastic bag. He takes it out. As he flips through the pages, Jody reads the notes some of his friends wrote, hopes and wishes for the future.

He opens the book to a page called "Trends."

Price of a hamburger: $1.40.

Favorite television show: Cheers. Hee Haw.

Popular jeans: Levi's 501.

Favorite band: Dire Straits.

What do I want for my future?

> All I want for my future is to live in my own place. I want to find a way to make the world better. And I really want to understand what Paul meant when he wrote his letter to the Romans. In the words of the Apostle Paul to the Romans, "All things work together for good for those who love God, for those who are the called according to His righteousness" (Romans 8:28).

Late that night Jody closes the book. He moves to the window, opens it to hear a cacophony of sounds. He lies down on the bed and stares at the ceiling. On the same bed he stares at the same ceiling he stared at all those years ago. Outside, the croaking increases. The sound of the bullfrogs is deafening. Jody lies on the bed, loses himself in the filtered light coming in through the blinds.

And asks himself again. Aloud this time, as loud as he can, he shouts out the question, to the ceiling and the floor and the walls, to the old dog John David standing in the doorway, his head cocked at a questioning angle.

"How did I get here?"

But no one answers.

"I'm here," he says aloud. John David bounds onto the bed, begins licking Jody Davidson's face. Jody nuzzles him back. "I'm here, John David. I'm here."

CHAPTER 30

Jody starts the long drive before daylight and doesn't stop for anything. At nine in the morning he parks the truck behind the large green van that belongs to his brother and all Scooter's strange friends from the large crumbling house on North Rampart Street. The side door of the vehicle is open and someone sits inside chanting, a man with long painted fingernails. He is listening to Chinese music on one of those long, flat cassette players from the seventies, the periodic sound of a gong crackling out of the old speakers.

A lanky man with a blank stare opens the door. He doesn't say anything but remains in the doorway. Jody pushes in. Half a dozen men and women sit on the floor of the living room, and he feels their eyes on him. On the wall hangs a framed poster of a woman holding a baby, its mouth cupped at her breast. The one who answered the door rejoins the circle. Jody hears muffled conversations, bits and pieces. They are talking about grocery shopping.

"I hate carrots!" a red-haired girl shouts. "My mother stuffed carrots down us like we were baby rabbits after my father left! She was too depressed to cook and all we ate for a year was carrots! I hate them! I hate them! I won't eat carrots! Just saying the word makes me cringe!"

"At least you had a mother," a pockmarked guy says. He wears a worn army jacket with a sketch of a skull and crossbones drawn in permanent marker on the back.

"Excuse me everyone," Jody cuts in. Only carrot girl looks at him. "I hate carrots too," he tells her. She blushes, smiles at him like a little girl proud of herself.

"Someone please tell me where I can find my brother. Our father is dead and I need to find him." They all look about, not at each other or at him. Army jacket gets up and walks into another room.

"I didn't come to interrupt your business. I'm just here to find my brother, I know he's around somewhere and I'm going to find him. Somebody please show me where so I don't have to dig through this place."

"Hey, man," army jacket replies with a practiced lilt. "We don't need your, like, imperialist, like, aggression here, dude." He returns to the room, takes another two steps toward Jody. "This is, like, a house of peace, *hombre*."

"Okay, *amigo*. Where's my brother?"

"Whoa! Dude! Chill out! Maybe you didn't hear me. This is a house of peace." He sticks a finger deep into one ear, takes another step closer.

"Tell me where my brother is. Unless you want a *piece* of me."

Army jacket throws his hands up, quickly steps back. He pushes the air in a slow-down signal.

"I can see you're rattled, dude. Just take it easy. Take it easy."

"I'm just looking for my brother. What is this place?"

"This is our home, Jody," carrot girl says. He looks at her quizzically.

"Scooter told us your name. He talks about you a lot."

Jody just looks at her.

"We live here and learn about ourselves here."

He is floating, turns toward every sound. "And Scooter too? He's actually a part of your group? Not just a tenant here? Why isn't he at this meeting?"

"Definitely, well, normally he would be here. I mean, we all know Scott went to prison. But all of us, in one way or another, have been to prison. All of us have been through trauma, some form of separation or something." She gestures with her hands as if she practices washing them. "We're all looking for answers. Most of us grew up in churches, like Scott did, but neither religion nor anything else was ever enough to make us feel a part of something. But this program does."

"And he's part of the program?"

"Absolutely."

"So does anybody know where he is?"

"I'm right here," Scooter answers from the top of the stairs. Scooter runs his hand down the back of his head, rubs it all over like a ball. All the hair on his face and head has been removed. For an instant he looks like the teenage brother Jody lived with in another life.

"He's gone, Scooter. Daddy's gone. His funeral is tomorrow."

"I know." He runs a hand over his head again. "I did it for Daddy. Just a minute." Scooter moves away from the banister, disappears. Carrot girl looks at Jody, raises her eyebrows hopefully. An Asian kid stares at the floor, and army jacket whispers jokingly with another guy Jody can't see. The two of them giggle intermittently.

Scooter walks down. He carries a bag in his hand. He goes out the front door to the passenger side of the truck. Jody follows. Scooter opens the door and gets in. Jody enters and sits down.

Scooter stares ahead. "Just a minute. Before you start it up."

"All right." Jody takes his hand off the key.

"What good's it going to do, Jody?"

"What's that?"

"Me going back up there. There's nothing up there for me."

Jody sighs. "It's just what you do, man. It's what you do when people die."

"There's no point to it, bro." Scooter rolls down the window, taps his fingers on the outside of the truck door. "I mean, I've got a pretty good deal right here. There's no reason for me to go up there."

"Your friends won't be here in a couple days?"

Scooter begins to rock in the seat. "There's no point. I'll just have to ride the bus back down here. On top of that I'm supposed to work this afternoon. Won't look good, me not showing up. I just started this job."

"Where do you work?"

"Bookstore."

"We can't get away from the paper, can we?"

"Paper's everywhere, man. But seriously. Thank you for coming." He opens the door.

Jody reaches out to him. "Stay in the truck, Scooter. I don't have time for this. We've got a long drive."

Scooter steps out. Jody grabs him by the arm. Scooter jerks away. He stands outside, looks in.

"Come on, Scooter. Let's go."

"I'm not going."

"Scooter! Why in the hell did I drive all the way down here! Come on!" He runs around and tries to shove his brother in the truck. Scooter resists, pushes against the doorframe.

"I didn't tell you to come down here, Jody. I didn't make you come and look for me."

"Get your ass in the truck."

Jody rears back then, slams an elbow into his brother's face. Scooter reaches for his lip, pulls his hand away to look at the blood. As suddenly as the rage had filled him, Jody deflates.

He feels a hissing, like air going out of a tire. He backs away from his brother.

Scooter guffaws then, one quick snort. He looks at the blood on his finger. "Unbelievable. Unbelievable."

"I'm sorry, Scooter."

"You know." Scooter shakes his head with disdain, spits a gob of blood onto the street. "I didn't want to have to say it like this. But while we're on the subject of what a screwup I am, don't forget if not for me you'd be nothing but dust by now. I did my time doing what I didn't want to do. I did my time. You went and did your own thing. So just go on."

"I'm sorry, Scooter." Scooter reaches up to the blood again, continues shaking his head. Jody squeezes past him, suddenly exhausted, sits down on the passenger side so he doesn't collapse.

"You sure about this?"

Scooter wipes his hand on his pants, makes a tinted smear on his leg. "I'm not sure about anything. That's what makes me who I am."

"It sounds so sad when you say it that way."

"It is what it is, man. I never had a mother one day of my life."

"You know I lost her too, Scooter."

"Yeah, and you know what? You got what you got. I got what I got. You've had your life. I've had mine. But there's something you may have forgotten.

"I killed that man, Jody. All I wanted was for her to love me. And I killed him. I think about it every hour of every day of my life. When I open my eyes. When I close my eyes."

"It was an accident, Scooter."

"Was I there with his wife? Yes. Did he come at us with a gun? Yes. Am I glad I took it from him? Yes. Did I mean to kill him? No." Scooter's face as he talks is beautiful, softened by the bluish light of a cloudy morning.

"But those are just the facts, man. There's what's out

there"—he sweeps a hand across—"and there's what's in here"—he pokes his chest, as if he could stick a finger through, into his own heart.

"Just leave me my peace, Jody. Just let me go now. Come back when you have more time. I'd love to see you, brother. I would. Just not under the circumstances."

"Are you sure about this?"

"I already answered that. Come back when you've got more time. You know where to find me now."

"I guess so."

"You always did."

"Scooter?"

"Yeah?"

"Girl in there said you talk about me a lot here."

"I do."

"What do you say?"

"I just say the truth."

"The truth?"

"You were always good to me. You tried to look out for me as best you could."

"I did. I tried."

"I know." Scooter cups his hand to his older brother's neck, a gesture so intimate that Jody instinctively leans in toward it. For once Scooter seems like the older one.

"And I tell them I miss you."

Before Jody is out of New Orleans he turns around three different times. Three times he exits the highway and drives for a mile or two back toward Scooter's house, each time thinking of something new to say he is certain will get his brother to the funeral. But each time, before he reaches the exit, all the arguments are played out in his mind, and each time he turns the truck around again and points it back toward Branden.

CHAPTER 31

Karen paints. She works in the morning, before the dolor of afternoon begins its predictable creep into her body. Today she skips the kimono, wears only Jody's blue tee shirt, as she works. She tells herself to try and think like him, to paint the way he would paint.

She stares at total blankness. Every wall in the place is white now, since she decided to start over yesterday, to go back to the beginning. She opens all the cans, dries her brush on a rag, then just stands there and stares.

Just try something different. She adjusts his shirt and decides that's what she'll do. *Look outside yourself.*

Karen stares at the blue, thinks she'll start with a big circle in the center. Instead she stops, considers. She moves to the green. Instead of painting large, as she normally would, Karen begins with small shapes of things in a corner. *Try something different. What you're doing isn't working anymore.* She works for an hour, stopping herself before each move and asking if it's what she really wants to do.

Eventually, a pond begins to take shape, with two trees on the bank and a lone duck floating in the water. Jody had described this scene to her when he told her about his father's house, when he called to tell her about the funeral and asked her to come for a visit.

She talks to herself out loud, looks at the picture as if through his eyes. Karen smiles.

"Not bad. Not my normal thing . . . It's different. Comprehensible."

Just to see where I came from. The place that made me who I am.

"Even if he didn't know me. He might understand this." She adds details to the picture, flowers on trees, baby ducklings on the water.

"But he does know me," she says aloud. She pulls the collar up to smell his shirt. His scent is fading, and she decides she'll take him up on his offer to see Louisiana, to get her fill of him again.

"Yes. He knows me." Karen beams. Of this, if only this, she is certain.

CHAPTER 32

The drive back is beautiful, peaceful. He has the sense, as he drives, of a world that's opening, of a sky that goes on forever, of sunshine pouring eternally through his window. The sights keep changing, but his feeling remains. He vaguely recalls something from the Bible. *The heavens will stay above the earth.* He looks out the window, first up, and then down. And sees, once again, that things are as they should be.

He arrives back in Branden at dark, drives straight to his old school. Alone, he walks the campus, looks in the windows of classrooms where he spent so much of his young life. Then, at the back of the property, he comes to the baseball field. He walks around the bases, looking up at the stars. He circles again, this time faster. At the plate he starts around them yet again, only now he is running. He finishes a third time and he still hasn't had enough, so he runs full speed into the outfield. He feels suddenly light. He picks up speed. He sees the old hog wire fence approaching and he jumps it without slowing, runs into the trees beyond the field and keeps on running, crashes into the understory and the dappled moonlight and all the creation he can see.

CHAPTER 33

Vernon looks good at the gathering in the morning before the funeral. He is already there brushing lint from his suit coat when Jody arrives. He is not alone. When Jody approaches, he grabs his chest in mock surprise at the sight of Uncle BF, who doesn't look a day older at ninety-two than he did the last time Jody saw him before he was even eighty. BF tells Jody he made the four-hour drive there from Texas by himself, which required him to leave home at five o'clock in the morning. He says he still loves to drive and gets a new Cadillac every other year. The old man leans on a walking stick. He wears a gray cowboy hat like Larry Hagman from *Dallas*, rose-colored sunglasses. He pulls Jody to the side, unbuttons his dress shirt to reveal an "I shot J.R." tee shirt underneath. His hands tremble as he works at the buttons. The skin on his liver-spotted face is smooth as glass.

"I figured your daddy would appreciate this," he says. BF chews gum, which cracks when he talks, and he smiles like a mischievous boy, his dentures reflecting the room's light.

"Yes he would. I know he would." Jody reaches an arm around the old man.

"So how you been, Uncle BF?"

"Oh, well. My sweet Earline passed away five years ago now. I've got a lady friend now, she's a young woman not but eighty-two. She's a baseball fan, in fact she had tickets to the Rangers game today and couldn't come. She never did meet your daddy, though. Besides that she likes to sleep late, she's probably not even awake yet." He shakes his head. "I can't believe Leonard's gone."

"He was too young. I'm glad you made it. How's Eddie? Is he still a preacher?"

BF picks up his cane and points across the room at a man standing alone.

"That's Eddie? Looks like he's grown his hair back."

"The Lord works miracles, don't he?" BF smiles and cracks that gum again.

"I thought you said you drove over by yourself."

"That's a four-hour drive. No way he's riding with me. He may be my son and may be a preacher. But he talks way too much."

Vernon stands in a corner with an unfamiliar man. The man talks to him and Vernon nods, wipes at his face with a handkerchief. His eyes are wide and red. Jody is about to approach but decides to leave him alone.

Everyone comes in and sits down. Brother Herb from Leonard's church opens the service.

"Good morning, everyone." The din hushes, a dying wave. "We are here to celebrate the life of a fine and distinguished man whom all of us knew as Leonard Davidson." He never looks down at any notes, just glances around the room and talks.

"Leonard Davidson was the middle son of the late EL and Hazel Davidson. He was born right here in Branden Parish Hospital on September the 26th, 1940. He was fortunate enough to be born to some fine parents who loved him and looked after him and raised him well, educated him in the ways of our Lord, taught him to love and be kind to his fellow human beings. He was also lucky to be brought up here in what everyone in this room knows is land that belongs to God Himself"—at this he stretches out his hands, a murmur spreads through the room, along with a few nods of agreement—"at a time when life was maybe a little bit simpler than the one we face today.

"After eight years serving his country, including time in Korea and the Philippines, Leonard married his high school sweetheart, Sybil Anderson. After a few years of waiting for their reward, they were blessed with two fine boys, Jody and Scott. The Lord had a different plan for Sybil, and she was taken from Leonard and this life when their second son was born. But Leonard was a man deep of faith and strong of heart, and he took on the task of raising his two boys by himself while working as foreman at the paper mill and while fulfilling the responsibilities of deacon in our church. He held the job of foreman until he retired three years ago, and held the job of deacon right up to the end. The world was a better place because of him, and all of us in Branden Parish and First Baptist Church were blessed that our God put him in our midst and set him free to walk the earth with us.

"When he found out he was sick he called and asked me to see him. It wasn't that long ago. He kept his good spirits even though the doctors didn't give him much hope. I visited with him quite a bit in his first few days in the hospital, and he told me stories about his own life which I was fortunate to hear about. I felt blessed to have a chance to get to know him a little better. And though all of us who knew him will miss him, I know that Leonard would like us to rest in the comfort of knowing that he was excited about the next stage of his life, about the chance to go home with the Lord and see his beloved

Sybil, his mama and daddy, his brother, and his old friends and family members again.

"Leonard Davidson was not a saint. Leonard Davidson was not a sinner. Leonard Davidson was a human being. He had his struggles in life just like all of us. But I for one am happy to know he's gone on to a place where he won't have to struggle anymore.

"If you would, I'd like all of you to join me now. Could we please bow our heads and have a moment of silence to honor the passing of a great man, Leonard Robert Davidson."

When Brother Herb clears his throat, everyone begins to stir again. At first only a few mutters can be heard, then the talk starts again in earnest, the smell of perfumes and colognes mix in the air. Jody sees his uncle talking to the man again. The man's hand is on Vernon's shoulder and Vernon is nodding, wiping his face and eyes with a handkerchief.

Brother Herb calls them all to attention again. "Burial today will be out at Sweetwater cemetery. In just a few minutes the hearse will be ready, and of course we've got a police escort. So everybody please be patient, remember to turn your headlights on, and we'll all meet out there."

Everyone stands. Jody approaches an ashen Vernon.

"Vernon. How are you today?"

"Jody. Son." Vernon wipes his face again.

"I'm Vernon's nephew. I'm Jody."

"David Adams. I didn't know your father, but he sounds like a wonderful man."

"Thank you for coming. You want to ride with me, Vernon?"

"I'm going to take off, Vernon," Adams says.

Vernon lifts one hand awkwardly in a sort of half wave.

The cars line up to get out of the parking lot. Ahead two deputies wait by the side of the road. A city policeman who looks about fourteen directs everyone out the single exit from the lot. Eventually Jody pulls out and joins the line. He switches on the headlights, as all the other drivers have done. Then the deputy cars pull onto the road, turn their flashers on, and one by one all the cars snake forward and turn onto the highway.

Vernon remains silent. Other drivers who meet the funeral procession pull to the side of the road. At the edge of town Pete Grady, a Branden old-timer and longtime friend of Leonard, stands out by the road, at the end of his driveway. Pete Grady was shot down from a plane in the Pacific and was fortunate to lose only a leg. He leans on a walker, wearing what he still can of his navy uniform, a white tee shirt stretched thin over his stomach, jacket thrown over his shoulders. A rifle is propped on the handlebar of his walker. As they pass he lifts the rifle in one hand, salutes the hearse with his other. Jody waves at him.

"Lots of things I thought would turn out different."

"Me too."

"You think Pete Grady feels that way?" In the rearview mirror Jody watches the old man turn on his walker and slowly move back toward his house.

"Probably wishes he hadn't lost his leg in that plane crash."

"I imagine so."

"On the other hand, he survived. I imagine he's happy how that turned out."

Jody and Vernon help carry the casket, place it on the stand by the pile of fresh soil. Everyone gathers. Men from the Honor Guard line up and begin to chant. They raise their seven guns once and shoot. The leader chants again and they lower their guns. Again he speaks and the seven guns fire BANG a second time. The leader chants again and again the men lower their guns. Each shot works like a magnet, pulls tears from eyes. Seven guns are raised a third time BANG, and then they are lowered and the cranking begins and Leonard Davidson is laid down into the hole in the ground.

Later, back at the church, the people eat cold cut sandwiches and potato salad, drink iced tea from Styrofoam cups.

"Well, Vernon. What now?" Jody and Vernon sit at a table alone.

Vernon squirms in his chair. "Me, I've got a couple more weeks of work, then I'm a free man. Don't know what I'll do, but I'll be a free man. How 'bout you? What's your plan?"

"I've got to get a few things straightened out here with the house. I'm just going to let it sit for the time being, get back down here to get it sold when I've got a little time this summer. Then I've got to figure out about John David. The guy I live with has a cat, and I don't think they'd get along too well."

"Well, I'm glad you don't have to hurry back. It's been real good to see you again."

"Actually, I do have to get back. My work needs me. I may even go in a couple days. I don't know. Boss is calling me every day, I know that."

Vernon looks all around, wipes his face with his hand, stares away. "You know what, Jody. I don't know what I'm going to do. I don't really have anybody else to tell that to. But I don't know what I'm going to do."

Jody squeezes Vernon's shoulder. "You'll be all right. Just be an adjustment."

"Yeah, you're right, Jody. Like it says in the good book, God protects the ignorant, right?" Vernon smiles big, as big as he can, but Jody sees right through it. His face is as sad as Jody's father's was the day he brought Scooter home from the hospital.

CHAPTER 34

Vernon doesn't feel his usual numbness when he pulls into the parking lot at work the next morning. Today his stomach is twisted in hollow knots. Maybe, he considers, he's just off from missing two days already this week. Vernon never misses work. For some time Vernon has found a way to manage himself from day to day, to feel even the most rudimentary hope each day as he drives to work. But today only the unsettledness remains.

He turns the corner of the lot toward his parking space, only to see the blue pickup truck parked there again. He waits for this to give him some sort of a rise, and he pulls to the side and sits for half a minute, just looks at the Confederate flag in the back window of the truck, expecting a wall of anger to hit him. But it never comes. He'll just have to let it go today. He parks next to the kid's truck, takes a few snorts, and gets out. The whiskey makes him groggy again, and he stops before going in the door to shake his head loose. But no matter how much he wants it, he can't feel the indignation he is waiting for. Finally, he goes on inside.

Caroline doesn't even say anything to him as he walks in,

just looks up and smiles, reaches out and touches his hand when he leans onto her desk to punch his time card. As he walks down the hallway toward the locker room, all the guys who pass him say something, "Sorry about your brother, he was a hell of a man," or maybe just smile. But he never says anything back, never "Thank you," never even smiles. Vernon feels a giant hollow spot inside his chest, like maybe his body is filled with helium and he is going to float away. And just be out of this place.

He goes into the locker room and begins to change his clothes. Everybody in there is silent, which isn't the usual course of things. But somewhere on the other side of the room, possibly even out in the hall, he hears Johnny Summers's baritone voice, making a joke or laughing about something. And for an instant the sound of it makes a little jolt in him, pricks him with the slightest little bit of irritation. Even in his state of unrest he knows, and thinks half aloud, that the jerk should have known not to park in his spot today.

Vernon finishes getting dressed and leans down to tie his boots. He registers again that his boots need oiling, but with Leonard and all he just hasn't taken them home to do it. That and the fact that he's almost done with this place. As he ties them, Vernon sees a few raised spots where the leather is really starting to wear, and one in particular on his left boot, where the material stretches over the steel toe, could break through soon if he doesn't watch it. For all of his career he has taken good care of his boots, has been fastidious about replacing them before the leather wears through. But, today, he just reaches down and rubs the spot, feels its roughness, smells the oil and old dried mud that has tried to work its way into his feet for as long as he has had this job. He probes with his index finger along the edges of the abrasion, runs a finger down the stitches that are trying to give way.

He sits there a minute, until his head begins to clear.

When he stands, Vernon feels a sudden bloat in his stomach and belches one time. What comes up from his throat is more than just air, and he feels the burn and tastes the bitter acid in the back of his mouth. He swallows it back down. He stands up and closes his locker, gently. As the whistle blows for the night shift to head out, he opens and walks through the door to do his work.

For the last couple months, since right after they finished the grueling three weeks of double shifts involved in the annual shutdown of the number three paper machine, Vernon's boss Charlie Haystack has been taking it pretty easy on him. And of course after all those long days, the first week or so of puttering around just doing little odd jobs around the boilers or greasing those machine parts that only had to be greased once a year was fine with him. But after the second week he was feeling back to his old self again, as spry and strong as any thirty-year-old, and for a couple of days had really resented being sort of sent out to pasture. But then things with Leonard got real serious, Jody showed up again, and just finishing out his time was working fine after all. For the two days Vernon has been at work this week, Charlie has had him working on building a little lean-to on the back side of the building that houses the number four boiler. Just a place to store some old rolls of rubber flooring and stuff. Vernon walks through the sticky heat of the plant to the back side of the building. When he gets out there, everything is right where he left it. All the lumber is stacked against the wall, the sacks of nails and the small toolbox Charlie checked out from central supply for him are wedged under the lumber.

Vernon picks up all the materials and tools and lays everything out the way he likes. A hammer on either end of the project, sacks of nails here and there, the toolbox laid open right in the middle. He clips the tape measure onto his belt and feels that rise in his stomach coming back, then again the reflux of whiskey and acid in his throat. He chokes it down. He stands back and looks at all the wood. After a minute he remembers exactly what his plan was. Just before quitting time the other day he had figured out the best way was to build the roof of the thing in eight-foot sections. After he gets done with those, he figures, he'll go find Charlie and get him or have him send one of the other guys down to help him start standing it up. Or maybe he'll just say the hell with all of them and do it himself.

He lays out the wood for the first roof section, lines it all up, and proceeds to nail the thing together. That takes him a half hour or so—Vernon has a good sense of time though he has never worn a watch—and then he lays out the next section and knocks it all together too. A few times as he's working he thinks about Leonard, sees the honor guardsmen raise their rifles, hears the crank as his brother is lowered into the humid earth. But each time he does, he shakes it off and keeps working.

As he lays out the boards for the third roof section, Vernon notes that he's short one twelve-foot two-by-four, though he does have two extra six-foot sections. He mutters to himself. "Shouldn't have cut that one back there. I knew that wasn't right." He reaches down and picks up one of the six-foot sections, doesn't know why he does this but he just does, and when he stands back up he gets that reflux in his throat again and this time it really hurts and he leans over and throws up a little bit. A wave of heat crawls from his neck up both of his ears. He tastes that bile in his mouth again and just spits it out as hard as he can. And still the taste won't go completely away.

Vernon walks back toward the central supply room. He knows it's a long walk, and knows it's a waste of time for him to be doing this, that he had all the materials already and if he hadn't screwed up he'd be done with the roof frame and ready to have Charlie get him some help down there now. He just wants to scream. As he walks he keeps having thoughts of his brother and he keeps fighting them down. He carries that board in his hand and slung over his shoulder like a rifle. He continues toward the supply room, past the number one and number two paper machines. Vernon passes Robert Millie in the corridor; they've never been friends really and Robert just says "Hey, Vernon" to him kind of nicely. Vernon never even smiles; he just glances for a second over at Robert, maybe nods almost imperceptibly, and walks on. Just like before, all the guys he meets as he walks lower their voices when they see him. Some of them say hello, some of them just nod. Most of them, he doesn't even know their names, but it all seems right to him; he doesn't feel too good but other than that everything is okay.

Vernon turns the last corner inside the building before he gets back outside to the wood supply room and meets Johnny Summers walking toward him in his gigantic hardhat. There's another young guy with him, his name is right on the tip of Vernon's tongue but he can't say it at that moment. The other guy pulls his hardhat off just as they meet and pushes his hair back out of his face, then slides the helmet back on. The door where the two of them walked in is still hanging open, and the wind is blowing pretty hard and Vernon hears it howling in through that door and smells the stench of the paper-making process blowing in. What Johnny Summers says to him catches him completely by surprise.

"You got something to say to me, old man?"

Vernon feels a tingle form immediately in his shoulder, and jump from there to his jaw. Then he feels that same tingling in his other jaw, like he's about to throw up. He chokes a little and the feeling passes, and he draws in a breath and regains his sense.

"I got lots to say to you, kid. But not today." Then, mumbling, "I'm gon' save it for another day."

Summers cackles loudly. "You gonna save it for another day! Save what for another day? What you got to say to me?"

Vernon feels a tightness in his upper chest, tastes that acid trying to climb up into his throat again. He sets the board down on end and leans it against the wall. He closes his eyes, rubs his temples.

"Like I say, save it for another day."

"Well, what's wrong with today? You got something to say to me, old man, say it today! Good a day as any!"

Vernon's face flushes hot. He jumps right back. "Kid, you're pushing your luck today. I'm sure you know my brother died yesterday and I'd just as soon not mess with you."

Summers looks down at Vernon with a look of pity, draws his breath in as if he's been practicing his lines. "Hmm. Your brother died yesterday, huh. Too bad. But old farts die. That's what happens. Screwworms got to eat too. While I've got you here, though, I've got something to say to you. I been thinking about it, and I'm gonna go ahead and take that parking space."

Vernon is dead silent. He stands perfectly still, feels his knees lock, his entire body almost freeze in place. For an instant his face flushes, but then it passes and his face becomes still too. A freshet of sweat bursts from his forehead and drips down onto his cheeks.

Summers turns once and looks over at his friend. The other man doesn't look back at him, only hangs his head toward the floor. Then Summers turns back to Vernon. "Yeah, I'm gonna take that parking space. That's gonna be mine now. Even if you get here first, I suggest you don't take it, if you know what's good for you. And as for your brother, I know he used to work here, but I guess I don't have to worry about him taking my parking space, now do I?" With that he turns again toward his friend and tilts his massive head back to laugh.

Until that moment Vernon had always given the kid the benefit of the doubt. Johnny Summers was young and stupid, an overgrown child with no idea of what the future held, of the agony life would, eventually, hand over to him. He was clueless of those things as Vernon himself had once been. But it is only this last, the bald contempt of his words, that brings Vernon, finally, unhinged.

The next sound Vernon hears is the riffling wind of the two-by-four, flat side forward in the air. The board cracks the Summers kid in the neck just above his gigantic shoulders. With the sound of the connection the other man takes off at a dead run toward the exit. The board snaps and the last third of it flies forward and clops on the concrete floor, skids across until it slides right out the door in front of the other man. Before his knees even bend, Johnny Summers falls straight down onto his face. From the floor he turns his bloody face up toward Vernon, but before he can think about getting up Vernon's boot is in his side. Vernon feels the pressure change in his foot, hears the sickening snap of bone and cartilage, smells the tangy ether of the blood slowly spreading across the concrete. Summers tries to turn and grab Vernon's foot but misses, and Vernon pulls his foot back and plants it now in Johnny Summers's stomach. Then Vernon lays what remains of the board in the middle of Summers's back. The kid lets out an enormous shout and Vernon kicks him again, then whacks him twice more with the stick just below his neck. Vernon looks down at him and screams.

"Do you think I'm dead! Do you think I'm dead you son of a bitch! I'm not dead! My mama and my daddy are dead, my brothers are dead, my son is dead, but I'm not dead you bastard!" Vernon feels the bile again, smells the iron scent of blood. Then, in an instant, he regains his composure, feels a swelling in his chest that pushes out any remaining confusion. He bends over the moaning mess of Johnny Summers. Again his voice is cool. There is a shudder in his throat. His lips draw tight and he breathes with labor through his nose. He leans

over the younger man and a single drop of Vernon's sweat falls on Johnny Summers's blue shirt and spreads outward in a darkening circle. Vernon belches and tastes bile again, and then again, and then it is more. Only in a last second of decency does he turn and throw up in the other direction, away from the bloody mess writhing like a run-over snake on the floor.

"I'm not dead yet," he half whispers now, then throws the board down next to Summers and it clatters across the floor as he walks out.

Vernon doesn't stop to speak to anyone. He walks directly to the parking lot, feels like he's going to explode. He moves in as straight a line as he can to his truck, gets in, and starts it up. When he slides his foot over to work the clutch pedal, a glint of light catches his eye and he looks down to see the steel of his boot peeking through the ruined leather. Before he can stop himself he tears backward out of his spot, then floors the gas pedal and slams full bore into the driver's side of Johnny Summers's truck, watches the glass shatter and hears the crumpling screech as he slowly backs away, leaving the bumper and most of the grill of his own truck scattered on the asphalt. Then he tears backward again, turns and flies out of the parking lot.

Later, when retelling the story, Vernon says he doesn't remember the drive home. He only guesses from the odometer that he drove straight there and didn't stop for anything. When he gets home he rushes into the house, squeezes the mustard bottle as hard as he can into his glass, fills the rest with Jack, slugs it down, then quickly makes another one. As he squeezes the mustard for the second drink, everything from the first round rushes back up out of his stomach and he vomits it all into the sink. Then he grabs the mustard jar, grabs the whiskey bottle, and slams them hard into the sink. The plastic mustard bottle bounces back out, but the whiskey shatters and the room is filled with the sullen smell. Without even undoing his bootlaces Vernon staggers over to his easy chair, falls into it, grabs the handle and slides it to recline, then quickly falls asleep.

CHAPTER 35

Vernon stands at the counter cutting slices from a brick of cheese the size of a lunchbox. He still has his work clothes on. As he had on the phone, when he begins to speak he sounds exhausted. He continues to cut slices from the cheese until John David begins to scratch on the door. Vernon puts the knife down, walks over, and lets him in. The dog jumps up onto Vernon's worn-out sofa, turns two circles, and lies down to sleep.

Vernon butters the bread on one side, then places the bologna and sliced cheese on the other side of half of the slices. He lays the remaining slices, butter side up, on top of the other, squeezes four sandwiches into his frying pan. After a minute the pan begins to lightly hiss.

"Not used to making four." He adjusts the sandwiches in the pan. "No room in the inn. I hope John David don't want one."

"He's sleeping." The dog snores loudly on the sofa.

Vernon reaches into the cabinet and brings down a bottle of whiskey. He looks at it for half a minute, appears to read the label. Then he cracks open the lid, sets it down on the counter, squeezes half an inch of mustard into his glass, pours in three fingers of the whiskey. He picks up the glass and looks at it, swirls the oily substance around. Then he sets it back on the counter.

Vernon turns the sandwiches, tends to them with his spatula. When they are finished he puts two on each plate, cuts them into triangles with a knife. He hands Jody a plate, picks up the other plate, and starts toward his chair. Jody sits down on the part of the sofa John David has left open.

"Oh, wait." Vernon retrieves two glass bottles of Dr Pepper from the refrigerator, pops the lids, and brings them into the living room. He hands one to Jody, who takes it and holds the cold bottle to his face.

"So what you got going, Jody?"

"I've been cleaning out the house today. Thinking about Daddy. Thinking about old times. I sure wish my brother had been there."

Vernon takes a bite, a long drink from the bottle. "You did what you could, Jody. He had his chance. Had it handed to him. You couldn't have made it any easier for him."

"I know. But still. I wish he had been there. Of course. There's a lot of things I wish."

"I imagine."

"You got something on your mind, Vernon?"

"Yeah. Had a little trouble at work today."

"With the guy I met?"

"That's the one. Afraid I had to show him what's what. He pushed me to where I didn't have a choice anymore."

"What happened?"

"I guess I'll see when I go back next week. If I go back." He raises his head, suddenly looks hopeful. "Hey Jody, I guess you're in charge now. It all right with you if I catch some fish at y'all's pond one day?"

"Of course it is. What made you think of that?"

Vernon shifts in his chair, takes on a rueful look. "I think about it all the time."

"About fishing?"

"Yeah. I guess I think about it more this time of year. In the spring. Me and Billy would be tearing up the fish this time of year if he was still here. We used to when he was a boy."

"I remember Daddy talking about that."

"I wonder if he'd still go fishing with me."

"What do you mean, Vernon? Of course he would."

"Oh. You never know. Things change. Maybe he would have moved off somewhere and married somebody and never would have wanted to see his old daddy again. I don't know."

"What I remember about Billy, I bet he wouldn't have gone far from here."

"Yeah, maybe. Look here, I wanted to show you something." Vernon goes into the kitchen, opens a cabinet, takes out a notebook, and carries it back to set it on the coffee table in front of Jody.

"I found this going through some things the other day." Vernon pulls a sealed plastic bag out of the notebook, unfolds it, and sets it down on the table. Inside the bag is a picture drawn in a child's hand. The paper is yellow with age, worn around the edges. Drawn in a faded blue are two stick figures, one smaller than the other, twists of hair drawn over the foreheads. The stick people, man and boy, hold fishing poles, butt ends on the ground, the tips extended over their heads, bent into hooks from the weight of the smiling fish hanging from them. The stick people also have smiles on their faces. Under the larger one is written, in block letters, *DADDY.* Under the smaller, *ME.*

Vernon reaches out to touch the picture with one gentle finger. "He brought that home from school one day. Must be twenty-something years ago now." Vernon smiles as if at something internal. "That boy loved to bait a fishing pole. Jody?"

"Yes?"

"You got a minute?"

"Sure. I've got all day."

Vernon moves into his chair. "Do you remember when Billy was born?"

"Not really. I was only a few weeks old."

"Oh yeah. Of course." Vernon leans back in the chair, methodically twists the Dr Pepper bottle on the arm of his chair, an eighth of a turn at a time. "Well, I was thinking about the day we brought him home. Misty and me. EL and Pearl and your daddy, they told me I wouldn't have to do too much with him when he was a baby." Vernon continues to twist the bottle.

"They said maybe when he was four or five I could start to talk to him when he was ready to play games or fish or do things like that."

"Sounds like something my father would say. EL too, from what I remember. But what would Pearl know about having children?"

"Pearl thought he knew about a lot of things. But I'm going to tell you something, Jody. It was a *real* surprise. I mean a real surprise how I felt about that little thing. I never did want to stop holding him. He'd cry at night and Misty would sleep right through it. But I'd be up like a flash.

"I was about your age when Billy was born. And I can still remember it like it was yesterday. Holding that little thing, him looking up at me with those pretty eyes. Squeezing my finger. There wasn't no reason for me holding him so much, really. I just enjoyed it and he liked it too. Your daddy and them said I was spoiling him, I was too easy on him."

Jody interjects. "Vernon. I've met all kinds of people brought up all kinds of different ways. In my work. The ones that do the best are the ones that know they are loved. That know they have a place in the world."

"Well, you know how EL raised us. But he never laid a hand on me for any reason."

"Daddy always said that."

"Still left a lot of room for improvement as a father, though. Anyway, maybe it was because Billy was an only child, he was always more mature, always wanted to talk about things with me. I didn't really know what to say to him. I just did what seemed natural. He acted mature, I treated him like he was mature. Like he could make his own decisions. A lot of people thought that was strange too, but his mother and I felt it was the best way to go. We just let him be who he was. Even after Misty and I divorced, we still talked and worked things out together. We tried to teach him right from wrong. We took him to church. Hey. You remember the time them pro wrestlers came down here?"

"I don't think so."

"Yeah. They came down here one time. Billy was about five then. Had a whole bunch of those guys you'd see Saturday afternoon on Mid South Wrestlin' on TV. Jake the Snake, Skandor Akbar, the Junkyard Dawg. The headliner, Andre the Giant, was supposed to be there. And I'm telling you, that little tyke was so excited to go see 'em fight. Even though of course it was all fake."

"Did you go?"

"Oh yeah." Vernon takes a long drink of his soda, empties it, then proceeds to turn the bottle in increments again. "But they had the show one Sunday evening after church, about seven o'clock. We tried to get him to take a nap that afternoon, but he was way too excited. Couldn't sleep. So we went over there and we waited and waited for Andre the Giant to come out in the ring. It got to be eight o'clock, then nine o'clock. Billy was just fighting to keep his eyes open. He was trying everything. The place was packed. We had pretty good seats down on the floor not far from the ring. I asked him if he wanted to go home, and he said no sir, he didn't. *Wanted to see the Giant.* Said he wanted to go to sleep down on the dirty floor and for me to wake him up when the Giant came out."

"Oh no."

"Oh yeah. And that floor was dirty. This one jerk next to us was chewing Red Man and had knocked over his spit cup on the floor. So I put my jacket down on the floor and he laid down there. And Billy hadn't so much as closed his eyes and here come the Giant. Son! I never seen anybody like it. Walked right down the aisle not as far as you are from me. Tall as that ceiling. Head twice the size of a regular man's. Big ol' flop of curly hair, made his head look even bigger."

"So you got Billy up?"

"Tried to. Tried everything. Set him in my lap, bounced him up and down. Slapped his face a little bit. I even had a paper cup of ice that melted and poured some of that cold water over his head! The things you do for your kids. But he never even opened an eye."

"Oh no."

"Oh yeah. So I just watched the show. It was fun. But stupid. Just as fake as it looks on TV. When it was finally over I waited for the crowd to clear out. I was walking and carrying him back to the truck and finally he woke partway up. Didn't really open his eyes, but he said a few words. *'Did the Giant fight, Daddy? Where's the Giant?'* Said it in that little boy voice. Voice as sweet as honey."

Vernon begins to cry silently now. He makes no attempt to wipe away the tears. "Do you remember how he died?"

"I remember."

"His eighteenth birthday. He asked me before if he and some of his friends could have a fire out there in the yard, have a few beers and camp out. And I told him it wasn't right. I didn't want him to start drinking alcohol and mess up his life. Everything was going so good for him. I didn't see how anything good could have come of it. He pleaded with me, said what's it going to hurt, we'll just be out there in the yard, nobody'll have to drive home until the next day."

"You know he was crazy about you."

Tears run like raindrops down Vernon's face. "Why was he like that, Jody? Why was he so good?"

"Because you loved him."

"No. No. I can't take responsibility. Not for that."

"You're right. Not completely. Partly it was just the way he was."

"But I was supposed to protect him. To take care of him. I was his father."

"You did your job, Vernon. Billy was a miracle. You did a wonderful job as his father. He was very wise. I remember that."

"Yes he was. You said it exactly right. He was a miracle." Vernon balls his hands into fists. He slaps his legs with his fists.

"I just wish I'd let him have his party here."

"It's not your fault he died, Vernon."

Vernon jumps up from the chair. He knocks over the coffee table, spilling dishes, and stands over Jody. "Yes it is my fault!" He slaps his hands on the back of his chair. "Yes it is! Yes it is!" He picks up a plate from the floor, grabs the empty bottle from the arm of his chair, flings them against the wall. They shatter in a shower of glass.

"I should have known not to teach him all those lies! I never should have loved him like that! Never! I never should have let that happen! But I did and look where it got him! Into the ground! Into the FILTHY GROUND!"

Jody grabs his uncle by both shoulders, bends down and under him to look Vernon in the face. Vernon fights, squirms out of his nephew's grasp. He tries to pick up his chair but Jody grabs him again from behind, holds on to him while he thrashes. Vernon cries in earnest now, great sobs and bursts of tears, and the salty water splashes onto Jody's hands. Vernon screams once, twice, three times. He screams as loud as he can, no words, only the sound. He thrashes in Jody's arms, fights to get away. He hooks a foot behind Jody's. John David jumps down quickly as the two men fall, held together, onto the couch, Vernon still screaming.

When he goes for a breath Jody speaks again, as calmly as he can. "It's not your fault he died, Vernon. It's nobody's fault. It just happened. It's nobody's fault."

In an instant, Vernon goes limp. He slides off the couch, slumps to the floor. Through the sobs he wails again. "He's in the ground! My boy is in the ground!"

For five minutes, neither says a word. Vernon sits slumped on the floor.

Jody bends again to look his uncle in the face. "He was a miracle, Vernon. He was. And now he's ready for you to let him go. Billy would want that. There's work left for you here."

Vernon just nods. For several more minutes they both are silent. Finally, Vernon gets up, walks to the back of the house.

When he comes out again he holds another drawing. He hands it over to Jody, sits back down in his chair.

Three stick figures play basketball. Two figures are standing, watching the basket, and the third has his arms extended.

"You know your cousin was quite a basketball player."

"I remember."

"Well, let me tell you. Nobody ever would have predicted it when he was little. When he drew that picture I think he was in second grade. He played with the other boys in a church league. Back when I was still part of the church. Billy was kind of skinny, he wasn't all that athletic when he was a little boy, he wore glasses. And if he ever got that ball in his hands he couldn't even get it up in the air, much less make a basket."

"Doesn't sound like my cousin."

"Well it was, at that age. So one day the coach was busy

after church and asked me to fill in. It wasn't much of a job really, just run around on the court and help the kids play. They were playing and the ball got loose and hit one kid in the leg, I can't remember his name, the kid was standing there at the top of the key." Vernon begins to laugh. "The boy wasn't paying attention, he looked like he was counting something on his fingers. Oblivious to the game. Ball caroms off his leg and goes toward the basket. Well, it must have gone right to Billy, and by the time I turned he was standing there next to his friend the Staples boy. Billy had his hands spread out like he had just shot the ball. The ball was in the air. It was a perfect shot. Nothing but the net."

"All right! Good shot, Billy!"

"I can't get that face out of my head. No matter how much I drink. I can't get the picture of his face that day out of my head."

"I understand."

"But at the same time. I'm scared to lose that picture. I'm scared to stop seeing that face."

"You know what I think, Vernon?"

Vernon only shakes.

"You don't need to forget his face. And you don't need to worry you might forget it. Billy's right here with you. He came to earth and lived the life he was meant to live. But he's still here with you. I believe that. And I have another idea."

"What's that?"

"Something I learned from another family I know. They lost a son too. A brother. Robert was his name. He was just a boy when he died. His father, his mother, my friends Robert's brother and sister, they say they still think about him all the time. It's been twenty-five years. But they do something special to remember him. On the day he passed away. And anytime they feel like it really. Why can't we do something like that for Billy?"

"I guess we could."

"I know what we can do. It's next week, right? His birthday?"

"That's right."

"Here's what we'll do. You come up to the house and we'll go down to the pond. Or we can go somewhere else if you like. Let's catch some fish. We can catch some fish for Billy."

When Vernon sees the flashing lights, he moves with purpose to the door. Two officers stand at the entrance when he opens it. Their arms are crossed. They both are young, barely beyond childhood, and Vernon feels a pinch of empathy for the boys, for the youthful certainty written on their faces.

He raises his hands. "I won't give you any trouble. I'm ready. I can go peacefully now."

CHAPTER 36

He wakes in his old bedroom, the first gray fingers of light feeling into the room along the ceiling. The night was short, spent late at the Branden Parish courthouse until Vernon was finally released on his own recognizance at three o'clock in the morning. He doesn't remember driving back, though it was only four hours ago. He makes coffee, takes it outside to sit in the tree swing and watch the day begin. A duck waddles out of the pond, makes its way across the yard. John David looks up from his slumber on the floor of the carport, then lies back down, less interested in the bird than the cool concrete. An old neighbor drives by. Jody never did know his name, only that he lives another mile or two up the road and that he never used to stop or wave. And still does neither. Absent from his time in the swing is Scooter's music, though a steady wind does blow through the spring leaves of the tree's branches, reaching like giant wooden arms toward heaven.

He gets another cup of coffee and sets out for a drive. He has no particular goal, and if anything he works to keep thoughts out of his mind. He shifts and turns and shifts and turns past fields of cows, pines that look to be a mile high, billowy clouds moving slowly across the sky, doing absolutely nothing to filter hotness from the face of the earth.

Art's call had woken him. Art had offered the car in exchange for his timely return. The road rolls by. *I've made a decision, Art.* In town, he passes through the parking lot of Walmart, taps the horn at Gary Wayne, who closes the door behind a lady getting into his car. Gary Wayne raises an arm and tilts his head, as if in deference. He continues past the mill, lowers the window of the truck to hear the giant machines' unceasing roar. As Jody passes over the track, Peterson removes his hardhat and tips it to him, shouts, "Hey, Leonard," as the young man carries on.

I saw my brother. He's all on his own now and he's doing just fine. Did I tell you about the tree swing? I'd like to sit there with you and tell you stories you've never heard before.

Jody drives to the edge of town, where plenty of kids in his youth thought the world just stopped. But today he sees only an expanse of blue and all the green of God's beautiful earth and a wide open future of promise, a grand scheme of time and possibility. All the radio stations are staticky except the closest one, a country station out of Ruston. The singer tells a tale of love and loss in a down-home voice; then the singing stops and he begins to blow a harmonica. Jody reaches for the volume. Not too high, not too low. The perfect sound for a song played just for him.

This is the thing we call life
Sometimes you win
Sometimes you lose
Sometimes you even get to choose

He drives until he's tired of driving. Then he turns the truck and heads again toward his house. The sun is setting now, and he passes through town as the lights begin to flicker on at the mill. Peterson is gone but his broom remains, leaned in place against the switching shack. Nearly home, he approaches the hill where they first saw the snow that night, he and his father, that night more than half his life ago but only an instant in the calendar of the world. He isn't sure what he'll find on the other side. But he knows it will be a scene of its own making, a mixture of what came before and the stunning particulars of this one God-given day. When he reaches the top he keeps going, on and on ahead, on a road that does not seem to end.

CHAPTER 37

At ten thirty Sunday morning, Jody parks at the end of Front Street, Natchitoches. Vernon reaches through the open window to pat John David on the head.

"It's plenty cool out here, so why don't you just leave the window halfway down and he'll be all right. Then come on."

"Where are we going, Vernon? You've had me wondering since you called me so early."

"Just come on. Before I lose my nerve."

Jody follows, as asked. Vernon heads straight for the front door of the church.

"Vernon. What are we doing?"

"Just follow me inside. I want to sit in the back row."

The sign above the door reads Enter Reverently. Vernon doesn't know the spring is broken, and the door slams against the back wall. In his long absence, the Sunday morning service has been moved from ten thirty to ten o'clock. So, when Vernon walks into the First Baptist Church for the first time in a dozen years, everyone knows it.

At the sound, heads turn. Vernon stands in the aisle, looks

around with a wild face on, holds the cap he has removed from his head in both his hands.

The church is silent. Then, slowly, a low murmur builds up, some shuffling of feet, hymnal pages turning, a few stray whispers. But not a soul exclaims. Everyone is waiting for the cue. For at pertinent points in a service, whether the end of a moving sermon, the final note of a schoolgirl's performance of a special song, or the baptism of a new member, there is silence. Until the proper person, whether chosen, elected, or self-appointed, gives the cue.

Jody scans the room for who it will be. Everyone in the place is looking, except for one mother who is shushing a crying baby. But the cries of a baby don't count. A little boy says he needs to go pee-pee, tries to force himself past his father into the aisle. But these words don't count either. Not the indiscriminate noises of children.

Finally comes the cue. "Ay-men," the voice booms. A chorus of ay-mens follows. The couple in the back slides down in their pew, and Vernon sits himself on the end of the row. Jody follows.

The young preacher David Adams had been in the middle of his sermon when they entered. Like the others he waits for the cue, and then, when the din dies down, he proceeds.

The minister removes the microphone from his lapel and sets it down on the lectern, then walks down two steps to the floor. He moves straight toward them. He steps into the row to stand in front of the entrants, places both hands on top of Vernon's head, whispers a few words only Vernon can hear. Vernon looks to the floor. Then the reverend moves his hands lower to both sides of Vernon's face, and pulls Vernon's cheeks upward to smile at him.

"Oh, Vernon. God bless you, Vernon." David Adams kisses the crying man on his forehead. Then he moves back into the aisle, makes his way to the lectern, and repositions his microphone.

Like our God, all of us have lost someone or something. A brother, a sister, a mother, a father, a daughter, a son. Our hearing, our sight. Our innocence. Our faith. Someone, or something we thought we couldn't live without. Maybe our lives have been changed by things or events we never, ever would have expected. Maybe we have found ourselves on the receiving end of love and good fortune we never felt we deserved. And maybe those things were lost to us.

But like our God, our job as those who remain is to carry on. And not only to carry on but to live with a higher purpose. To glorify God with our behavior. To be family to our family and to those without a family. To be friend to our friends and to those who have no friends. To find the place God means for us to be.

When God made the world, he had a picture of how he wanted it to turn out. Just like any of us does when we start a project or create something. Just like we all have ideas when we're young of how we want our own lives to be. Maybe some of you wanted to be athletes or movie stars in Hollywood. But there was one problem. God gave us the freedom to choose. And we didn't always choose well. Starting with Adam and Eve.

I know what some of you are thinking. And whatever you do, don't blame Eve. Adam was the one who opened his mouth and ate that apple. What happened next, all of us know. After a while there was only one way to fix the mess.

> *God sent his son to earth. His only son. Now friends, if God created this world, and everything in it, in his own image, do we really believe he wanted to have to send his son down to die for us? Do we?*
>
> *I don't think so. God didn't want his only son to have to die. And Jesus was a human being just like us. A person with normal needs, wants, wishes. But God's son had a place to fill and he chose to fill it. Maybe he wanted to do otherwise. But he found his place and he knew it, and he did the job he was sent here to do. God didn't want to lose his son. He didn't. But he did it for us.*
>
> *That's how much God loved us. How much God wanted us to live in his world.*
>
> *Sometimes we feel like we can't fill our places. I certainly feel that way. I'd be willing to bet that many of you do too. But here's a thought. Not an original one, but a good one nonetheless. During the hard times, let us all remember this. From the words of the Apostle Paul.*
>
> *If God is with us, who can be against us?*

David Adams reaches under his lectern, pulls something out. He holds it up, moves it back and forth, raps it with his knuckles. He runs a hand over it as if doing magic, then holds it up again.

> *Can everybody see what this is? It's a rock. A simple rock. And no matter what I do, what words I say over it, it's still just a rock. And neither I nor anybody in this room can do anything*

to change that. I can't turn it into bread. But through his son, our God turned a rock, a rock not much different from this one, into bread.

And fed his people. Now if God, our God, who works in us and through us can turn rock into bread, what can't he do? And with God on our side, what can't we do?

Nothing.

We sometimes feel like we've lived with too much.

That we've been given crosses too great to bear. For those of you who have children, I have a question. And even for those who don't have children, try to imagine. Would you give your child a task he couldn't bear? Would you make her withstand things you knew she didn't have the strength to withstand? Of course not.

In difficult times, friends, let us remember this. In God's eyes, we all are his children. And if we let him, if we don't squirm away, he will hold us in his hands.

We can never know all that life has in store for us. For there is more wisdom about what God intends for us as his children, there is more understanding of God's plan in a newborn baby with its mother's blood still on its face than in a hundred-year-old wise man who has been around the world and seen everything.

We will never know all our God has in store for us. We can only open our hearts to the mystery. And, in doing so, allow our love to flow like a river, to mix in the great river of love with those whose love surrounds us.

When the sermon ends, there is silence. Then, after what seems like minutes, the baritone man again gives the cue. Suddenly a chorus of voices can be heard, and just like that a general murmur erupts and everyone is standing up. Over the din David Adams speaks.

"The Lord our God said, my peace I bring unto you, I give you my peace. And let us greet one another with the sign of peace."

People from aisles around are on top of Vernon, everyone shaking his hand, patting his back, hugging him. Vernon can barely look at any of them but he does his best, blinking at faces through the fog in his eyes.

"It's good to see you again, brother," one says.

"Praise God, look who's back," says another. "The prodigal son."

"I'm glad to see you with your clothes on again, Vernon," someone says. Vernon tries to stifle his laugh, but he can't. He leans back and laughs and Jody stands next to the uncle that he used to know. All the hands and the prayers and the love surrounding him.

When everyone has gone back to their seats, more hymns are sung. People take turns raising their hands and making requests. An elderly woman asks for "The Old Rugged Cross." A little girl asks the congregation to follow her in "Jesus Loves Me." Then "Love Lifted Me" with a waltz beat.

David Adams stands at the podium. "Vernon? Any requests?"

Shakily, Vernon stands. "Doesn't matter. Just whatever y'all want to sing. Just something pretty."

"Oh well then, ladies and gentlemen, I know it is not our custom, I know we don't normally sing it here at the end. But I've got a real special feeling about this day, and about some of the things God has in store for us. Praise God, there's a lot of rejoicing among the angels in heaven this morning! Would everybody please join me in singing my own favorite hymn." The organist raises one hand to adjust her oversize glasses, then lays down three unmistakable chords.

Praise God from whom all blessings flow
Praise Him all creatures here below
Praise Him above ye heavenly host
Praise Father, Son, and Holy Ghost

After the postservice coffee, after the crowd has cleared away, after more people touch and shake and hug Vernon than probably have for all the other days of his life put together, Jody and Vernon stand talking in the park. The early afternoon rays are beginning to peek into the cab of Jody's truck. John David hangs his head on the windowsill. Finally Jody lets the dog out to run in the park. They each take a seat on swings, which hang under the double shade of a magnolia overpowered by a giant cedar tree. The air underneath is cool, damp. The canvas seats of the swings smell like earth. The dog tears around in the grass before stopping to bark at a butterfly. A boy from the church throws a stick for him and he races off to get it, brings it back, and drops it at the boy's feet.

"Jody, did I ever tell you about Dodson?"

"Who's Dodson?"

"He was an old sheepdog your daddy and Pearl and me had. Dang that was fifty-something years ago." Vernon kicks the ground, rocks in his swing. "Pearl and your daddy, they were always trying to fight him, roughhouse with him. He loved us all, believe me. And they never hurt him or anything."

Jody pulls a blade of grass, chews it. "So whose dog was he? Who would you say he loved the most?"

"He was mine. Like I say, them other boys were pretty rough on him, but me, I just loved him. We had a big hill out behind our house, I used to wrestle with him out there, roll around on the grass. And then he'd start pushing me toward the hill with his nose and I'd grab on to him and we'd roll down the hill. Rolling down that hill, over and over, all held together."

"No, I never heard about Dodson. Sounds like a part of the family."

"That he was."

"How are you feeling, Vernon?"

"I don't even know how to say it. I feel like I need a drink but then at the same time that's the last thing I want. But I'll get through it.

"You know I never cared for alcohol," Vernon adds. "I never took to it. I guess it's just helped me get through the days."

"I can believe that. I never cared for it either. Maybe I should come home with you, make sure you're okay."

"Can you come over in the morning?"

"Sure."

The dog runs over, panting, drops the stick at Jody's feet. Vernon throws it and John David tears off.

"Jody, there was something else I been meaning to tell you. When BF and Eddie were here for the funeral they told me the reunion is a week from Saturday."

"The Davidson family reunion? I haven't been there in a long time. Wow. It'd just be the two of us from this side. You think we'd still know everybody?"

"I think so. You can recognize your family by smell."

"Yeah, I'd love to go. Sounds like fun. So they still do the reunion on Saturday? I thought *Hee Haw* was off the air."

"Off the air? Yeah, it's off the air. But BF's got every episode they ever made on D-V-D. Says between that, *Dallas,* and *The Dukes of Hazzard* he watches one or two a day and still can't get through all of them in a year."

Jody laughs, picturing the old man leaning on his cane, bending over in front of the television to insert the disc in the player. "That's something. That's something. A ninety-two-year-old man taking pride in his DVD collection. But at his age it's good to have something to be excited about."

"Good at any age."

"You know, that may be the greatest television show ever made."

"Earline would have agreed with you. BF, he would say *Dallas*. Myself, I prefer that Bill Dance fishing show. Speaking of which. Can you still go with me on Thursday?"

"Sure. Are you coming to our house?"

"Actually I have a different place in mind, if that's okay."

"It's your day."

The two sit on the swings for a while longer, until John David gets tired of chasing the stick and comes over to lie at their feet.

"I'm getting hungry, Vernon. You want to go to Talton's with me? See if he's got any more stories to tell?"

"Oh, he's got stories to tell, don't doubt it. And those hot links do sound good on a fine Sunday afternoon. But I've got to get home to take a nap. I'm just whipped."

"Well, maybe I'll take John David out there, get him some. Like to see the look on his dog face when that hot pepper hits his tongue."

"I'm glad you said that, Jody. I've been meaning to ask you something. About John David."

"What about him?" The dog looks up, cocks his head at Vernon.

"Sounds like you're gonna be busy for a while, and I'm retired. 'Course he was Pearl's, then your daddy's. What do you think if he comes to live with me? I could sure use the company."

"Let's ask him." Jody walks to Vernon's truck, opens the door. "Hey, John David, you want to go stay with Vernon?"

The dog bounces up, tears across the grass, and jumps in. Then Jody closes the door and he hangs his head out the window.

"Looks like he's ready to go."

Vernon joins them, leans on the windowsill. "Well, all right. Don't he need to pack up or something? Anything I need to come up there and get for him?"

"No. He's packed. John David travels light."

"I thank you, Jody. You won't regret it. Your daddy and Pearl, this is what they would have wanted." Vernon reaches in and pats him, and John David turns to lick Vernon's hand. "Well, I'll be. First Pearl, then Leonard, and now me." Vernon smiles proudly, as happy as he has been in many, many years.

"Looks like John David knows where he belongs."

"So it seems."

"Looks like he's found his way home."

CHAPTER 38

Johnny Summers is so embarrassed at getting beat to a pulp by a man as old as Vernon that he insists on a cover-up. He drops all charges. To explain why he had to be carried out of the mill on a stretcher, Johnny has Charlie Haystack tell everyone he had a seizure, fell on his face, then broke his ribs kicking around on the floor. To keep Vernon's full retirement intact, Charlie Haystack sets out to fabricate timesheets dated for the six-week period before he actually started working in 1968. Haystack consults with Jody, who gives him a ream of a Gellert Specialty Papers product that, when baked at 350 degrees for an hour, yellows perfectly.

For a week Vernon stays home in bed. Dr. Spencer comes by with vials of sedative to help with the detoxification. Jody is with him around the clock, John David curled at the foot of Vernon's bed. Peterson drops in wearing his orange vest and hardhat, shares more tall tales with Jody as Vernon sleeps, until he finally has to get back to the train track for his afternoon sweeping. Talton Thibodaux stops over with cornbread and beans, a gallon of sweet tea and ice in a jar, and refuses to leave until Vernon eats and drinks. David Adams visits daily, lays his hands on Vernon's head, prays aloud that God in his great and bounteous wisdom and power return Vernon, healed, to the world of the living.

Vernon floats in and out of consciousness. His sleep is filled with dreams about Billy as a baby, as a toddler, as a boy, as a man. Each time he awakes, as Billy's life progresses, Vernon feels a peace about his son he has long forgotten. Each time he thinks about the crushing loss of the days and weeks and hours of his life Vernon stops himself, instead says a prayer as best he remembers how; for Billy, for Leonard, for Pearl, for EL. For himself. He sleeps through most of Billy's birthday. Jody assures his uncle that, when he is feeling better, the two of them will go wherever Vernon wants, to fish in Billy's honor.

Vernon has three tasks in mind when he is up again. He scours his house, takes out years' worth of junk, until the inside begins to look as clean as the outside. He and Jody drive into town, John David on the seat between them, to buy a washing machine. On the way back they stop at the nursery, bring home azaleas, marigolds, roses, hundreds of bulbs, a bougainvillea. Vernon spends afternoons outside, trimming, weeding, planting, and before long his yard is once again filled with color. As Vernon moves he works out mathematical rhythms in his head, thirty-two-note ditties to the tune of the Doxology. Each time he begins to feel a pang of sadness, a tug of desire for a drink, he recites one of the songs.

One day I'll see my son again
I'll do my work here until then
Lord keep your child who's left this world
Safe in your hands let him lie curled

The two drive north, headed for Big Boar Lake. In the back of the truck are their tackleboxes, a picnic lunch, rods and reels with shiny spinning lures already tied on. John David lies next to the basket, periodically lifts his head to sniff the bologna sandwiches inside made especially for him. Vernon points out the new sign at the Mt. Olive Church as they pass.

This is the day that the Lord hath made
Let us rejoice and be glad in it

"You like it, Jody? I bought that sign for them to replace their old one." Vernon smiles.

The two continue, cross the great Red River at Grand Ecore, turn onto the back route toward Branden. The road cuts through a soybean field, a couple of one-light towns, then again into woods, huge towering pines as far as they can see.

Vernon stares out the window, shuffles in his seat. "Jody? You in a hurry?"

"Not at all. It's your trip, Uncle Vernon. Karen doesn't get here until tomorrow afternoon."

"I think I'd like to run by someplace for a minute."

"Whatever you like."

The man walks out of the barn when they pull up the driveway. He is a large man and wears pressed blue jeans, a straw cowboy hat, black boots, a snap-front Western-style shirt. A smile spreads into dimples across his big, ruddy face when the two get out of the truck. He brushes horsehair from his clothes as they speak, his hands big as old-fashioned baseball gloves. He remembers meeting Vernon once, that one time after they bought the place, when Vernon stopped by with Billy. "With that handsome boy of yours," the man says. "I know it's been a long time, Vernon. I don't really know you. I heard what happened and I'm sorry for your loss. We lost a boy in Vietnam, so I know how you feel." The man's name is David. His wife is gone to visit her mother. He invites them in for tea.

The three go inside. Vernon and Jody sit in the living room

while David puts his hat on a rack in the foyer, goes into the kitchen. Vernon scans the room, looks back through the years. David strains the tea, pours in sugar, drops ice in glasses. He towers over the counter, nearly has to duck when he carries the tray in through the door. He asks Vernon if he likes retirement. David's been retired five years, says he spends most of his time now with his horses. David sits down, takes a long drink from his glass. The escaping fog clouds his face in mystery.

"Something I can do for you, Vernon?"

"No. Nosir. Just wanted to see the place."

David sets his glass down. "Well, boys. It's good to see y'all. Glad you came by. I don't get many visitors. I got a new Appaloosa this week. Need to let her walk a little bit. Would you fellows join me?" The three men stand, don their hats, go outside to the barn. David slips the halter and lead line over the filly, takes her into the corral. He scratches her jaw as he walks her out, talks to the animal in a soothing voice. He opens the gate, escorts her in, then exits himself, closes the gate, rejoins the others. They all watch the beautiful horse in the pen. David seems to be thinking.

"Vernon? Since I've got you here. Mind if I ask you a question?"

Vernon leans on the top rail of the corral, stares at the animal.

His hands shake.

"You know, there's something I've wondered about for a long time."

"Yes?"

"I never saw any sign of a horse here when we bought the place. Not a hoofprint, nothing."

"We never did have any horses."

David studies Vernon. "But y'all must have built this corral."

"My father built the corral."

"So he intended to get horses but he just never did?"

Vernon stares ahead. Jody and David both look on at him. Vernon purses his lips, squints.

"Y'all just never got any?"

"That was a long time ago."

David is stumped. He turns quizzically to Vernon, then away.

David slowly, deliberately folds up the cuffs of his shirt. "You got something on your mind, Vernon?" David squints against the sun, wrinkles in the corners of his eyes giving him a friendly look. His bittersweet smile lends weight to his gravity.

"Well. If Jeanie was here she'd say it sweeter, but . . . Vernon, I been around long enough to know when a man's got something on his mind."

Vernon's face is now a sheet of tears. He tries to force a smile himself.

"It's quite a story," he finally says.

David reaches a massive hand to touch Vernon's back, like the two are old friends. "Well, what is it, man? You've got me curious now. I'm all ears." Then adds, "You just go on and cry. I've been crying thirty years over my son. I'll wait."

Vernon blows out. The Appaloosa wanders, then goes to a bucket of water hanging from the top rail and noisily drinks.

"Like I say, it's quite a story."

"Well, Vernon. Here I am. Jeanie'll be gone all day. Y'all know how women get to talking."

Vernon wipes his face over and over, as if stalling for time. "Do you really want to hear about it?"

David throws his hands up. "If I was a cat I'd be dead by now. Do I look like I'm in a hurry? Hell, man. I'm retired." David laughs once. As if given permission, Vernon does too, feels everything inside him begin to settle.

"Did you ever meet my brother Pearl? Did he ever stop by here?"

"Kind of a short fellow? Bowl haircut?"

"That's Pearl."

"He came by a couple times, years back. Didn't want to come in the house, just wanted to stand out here like we are now." David adjusts his hat. "He wouldn't even tell me his name, just said he wanted to see the place. But I knew something was going on with him. He seemed kind of nervous."

"That was Pearl. He never told you anything about this corral?"

"No, but I never asked him anything. If he had come in the house, Jeanie would have asked him all kind of questions. Like I say, she's a lot better of an asker than I am."

"David. Is it all right with you if we go inside?"

"Sure. If y'all want to. I'm parched. I could use some more tea. Jeanie's a good cook but her tea's not as good as mine."

"If you don't mind. I've been wanting to come by here for a long time. And if you've got a minute to sit down. You seem like a kind man. There's some things I'd like to tell you."

ABOUT THE AUTHOR

Brian Holers was born in the Midwest and raised in the Louisiana Bible Belt, where he played baseball, fished, and made up stories for entertainment. He's lived in the Pacific Northwest for more than thirty years. Currently he lives in the suburbs of Seattle with his dog and cat, Rexy and Roxy. Learn more at www.brianholers.com.

CPSIA information can be obtained
at www.ICGtesting.com
Printed in the USA
JSHW022355241022
32050JS00003B/3